Reforming
LORD NEIL

A Regency Romance

Inglewood Book Five

SALLY BRITTON

To My Children, For Their Love and Support

Chapter One

AUGUST 1815

Many in Suffolk county doubtless enjoyed a summer's rain. Teresa Clapham, however, heard the first drops upon her window and bit her lip to keep from crying. Even alone in her small bed, in the sparsely furnished upstairs room, she could not make a sound. It would not do for her mother, in the room next door, nor her daughter across the hall, to hear sounds of her distress. Not when they depended upon her to remain composed and cheerful.

Several hours remained until she needed to rise, around the same time the sun would come up from the sea, hidden by the clouds. If she roused too early, she would wake the other occupants of the house and throw everyone's day into confusion.

Teresa pulled in a deep, shaky breath. Practicality had to win out over emotion. If she gave in to tears, she would give herself a headache. That would only make the day ahead more miserable. She breathed slowly, counting backward from one hundred in French; the process usually calmed her.

Then she heard the first drops of rain fall into the bucket she kept in the corner of her room. The water hitting the thin metal made a tapping sound, harsh and echoing through the quiet room. The leak had grown worse. A month ago, it could rain fully half an hour before a single drop came through.

The roof needed repair. If that was the least of her troubles, the rain might be shrugged off, ignored for a time, but it was one of a hundred things that needed attention.

The tears would come if she did not move. She had to busy herself, and counting was not enough. The heavens wept enough for the time being. She need not add to it.

But the dripping had pulled her away from sleep for the remainder of the night.

Finally, she gave up and rose from her bed. The ropes holding the mattress creaked, as did her bones. Were the bones of a thirty-year-old woman supposed to creak? The ropes must need tightening. She had performed the task before, but she could not recall where she had put the tool for twisting the ropes until they were taut enough.

Her bare feet eased onto the wood floor. She felt about for her worn bedroom slippers, but gave up after a moment. Most likely, Caroline had borrowed them. Though only eleven years old, Caroline had grown alarmingly over the spring and could very nearly wear her mother's shoes as comfortably as Teresa wore them. The child certainly outgrew her own faster than Teresa managed to keep up with purchasing new pairs.

Yet another thing to add to her list. Caroline needed new boots soon. Unless Teresa gave in at last and let the girl spend what remained of summer barefoot.

With a shawl around her shoulders, and her black hair still in its braid, Teresa left her room as quietly as possible. She went down the uncarpeted corridor, the narrow staircase, and to the back of the house where the kitchen might offer her distraction.

A light beneath the kitchen doorway gave her pause before she pushed the door open on its whining hinge. Perhaps there was oil in the barn she might use to silence that sound. She added that to her list of tasks.

Mother sat at the table, white cap upon her head, shawl around her shoulders, and her hands wrapped around a teacup. Louisa Godwin smiled through the lamplight at Teresa. "What woke you?" she asked quietly. "The rain or the bucket?"

"The rain." Teresa shared her mother's tired smile. "May I join you, Mama?"

"Of course. Pre-dawn tea parties are never enjoyable without company." Mother nodded to the teapot on the table. The tea things were too fine for the old wooden table, and the humble kitchen. The set had belonged to Teresa when her life had consisted of beautiful, delicate things. The cups, saucers, plates, teapot, and the other trappings sprayed with pink rosebuds had been a wedding gift from her late husband.

Teresa poured herself a cup of herbal tea. They could not afford tea leaves, but dandelions, rosehips, chamomile, and every herb they gathered and dried themselves had been tried and tested in various combinations. Sweetened with honey instead of sugar, accompanied with milk on occasion. It was simple fare. But enough.

When Teresa settled across the table from her mother, cup in hand, she released a weary sigh. "It will be a long day for both of us now."

Mother shrugged. "We will come through it fine, I dare say." Despite her fifty years, Teresa's mother still held herself with grace, and had retained beauty in her maturity. Her frame was neither spare nor plump, the only wrinkles near her eyes and at the very corners of her mouth were from years of smiling, and though the silver strands had increased their appearance in her black hair, nothing quite gave away her age.

"We always do." Teresa sipped at her tea, listening to the wind and rain. She shivered and pulled her shawl tight with her free hand. "I need to find a way to get the roof repaired. I thought I would wait until the end of summer, but the leak seems to be growing the longer I leave it undone."

After a thoughtful nod, Mother added, "We ought to check

for leaks in the barn, too. Any there could cause problems when we bring hay in for the winter."

How their lives had changed; Teresa used to be a creature of the moment, never worrying about winter rain and snow when summer was still underway. But over the course of two years, the first living under the grudging charity of her brother-in-law and the second in her inherited cottage, Teresa had adapted.

The kitchen door made its awful squeal again, and Teresa turned to see Caroline standing there, wearing Teresa's slippers.

"It's raining," Caroline said, lingering just outside the room as though uncertain of her welcome.

Teresa exchanged a knowing smile with her mother. "Come in, dear. Have some tea."

Caroline's eyes brightened in the darkness, and she hurried forward. "Thank you." She retrieved a mug from one of the shelves. Teresa felt the familiar softening of her heart when she saw how easily her daughter reached what had, a year ago, been too tall a shelf for her.

"Caroline," she said, and her daughter turned with mug in hand. "Take a tea cup. It is a special occasion."

"It is?" Caroline sounded surprised, but quickly did as she was bid. She settled in a chair next to her grandmother. "What occasion?"

With a laugh, Teresa pushed aside her worries for the moment. Her daughter needed moments of sunshine amid the hardships they faced. "The occasion of us all waking up far earlier than we should."

"Let us hope such occasions are rare in the future," her mother said. "But if you will fetch some bread and jam, grand-daughter, we can have a little celebration."

Small joys kept them all hopeful of better days, though Teresa saw none on the horizon.

Hours later, the teacups were drained, and the rain had finally stopped. Wearing a dress that had once been as blue as the summer sky but had faded to a more gray-like color, Teresa went out to milk their old dairy cow.

Milking a cow. What would her late husband have thought, if he saw her perform the undignified chore? Yet every time she sat on the three-legged milking stool, Teresa offered up a prayer of gratitude for the animal and the farmer's daughter who had taught her how to go about milking.

After that chore, she went to weed their summer garden, leaving her shoes off rather than coat them in mud. It was easier to clean her feet than scrub at mud-caked shoes. Gulls had already been and gone, picking at the bugs that had come out to nibble on cabbages and vines, before making their journey to the sea. It had surprised her to see such large birds taking notice of her little garden, yet she expressed her thanks for them, too. The smaller birds were still hopping about, finding tinier creatures that threatened carrot leaves and chamomile petals.

By the time Teresa finished in the garden, Caroline had already fed their six chickens and gathered the eggs. She waved to her mother from the barnyard and went on her way with her basket of eggs.

Teresa wiped a line of sweat from her brow and walked to the fence separating her property from the road. Though tired, she ducked beneath the long rail and started up the path. It curved over a hill, then turned eastward and upward, taking her above the sea.

Dunwich lay to the south of where she stood. All Saints' church tower, crumbly as it was, poked up from the cliff side. She shuddered and turned from that somber sight. Instead she turned her face to the east, where the sun rose steadily.

"We will make it through today," she said quietly. "And this week, and this month, and this summer. We can make it through winter." They had already done it once.

Yet even as she spoke, lifting her hopes and eyes heaven-ward, a weight dragged at her heart. Her meager income would barely keep them alive. How would she find a way to pay for repairs? For any help at all? If she were a man, it would be enough. A man could climb atop thatched roofs to repair them, till more ground than she could, swing a hammer, chop wood, and do all manner of things she had to hire out.

But if she were a man, she would not be in her predicament. She would have inherited from her father, for one thing. Never married and thus kept the eight-thousand pounds of her portion away from her husband.

The familiar anger surged, quickly replaced by guilt. "I am not angry at you, Henry," she said softly to the sea. "I only wish you had told me, that I'd had some warning." She had never even suspected her husband had a weakness for cards. He had treated her with such tenderness and love. He had been a present and compassionate father. There had never been anything to make her worry over his conduct or their marriage.

The revelation bestowed upon her when her brother-in-law had told her of her husband's debts had nearly shattered her good memories of Henry. She could not imagine her husband stealing the funds that ought to have supported her and Caroline upon his untimely death. The reality stung deeply.

She wiped away the tears she had thought conquered that morning. Squaring her shoulders, she forced a smile. Likely had anyone seen, they would have found it a grim expression.

Man or no man, she would find a way to make every farthing count. They would be warm and well fed come winter.

Somehow.

Chapter Two

No one hated the Marquess of Alderton the way his third son hated him. Lord Neil would rather fling himself off the second-floor balcony than spend more than an hour in his father's company. The entire household knew it, and so everyone from Lady Alderton to the lowliest scullery maid kept away when the two men were in the same room.

That meant that the family members at home rarely sat together after dinner. But that evening, Lord Alderton had commanded they all retire together to one of the parlors. Apparently, he had something on his mind.

Neil glanced at the doors leading to the balcony, wondering if he vaulted over the rail whether or not the shrubbery below would break his fall.

"This family has come under scrutiny," his father said in his deep, cool voice. "I am positioned to lead my party, should things go according to plan next Season, and I have the support of the Regent."

Of course he did. The marquess and His Royal Highness

were often seen in each other's company. Neil kept his mouth closed, and his eyes on the doors.

"Behaviors must alter. After the way Olivia nearly exposed herself to public scorn, I have decided I have given all of you too much of a leash."

Olivia, from her place on the settee next to their mother, gasped aloud. She shook her head dramatically, her golden curls bouncing. "Father, you cannot still believe those lies. I explained what happened, that Sir Isaac—"

"Enough, Olivia." Their father did not need to raise his voice to silence her. His power in their family, in the kingdom itself, was well known. "I know you well enough to recognize your manipulative explanations, your deceits. I have seen you practicing your wiles since childhood."

That drew Neil's full attention to his family.

Lady Alderton gasped and put an arm around Olivia. The two of them looked very alike, and Neil had also inherited his mother's coloring: fair hair and eyes that never quite settled between green or brown. "Alderton, what a thing to say—"

"We both know where she gets it," the marquess said with a careless flick of his hand, directing it to his wife. When Neil's mother paled and began to protest, the marquess laughed darkly. "Stop your sputtering, my lady. You have taken more lovers than I these past years."

Neil clutched at the arms of his chair. Whether his father's accusation was true, his mother did not deserve such disrespect in her home, before her grown children. Yet lashing out at the man would worsen the situation.

"All of you are a disappointment to me," Alderton went on, turning his back to them. "At least I have two worthy heirs. And two children I know to be mine."

"Alderton—" The marchioness stood. "Stop. I will not have you bring up those old accusations here. You have made your point."

Neil rose slowly to his feet and walked, as though bored, to stand behind the settee where Olivia still sat, quietly fuming.

"Oh, but I have only begun to make my point." Alderton turned, his cold stare sending a shiver down Neil's spine. "I have already spoken to Lord Brunfield and Captain Duncan," he said, referring to his eldest sons by titles rather than names. "They understand their responsibility to this family. Brunfield has managed to have three children, two sons, to continue the line. Captain Duncan has forged powerful political alliances. But the three of you"—his lip curled with distaste—"a marchioness taking lovers, a son as useless as he is lazy, and a daughter without a shred of virtue, without the decency to even marry, are no more than dead weight to a man with my political ambition."

Olivia put a hand to her throat. Neil moved his hand from the back of the settee to her shoulder.

For her part, their mother raised her chin higher. "My lord, if we are going to point out reprehensible behavior, perhaps we ought to start with the head of the family. Your many indiscretions do not paint you as an honorable man. Perhaps we have all followed *your* lead."

The marquess moved forward, quick as lightning, and grabbed his wife by the shoulder. Neil tensed, ready to spring over the furniture to go to his mother's aid. It had been years since his father had dared strike a member of the family. Not since the first time Neil had struck him back.

Neil's movement, though small, was enough to attract his father's eye. "Ah. Think you to challenge my authority in my own home, Neil?"

"My mother does not appear comfortable in your grasp, my lord," Neil answered, keeping his tone even. Not challenging his father. Not yet.

"Your mother is hardly a lady." The marquess released her, and her golden head bowed. "I am discreet in my pursuits, wife. You, however, have been *seen*."

"What?" she whispered. She took a step backward. Olivia rose and put her arm around her mother. That left Neil alone, the couch between him and the rest of his family.

"Discretion is all I asked for," the marquess snarled, pacing back to the fireplace. "My wife is seen bidding a lover farewell, my daughter's attempts at luring a man into her bed are exposed, and my useless third son does nothing of note but spend my money."

Neil's hands curled into fists. "I never spend more than you give me. Unlike my eldest brother. Tell me, Father, are Brunfield's gambling debts acceptable?"

The marquess glared over his shoulder at Neil. "Gambling is acceptable behavior for a man of his standing and wealth. He has to do something to amuse himself. His debts are small, considering what he brings to this family as my heir. You, on the other hand, are entirely expendable. You could have had a career in the church, and that might have been of some use. One could always use a bishop in the family. Or you might have gone into the law. But instead, you are a lazy, idle leech. That changes now, Neil. If you expect to receive your allowance, you will do as I say."

Neil tipped his chin upward. "And what is it you say, my lord?"

"Your lack of a wife has given me reason to suspect you lack passion, but given the way Inglewood reacted to your wooing of his countess, there may be more to you than I thought. I have considered how I might use your hidden talents." The marquess's eyes gleamed. "I have a political opponent with a wife who may very well fall for your charms."

The hypocrisy his father displayed turned Neil's stomach. His reasons for seeking out the Countess of Inglewood had been his own. She was the first, and only, married woman he had approached and he had failed to secure more than her pity. But his father demanding Neil abase himself to spy on another man, while tearing apart his mother and sister for similar behavior, disgusted him.

"I might be a useless third son," Neil said slowly, "but I will not seduce anyone at your command."

The marquess smirked. "No? Then you continue to prove useless. Of course, I am not surprised at your disobedience. You have ever been a disappointment." He looked to his wife, still standing with her head bowed. "My lady, do you still claim this man is my child? I see more evidence every day that he is not."

Neil came over the settee and placed himself between the marquess and his mother, who had appeared to flinch away from that accusation.

"Take back your slander, my lord. Father or not, no one speaks to my mother in this way." Neil kept his hands at his side, though he was ready to fight with his hands if need be. He had never struck a man other than his father. His brothers, of course, but fighting during youthful disagreements did not count. Yet he was ready to swing at his father in defense of his mother.

Perhaps it would prove refreshing.

"Neil." His mother's hand landed on his shoulder. "Darling. Stop. Fighting will solve nothing."

"Neither of them are mine, are they?" The marquess looked from Neil to Olivia, who made not a single sound. "That is why they look nothing like me, and why they behave without a shred of respect. Disobedient, unnatural children."

Neil took a step forward. "You will not speak to my mother and sister that way. Not before me."

The marquess folded his arms, appearing as relaxed as though he had done no more than share his opinion on the tides. "Then you are dismissed."

"My lord—" His mother started to speak, but Neil would fight his own battles.

"Dismissed? I have yet to hear your grand plan for taking up leadership of your party." He laughed, coldly. "It sounds as though it will go as well as this little family gathering."

"You forget yourself, Neil," Lord Alderton said, voice lowering. Neil recognized danger looming, but had yet to discover what shape it would take.

"I forget nothing. You raised me to be this way. No matter how you deny it, your influence has turned me into the man I am. Are you not proud, Father?" he asked, flashing an impudent grin at the man he hated.

"Not at all. I am disgusted." The marquess narrowed his eyes. "And I am finished with you. Remove yourself from my sight."

"Gladly. Come, Mother. Olivia." Neil took his mother's arm and turned to leave the room.

"You misunderstand," the marquess said, voice hardly more than a whisper. "I never want to see you again. You are to remove yourself from my sight, my house, my lands. You are to take nothing that belongs to me or to the family with you. No horses, no dogs, no funds. You have a quarter of an hour. If you are still here, I will make certain you regret it."

Neil whirled around, shock turning his blood to ice. "You cannot be serious. I have done nothing—"

"Precisely," his father said, a snarl in that single word. "Nothing. You are useless. You are nothing to me. I will spend no more effort, no more of the family money, on such a poor investment as you have proven to be." He pulled a watch from his waistcoat and flicked open the cover. "Fourteen minutes."

"Alderton, you cannot—"

"Father, please, not Neil—"

The pleas of his mother and sister would not be heard. His father's behavior had been volatile before. He'd once whipped an eleven-year-old Neil with a riding crop for naught more than a minor infraction.

Neil stormed out of the room, the women following behind him.

Olivia's shrill voice called after Neil. "You cannot leave—"

"I must. But the two of you should lock yourselves in your chambers, Mother. He is in a mood."

"I would call it more than a mood," his mother muttered. They stopped at the top of the stairs. "Where will you go?" she asked. "You must send me word. I will keep in contact and tell you when he's ready to forgive you. This has to be some sort of plan, turning you into a prodigal."

"Perhaps." Neil did not have time to think over his father's scheme, but the marquess never acted hastily. That thought alone reassured Neil when his mind wanted to give way to anxiety. The marquess had set everything up, before they had even walked into dinner that night. Neil would bet on it, if he gambled the way his eldest brother did. "Keep yourselves safe. I will send word when I have found some place to weather his displeasure."

"Take this." His mother took off the necklace she wore. It was studded with rubies. Then she pulled off her earbobs and put all of it in his hand. "They are mine, not the family's."

Olivia's worried expression changed into a scowl. "And he wonders why I will never marry. Bah. Giving another man that sort of power over my life." She jerked her chin upward. "Come, Mother. My room has strong bolts."

Their mother shook her head. "He will not harm us, Olivia. This was all done for Neil, though I cannot guess why. Retire to your room. I will go to my own."

Olivia glowered at Neil. "You had better fix this." She turned on her heel and stormed down the corridor toward the family wing.

Neil looked down at his mother, her green eyes full of sorrow. "I will be fine, Mother. There will be a friend with a spare room somewhere. I will be away only until he comes to his senses."

"I have been married to that man for forty years. He is playing a game. Though I do not know what it is. Be careful where you go. He has spies everywhere, and too many powerful people who owe him favors." She put her hand on Neil's cheek, her brow pinched. "Neil. I will say this once and only once, and you will never repeat it to your sister. But you are *not* that man's son."

Neil pulled away from her, nearly dropping the jewels she had given him in his shock. "Mother, what do you mean?"

"There is nothing, absolutely no reason, why you must be like him or why you cannot escape him," she whispered harshly, her expression fierce. "Go. Before he turns your own precious dogs against you."

She turned and went away, too fast for Neil to even attempt to grab her wrist, to stop her and demand an explanation.

His time was nearly up. And the last thing Neil wanted was for his father to turn the dogs on him. Despite his care for the animals, they were well trained to do as the kennel master commanded. Being chased off the property by the animals he loved would prove the greatest humiliation.

Neil stuffed the jewels into his coat pocket and fled the house, out the front door, and away from the only family he had ever known.

Chapter Three

Three days of being turned out of houses and away at doors by those he had considered friends had altered Neil's perspective on how easy it would be to wait out the marquess's wrath. Once he had shared his story, the noblemen and gentry had politely rescinded their hospitality.

Whether they declined him as a guest due to fear of the marquess's displeasure or disgust that Neil no longer had full pockets, they did not say. He wandered up the coastline, his hope waning as his list of friendly acquaintances thinned.

He'd traded one of his mother's earrings at one house for a horse and a bag of coin, but that was all the help he'd had. The horse wasn't a particularly fine specimen, either, but it hadn't seemed to mind wandering down the road.

Soon, he would need to turn westward. The next gentleman he meant to try was a third son, like himself, who lived near Saxmundham. At least, that's where Neil thought the man said one could find him.

He dismounted the gelding and walked upon the road, giving his legs a much-needed stretch. His first instinct upon leaving his father's house had been to seek out Lady Annesbury or Lady Fox. But he could not step foot upon the first lady's lands without angering her husband, and the second lady was not at home. Having recently married, she and her irritating husband had gone on a wedding trip.

The knowledge that his immediate plans had been to run to women with whom he shared naught more than friendship stung his pride. There was no lover to seek. No gentleman who thought highly enough of him to risk his father's wrath by offering shelter. The men who owed him favors were few, and not exactly near neighbors.

What was a man to do, without more than a small purse of coins to his name and no place to go? Perhaps this had been the marquess's plan, to force Neil into recognizing how much he depended upon his lordship's good graces. The marquess had always been manipulative. There must be more to his reason for turning his third son out. A man did not invite that kind of public scrutiny without reason.

Or perhaps the marquess had only tired of throwing money away on a child he had rightly suspected was not his own. Neil cast that thought away. He was the natural child of another man. In the hasty seconds his mother had shared the revelation, he hadn't asked who the man was. Did it even matter?

Why had his mother even told him? Perhaps she wished to spite the marquess. Instead, she had thrown Neil into confusion. He couldn't think on that. There would be time to spare on that mystery another day. A day when he had a roof overhead and a bed no one would turn him out of when they discovered he had angered one of the most powerful men outside of the royal family.

Neil glared up at the sky, noting patches of cloud everywhere except before the summer sun. He took his hat off and wiped at his brow with the back of one gloved hand. That was another thing. His attire was ridiculous. He had been dressed for dinner when he'd fled without clothing and was offered none by any he had met. He'd already stuffed his white gloves away in a coat pocket, but his trousers and shoes were not meant for riding and were certainly ruined.

All his clothing came from tailors, most from London. They were expensive, perfectly fitted to him. Finding the appropriate attire in his current circumstances would prove difficult.

Neil glimpsed a flash of movement to his right, behind a low gate, and turned more out of instinct than interest. A woman stood from her work in her garden, a basket tucked against her side, and stared at him with her head cocked to one side.

Replacing his hat, Neil went to the fence. The day was hot. He and his horse needed refreshment. "Pardon me, madam. Might you know where I might find a public house? My horse is thirsty, and I am similarly afflicted."

She blinked at him, perhaps at his overly formal words. Yet he found impressing commoners with charming smiles and flowery language usually made them more compliant. Perhaps he had overestimated her vocabulary.

"The nearest public house is in Dunwich, behind you about four miles. But you are welcome to water your horse here at our trough. If buttermilk will cool your thirst, or dandelion tea, I can offer that as well." She spoke with the accent of an upper class gentlewoman, despite the smear of dirt on her cheek. He had to blink, the incongruity forcing him to reconsider his response.

"That would be most welcome. Thank you, Mrs.—?"

"Clapham." She nodded up the road. "Our gate is around the next bend."

"Thank you," he repeated stupidly. He offered a small bow as an afterthought, then remounted his horse.

The woman started walking in the same direction, disappearing behind the hedgerow lining that side of the lane.

The shrubbery and fence broke after he went around the slightest curve in the road, revealing a dirt path that took him to a small house. The ground floor appeared to be made of gray stone, the above floor wood, and the roof thatched. There was glass in the top windows, but the bottom had none, only shutters thrown open to let in the breeze.

The woman arrived near the house, but she gestured to a small barn made entirely of wood, with a similarly thatched roof. He saw the trough outside of it and rode closer before he realized it was empty. The woman had gone to a pump located between the house and barn.

He dismounted and affixed the horse's lead to a rail apparently meant for that purpose, positioned as it was just above the trough.

Mrs. Clapham, a comely woman he supposed, were it not for the well-worn clothing she wore, positioned a bucket beneath the pump and began to work the contraption, water pouring out to fill the pail.

Neil shifted uneasily. Everything he knew about etiquette would have him preventing a gentlewoman from performing such an action on his behalf.

Obviously, she is not a gentlewoman. No matter how she sounds. He adjusted his stance, looking away from the uncomfortable sight to take in the chickens pecking at the yard. Though the buildings and grounds were humble, there was an air of cleanliness about it. There were flowers planted along the side of the house. No rusted tools or discarded objects about the yard.

The woman came to the trough, holding the bucket at one side, though she used both hands. She dumped it, then went back for another. It would take several trips to fill the trough. Neil shifted again. Should he wait for her to finish? Perhaps he could amble away to avoid the discomfort.

He shifted his attention to a tree near the corner of the house and went toward it. He inspected the slim trunk, looked up into the branches.

A child peered down at him, all wide-eyed and shadow-speckled. She was frozen, her bare toes curved around the slim branch, her arms wrapped around another at her waist, where she bent and stared down at him.

"Good morning."

The girl's eyes widened and she turned as though to see the woman through the branches.

Neil leaned a shoulder against the tree and checked the progress of Mrs. Clapham. "She is at the pump. Shall I call to her for you?" He glanced up to see the girl shaking her head back and forth anxiously. "Ah. You are climbing the tree in secret."

She nodded.

Neil chuckled. "Very well. I will not give you away, miss." He lowered his eyes, watching the chickens instead. "Do you live here?"

No answer came, so Neil sighed.

"I'm not looking anymore. You will have to answer aloud. A whisper will suffice."

"I live here," she whispered. "That's my mother. I'm Caroline."

"A pleasure, Miss Caroline."

There was a long pause before the girl responded. "What is your name, sir?"

"Neil Duncan."

"Oh. A pleasure to meet you, Mr. Duncan." There was a rustle above him and when he looked up he saw the girl had tucked herself closer to the tree trunk, her footing more certain. "My mother does not like me climbing trees," the child said. "It isn't ladylike."

Interesting. But it was none of his concern who the woman was or how she knew what was and was not ladylike.

After his horse rested, he would be on his way. Even if he wasn't certain of his destination.

The door at the front of the house opened. Neil looked over his shoulder, and then he moved away from the tree. The woman standing in the doorway with white cap, iron gray eyes, and a stern glare, commanded his immediate attention.

"Madam." He bowed, the movement slight. A marquess's

son bowed low to very few. At least, a man raised in such a station need not lower himself overmuch for a countrywoman.

She took his measure with one appraising glance. "Sir." Then she directed her eyes to the tree. "Come down, Cara. We have yet to study geography."

A bare-footed, tree-climbing child had geography studies?

"Yes, Grandmama." The girl's voice lilted sweetly in her obedient answer, and Neil looked up in time to see her stepping down from one branch to another with as much grace as a fully grown woman descending a stairway. The last limb was several feet high, yet she jumped down as though it was nothing to worry her.

Miss Caroline grinned most impudently up at him, bobbed a curtsy perfectly adequate for a child of her age, and hurried by him and through the door to the house.

Her grandmother stayed outside the doorway, her eyes fixed upon him. "You are oddly dressed, young man."

Young man? He doubted whether he was more than a dozen years her junior. Then again, there was some gray in her hair. She might be older than she looked.

"I am dressed for dinner." He held his arms out, not at all self-conscious of his odd apparel. Best to accept his circumstances, after all. "Yet I find no one will ask me to the evening meal."

The woman pursed her lips. "My daughter is caring for your horse?" While nothing in her manner was precisely rude, her tone struck him as somewhat commanding.

Neil adjusted his coat. "If your daughter is Mrs. Clapham, then yes. I am—" He stopped, considering the woman before him and the recent revelation in his parentage. The child had assumed a title when he had not told her he was a lord. Might the grandmother do the same? "I am Neil Duncan."

"Mr. Duncan." The woman curtsied, barely dipping. "Consider yourself invited for dinner." Then she walked into the house, closing the door behind her.

TERESA DID NOT MOVE, AS SHOCKED BY HER MOTHER'S hasty invitation as the stranger. She had come up behind him, ready to offer him something cool to drink, when she'd heard her mother's pronouncement.

Though prone to trust more readily than most, Teresa had not thought to extend more than a moment of respite to Mr. Duncan. What was Mama thinking? Inviting a stranger to dine with them, unusual as it was, might prove dangerous.

"You need not stay, Mr. Duncan," Teresa said softly from behind him. He turned around to face her, the surprise still as evident upon his face as it had been in his posture. "It will be humble fare upon our table." She looked over his clothing again, noting that while it was highly unsuitable for riding, the cloth seemed fine, and it all fit him with a precision that indicated an exceptionally talented tailor had seen to the task.

His expression cleared, though Teresa knew the charming smile he bestowed upon her was not exactly sincere. "When a man is hungry, Mrs. Clapham, he takes his dinner where it is offered. If your husband does not mind the invitation, I will be happy to be a guest at your table."

Her stomach tightened, though not from grief. Not anymore. A year and all that Henry's thoughtless actions caused had made the mourning process short-lived, and his memory pained her less if only because she refused to think upon him.

No, it was nerves. Despite the man's words, she doubted that a thick lamb stew and slices of dark bread would appeal to him.

"There is no husband to mind, Mr. Duncan." Ought she have said so? Perhaps she should have pretended her husband would be back too late for dinner. Her mother always told her she was far too trusting. Teresa gestured to the door. "If you would like to pass your time in the house, you may, but dinner is yet two hours from ready."

"I see." He looked to the door, then to his horse. "I should tend to my animal."

"There is a paddock behind the barn, where the cow is passing the afternoon. If you like, your horse may join her there."

"Excellent idea. Thank you, Mrs. Clapham." This time when he smiled, she caught the edge of another emotion entirely. He almost seemed tired.

Teresa began walking that way. "The easiest way is through the barn, if you wish to follow me."

Mr. Duncan kept pace behind her, and she paused when he fetched his horse. The large beast had apparently quenched its thirst. She led the way through the barn door, tall enough for the horse but with barely the width needed for man and beast to pass through side by side. At the rear of the barn was a wide door which had been divided to allow the top to swing open without letting the cow back inside. Teresa unlatched and opened the bottom, then stood aside. Once the man and horse went through, the cow barely glancing up from her chewing to see the newcomers, Teresa swung the door shut.

The gentleman, for surely dressed as he was he had to come from at least that station in life, began undoing buckles to release the horse from saddle and bridle. He hummed as he went about the work, his voice pleasantly low though not deep enough to be considered a baritone.

Teresa had chores to do. Gawking at a stranger, as though starved of company, was unbecoming. Never mind that the last man she'd had contact with was a fishmonger who liked to argue with her over the price of his catch with more vigor than she did.

Turning around, Teresa went to her next chore. She had picked what vegetables were ready for the table, as well as several shallots. She went looking for her basket of the garlic and onion bulbs. With the intermittent rain, she would need to dry them beneath cover.

With her mind set to a task, Teresa managed not to think about the stranger for nearly a quarter of an hour. Until he found her outside the kitchen door, snapping the long green beans she had harvested for their stew.

He approached with his hat in hand and with all the confidence of a man born to privilege. He was studying the back of the house with a deep frown, as though it had somehow offended him.

"Are you ready for your refreshment now, Mr. Duncan?" she asked, drawing his attention to where she rested on one of the spindly-backed kitchen chairs. Teresa dropped the last halved bean into the small bowl near her feet before standing and wiping her hands on her apron.

He stopped several feet from her and gave her the same look he had given the house. "I do not wish to interrupt your work, Mrs. Clapham."

Teresa laughed, despite herself. When was the last time anyone had spoken to her with such deference? "You are a guest, sir." Despite her merriment, his frown deepened. He looked away, at the barn or over her small vegetable field.

"Not everyone would be so kind to a stranger."

It was difficult to tell if he was speaking to her or to himself. Teresa decided to answer anyway. "It was not long ago that I was a stranger here. The kindness of others is all that kept us from giving up." She had no thought to share more of her personal life with him, but that much was enough to explain their humble generosity.

The gentleman's expression changed from one of confusion to something softer. Almost understanding. "Your circumstances were not always what they are now, I take it." He had an interesting way of speaking. His words were not clipped, but spoken slowly, almost silkily.

Teresa folded her hands before her, unwilling to share more. "No. They were quite different for most of my life."

He nodded, almost thoughtfully. "My circumstances have recently changed, too, Mrs. Clapham. Most drastically."

What did one say to that? Here they were, complete strangers, admitting to reversals in fortune that most would deny or hide. Of course, her fortune was plain to see, given the dirt upon her hem and the apron she wore. But his must be new, and had likely come upon him suddenly, given his manner of dress.

How did a man's lot change enough that he still wore expensive clothing while admitting to it?

Only one thing came immediately to mind. Gambling. Fortunes were won and lost at tables in England. Hadn't her own disappeared due to cards in her husband's hands? Though she did not know how long it took Henry to lose her fortune and everything not part of the entailment, given how well they had lived up until his death, she did not think it had happened gradually.

She shivered, despite the warmth of the August sun streaming through the clouds. Mr. Duncan raised his eyebrows at her.

"Excuse me. I will fetch you refreshment." She curtsied, out of habit, and hurried into the kitchen.

Mother and Caroline were in the kitchen. Teresa closed the door behind her and cast a glance at Caroline, quietly doing sums on a slate. The girl's face was wrinkled in concentration, her tongue sticking out at one corner.

"Where is Mr. Duncan?" Mother asked.

Caroline looked up, meeting Teresa's gaze. Teresa forced a smile. "Oh, he is outside. Have we anything cool to offer him?"

Mother went to the table. "The dandelion tea has cooled. Here." She poured some tea from the pitcher where they kept it after it cooled. Most preferred tea hot, but the herbal varieties still tasted delicious. Especially when they added fruit and honey to it. Several berries had been crushed and added that morning, while the tea was still hot, giving it a tartness akin to lemonade. But Caroline had stirred honey in, as well. The ladies found it most refreshing.

"Let us hope he does not mind our odd tastes." Teresa poured some of the tea into a tin cup. Then she hesitated. "Caroline, will you take it out to him? I need to speak to your Grandmama."

Caroline fairly leaped from the table, clearly happy to leave her mathematics behind. "Yes, Mama." She took the cup in both hands and grinned. "I will tell him all about how it is made, then he will have to appreciate the taste."

"Thank you, Cara." Teresa placed a kiss on her daughter's forehead—an easy feat, given how little she had to bend to accomplish it. Caroline disappeared out the door.

Mother gave one last stir to the warming stew, tapped the spoon on its side, then turned to face Teresa. "What do you think of him?" Mother asked before Teresa could say a word.

"Why do you ask?" Teresa wiped her hands down the front of her apron, somewhat nervously. "You usually tell me I am too quick to trust people."

"Yet you have never been wrong, that I recall, about people's character. You have a unique gift." Mother smiled gently, the praise offered with a smattering of pride.

Teresa shook her head and lowered herself to the bench beside the kitchen table. "We know that cannot be true, given what Henry did to us."

"Henry was a good husband while he lived," Mother argued, her eyes softening. "We cannot know what led to his mistake at the end. Your brother-in-law did not tell us enough to know for certain what drove Henry to gambling away your portion."

"Frederick told us what he could." Though she had never quite trusted her brother-in-law, when he brought paperwork written up by the family solicitor, she could not doubt what he had told her. Teresa approached her mother on the pretense of looking into the dinner pot. "What do *you* think of Mr. Duncan?"

"I think he will make an interesting dinner guest." Mother took Teresa by the shoulders and smiled softly. "My darling, we must look for sunshine amid the clouds all our days. Let us be grateful for the entertainment a visitor offers and return to our work tomorrow."

Teresa sighed and hugged her mother. Together, the two of them had accomplished a great deal. They had moved to a house far from what either of them knew, repaired as much as they could with her mother's funds, and lived a simple life without servants to wait upon them as they had both once done.

"Very well. I look forward to this evening, then." Teresa went to the door and opened it to find Caroline chatting amiably with Mr. Duncan as he sipped at his tin cup, nothing in his expression showing disappointment in their special concoction.

Perhaps the gentleman would not mind their dinner so much, either.

Chapter Four

Never in his life had Neil prepared for an evening meal by waiting outside of a house for dinner to be served. But as the ladies of the household had disappeared inside, without inviting him in, he went looking for things to occupy his time. If he sat still, he thought on the marquess's cruelty as much as he wondered after his own parentage. As he could do nothing about either circumstance, dwelling upon them would do nothing for him.

It was best to stay busy.

He had walked about the paddock where his horse grazed on long grass and dandelions alongside the black cow. He found a few slats of wood that appeared loose, the nails holding the board in place sticking out at odd angles. There had been a variety of tools inside the barn. Perhaps, to secure his animal's safety, he could correct the problem.

It might silence the thought in his mind that he had watched a gentlewoman fetch water for his horse, while he stood about like an imbecile. Doing a good turn for Mrs. Clapham would restore the balance of decorum he had unknowingly upset.

Upon entering the barn, after his eyes adjusted to the

dimness, Neil searched out the tools he had seen. The hammer found, he took himself back outdoors. The first nail he worked upon bent horribly out of shape with his strike. He glared at it, adjusted the angle at which he held the hammer, and swung at the next protruding bit of metal.

That one went in straight.

Neil repeated the action on as many boards as he found that needed it, then tested the work by shaking the boards. Several of them appeared rather old. Likely in need of replacement.

It took very little time, and the work was oddly refreshing. Sweat beaded upon his brow, and the muscles in his shoulder tensed and released with each swing. It was almost a shame when he could find no more nails to fix in place.

With hammer in hand, he returned to the barn. He noticed straw upon the ground, and a broom standing in one corner. Straw didn't generally belong on walking paths, he knew well from his own father's barns and kennels.

In his youth, he had once been punished by the kennel master for smuggling treats to the dogs. The master had kept the animals half-starved during fox hunting season, claiming it made them better hunters, and Neil had attempted to feed his favorites scraps of bacon from his own breakfast. When the master caught him, he'd given Neil the singularly disgusting task of cleaning out the straw in the kennels, from where the dogs lived to the main aisle.

The punishment had taught Neil two things. The first, of course, was how to properly go about disposing of filthy straw. The second was how to better sneak past the kennel master. His favorite dogs had not starved before the hunts that year.

Taking off his coat, Neil surveyed the stalls and the barn. It was not in desperate need of work, but the building did need more attention. He could take care of one more small thing to show his gratitude for the women's kindness. And hammering home a few loose nails was not, perhaps, enough to make up for her waiting upon him.

Neil found a rake suitable to the task and started moving the straw out the door. If he put it into a pile, it was something to do, and Mrs. Clapham might use the straw either in garden beds or burn it. He cared not. He merely needed to occupy his hands and mind.

His horse came to stick its head over the door, staring at him as though surprised Neil had lowered himself to a laborer's work.

"It is odd," he said to the animal as he raked the straw into a pile at the center of the barn. "But I cannot allow myself to be indebted to these women." No one ever hung a debt over Neil's head. He was the one who claimed favors, not the other way around.

Not that it had done him any good of late. As word of his father's anger traveled, the people who owed Neil anything would be less and less likely to settle with him. Without the marquess's backing, Neil was as powerless as a pauper.

The horse nickered at him. Neil glanced over his shoulder, then shrugged. "They are alarmingly trusting, are they not? Three females alone, letting a man into their midst." Were all people in their poor circumstances so generous? Neil doubted it.

"Foolish women," he muttered. "What if I wished to rob them?" Though it did not appear they had much of value, given their clothing and lack of servants.

How had gentlewomen fallen so low as to fetch water for a stranger's horse and snap beans in the kitchen yard? There ought to have at least been a man of all work about to look after them. Such a servant could not require much in payment.

They sent the little girl out to tell him dinner was ready. She came with a bounce in her step, and shoes on her feet. She had changed into a different dress, her hair was down, and she smiled brightly at him.

"Mama said you ought to wash with the bucket, by the pump. We haven't anywhere else prepared for guests to clean up before a meal." She looked at his pile of straw with interest. "Did you do that?"

"Merely to pass the time." Neil fetched his coat from where he had thrown it over a stall door. "I will wash and be in directly, Miss Caroline."

She stared at the straw a moment longer, then looked up at him with a smile upon her face. "Thank you for doing one of my chores." Then she skipped away, directly for the kitchen door.

Neil had never washed up for dinner in a bucket before. He had never prepared for any sort of dinner without a servant to adjust his cravat and help him into his coat. What had become of Benton, his valet? Had the household found another use for the young man, or had he been dismissed entirely?

It was dashed difficult to find a valet capable of caring for Neil's things in the way he preferred. They better not have dismissed him. The man could put a shine on boots that was unequaled in even the royal court.

Neil took his gloves from his coat pocket and examined them. They were dirty. No longer white, really, and completely out of place among present company. He sighed and tucked them back into his pocket. Then he went to the kitchen door and knocked.

He had never entered a house by a kitchen door in his life. His mother would have a fit if she could see him at that moment. That thought put a smile upon his face just as Mrs. Clapham opened the door to him, her own expression one of welcome. She wore a different dress, less faded and worn than the first, though its drab gray color made it appear more like an old mourning gown than something one would consider wearing to dinner.

"Mr. Duncan, do come inside." She gestured to a table on the far side of the kitchen. A simple cloth was upon it, the color some indeterminate shade that was neither cream nor yellow, with only a handful of dishes upon it.

Mrs. Godwin stood at one end of the small rectangular table,

Caroline on the side opposite where he stood, and then Mrs. Clapham went to the other end of the table. That left Neil sitting across from Caroline. When all were near their chairs, the women sat as one, and Neil followed suit.

The matron of the family spoke first. "We are having lamb stew, rolls, and some fresh cherries that Caroline gathered for us this morning. Would you like cider or dandelion tea with your meal, Mr. Duncan?"

Though the tea had not revolted him, Neil could not say he looked forward to ever having such a beverage again. When the child gleefully told him how the sweet, grassy-sort of drink had been prepared, he drank out of politeness and a real thirst, trying to ignore the taste.

"Cider, if you please, madam."

The woman poured from a pitcher at the table, then handed the cup to him. At least it wasn't tin this time. In short order, Mrs. Clapham had a bowl of stew and a plate with cherries and a roll before him. He had never had such an odd dinner. But his last meal had been no more than a meat pie procured at a road-side inn that morning, so his hunger prevented him from turning up his nose at the food entirely.

In truth, it all smelled adequate, and then surprised him by tasting a great deal better than the food at the inn.

Mrs. Clapham stirred her stew, her gaze still upon it when she spoke. "Mr. Duncan, Caroline said you have raked the straw in the barn. I thank you for that. It was not necessary."

Neil kept his back rigid, his manners exact, more out of habit than anything. But he noticed the women at the table sat more like fine ladies than commoners. However long they had been poor, it had not been long enough to remove the more genteel habits from their behavior.

He spoke with careless indifference. "I merely wished to express my gratitude, Mrs. Clapham, and that seemed a better way to do so than penning a letter."

"We never get letters," Caroline said from her side of the

table, then sighed. "And I never get to write any, so I do not see why I must practice penmanship so much."

Neither woman showed signs of sympathy, though mother and grandmother both smiled over their stew.

Neil took it upon himself to address the child, out of curiosity rather than interest. "But suppose the time comes, Miss Caroline, when you do receive a letter and must pen one in response? An elegant hand will serve you well on that day."

She wrinkled her nose at him. "That is what Mama says. But I cannot think of anyone who would write to me." Then she cast an exasperated look at her mother. "Or speak French, Prussian, or Spanish to me, either."

Did the child have an education which included modern languages? Neil rested his spoon against the edge of the bowl. *"Je vais vous parler en français. Si tu veux."*

The girl's eyes widened. *"Parlez-vous français, monsieur?"*

Her mother laughed. "I should think it obvious that he does, my dear." She turned to Neil and explained, in French. *"My daughter has never spoken the language to anyone other than my mother and myself."*

Neil sighed dramatically and met young Caroline's eager gaze. He spoke in French, slower than normal for her sake. *"My mother forced me to learn French. We were not allowed to speak any other language before noon."*

She answered hastily, her accent certainly English though not too harsh upon his ears. *"Please, do not give my mother that idea. I only have to speak French on Sunday."*

He nearly forgot himself and laughed at the girl's pained expression. He remembered well the years of learning, of speaking a language he never thought to use outside his home. The war with Napoleon had made the idea of speaking French almost traitorous to many. "It is a beautiful language, Miss Caroline, and you speak it quite well for one your age. Your mother must be a marvelous teacher."

Caroline colored, but from the corner of his eye he saw an

identical blush in her mother's cheeks. A woman of her age, blushing? It was almost indecent. The woman must be near thirty, to have a child of Caroline's age. While he had known handsome women upwards of three decades, they usually had long-since lost the innocence and sweetness required to blush. Rouge became the only way they brought color into their cheeks.

Were Mrs. Clapham not so browned by the sun, she would likely appear quite pretty. His tastes did not run toward women with such dark hair and eyes, of course, or one whose stature made her appear rather sickly. The woman was thin and shorter than his sister, Olivia, by half a head at least.

Yet she had hauled a bucket full of water across her barnyard with relative ease, proving her delicate structure had no bearing on her abilities.

What a shame one as daintily built as she had been reduced to farming.

His eyes went to her hand, holding a spoon to her lips. The skin there was tan, and her hands did not appear fine and smooth, despite the well-tapered fingers. They were on full display, too. None of the women wore gloves, nor any other ornament.

"Mama," Caroline said. "The cherries are nearly ready to be picked. Are we going to hire someone from the village to help this year?"

Mrs. Clapham shook her head, not lifting her eyes from her bowl. "Not this year, darling. I am afraid we must do most of the harvest work ourselves."

The little girl's head tipped to the side. "But last fall we paid people—"

"And we have since learned how to manage ourselves. Besides, one cannot pay hired men in biscuits the way I can my daughter." The woman's swift interruption, and the somewhat playful remark on payment, was enough to make the girl giggle.

Likely the matter was less about the ladies being capable alone and more about paying hired hands.

"Mr. Duncan." The grandmother addressed him, her tone almost business-like. "My daughter tells me you have experienced a recent change in fortune. While I have no wish to pry, I would like to ensure you are on your way to experience greater hospitality elsewhere. Do you travel to visit friends or family?"

A lesser man might have evaded the question, or stammered an answer. Neil pasted on a confident smile instead. "I have recently discovered I have no friends, at least in this part of the country, and it is family that has left me in my unfortunate circumstances. But I assure you, madam, that I am certain my situation is temporary."

"Temporary?" Mrs. Clapham asked, and he gave his attention to her, seeing her frown. "Have you better fortune to look forward to, Mr. Duncan?"

"Eventually." He shrugged. "Though I cannot say when."

Mrs. Clapham looked from him to her mother, then back again. "Where will you go when you leave here?"

"I had thought to try my luck in Saxmundham." His fingers tightened upon his spoon, but he made certain his tone stayed light. "Though that might prove as futile as the rest of my inquiries."

"But you were riding north, Mr. Duncan," Mrs. Clapham said. "Saxmundham is southwest of here. I think it would be just above ten miles from our home."

"Ah." Neil forced his tight-lipped smile larger. "Then I shall make it by midnight, perhaps."

The women exchanged another glance. "There is no moon tonight, sir," Mrs. Godwin said softly. "And it is not a safe journey to make at night, without a lantern."

They were correct, of course. Neil put down his spoon and thought on the matter a moment. What was the name of the little village nearby? "Dunwich, then. I will find the inn."

Mrs. Clapham was shaking her pretty head before he had

finished speaking. "There is no inn. The public house is rather small, and the family lives above it. I cannot think of anyone who lets rooms in Dunwich." She shifted in her chair, drawing a hand to her neck as she thought. "Walberswick is a mile north of here from the beach; if you take the road it is two miles. But it is difficult to get down to the shoreline with a horse."

Neil gritted his teeth. Though a small thing, something he would have laughed at in days past, finding himself ill-prepared for a simple journey served to further strain his nerves. "Have you ladies any suggestions? I find myself in need of guidance in these strange lands." He heard the strain in his voice, despite his efforts to remain amiable.

"He could sleep in the barn," Caroline said brightly, her eyes glowing. "I did that once."

Both mother and grandmother turned to the child, the mother with her lips parted in a gasp and grandmother with narrowed eyes.

"Young lady," her mother said, tone firm. "When did you sleep in our barn?"

The child ducked her head. "Last week. Jill Martin wagered me a kitten that I would not do it."

"Jill Martin?" The grandmother raised her eyebrows. "I doubt her mother knows about this."

Mrs. Clapham's voice was softer, almost sad, when she spoke. "A wager. You slept outside, without my knowledge or permission, for a wager? Caroline Clapham, you are excused from the table and will go to bed."

Caroline's brows lowered mutinously. "But I have not had my cherries—"

"And you will not have them tonight. I will speak to you before I turn in this evening. Go to bed. Now."

The girl stood, frown nearly comical in its intensity. She dipped a curtsy without meeting anyone's eyes, then fled the room. Neil heard her footsteps on the floor, then a pounding up steps somewhere beyond the kitchen, before the steps hammered above them.

"I apologize for my daughter's conduct," Mrs. Clapham said quietly, drawing his attention away from the ceiling boards and back to her. She appeared rather tired as her shoulders slumped, two dark circles beneath her eyes. "We are not usually so dramatic at the dinner table."

Neil had no wish to distress the woman. She obviously had enough in her life to cause her difficulty. His own issues would solve themselves in time, he was certain. As long as his father relented before Neil's money ran out. Hopefully, the necklace and the other earring he still possessed would keep him from too much discomfort. For a time.

"The apology is not at all necessary, Mrs. Clapham. I am afraid I did far worse than sleep in a barn at her age." He tried for a confident, teasing smile, but when she only sighed and rubbed at her forehead, he wondered if he had lost his ability to charm as well as his fortune.

The grandmother cleared her throat. "Mr. Duncan, thank you for your understanding. Though I would not usually countenance such a thing, Caroline's suggestion might be the only one we can offer you this evening. The barn has a loft, sir, that is clean. Sleeping there this evening may be your best option."

Had he really descended so far beneath his station as to consider sleeping in a barn? His smile slipped away at last. Where else would he go? There were no nearby inns. Without a moon, travel at night would be dangerous for Neil and for his horse. Sleeping out in the open did not sound pleasant, either.

Neil put a hand around his cup, wishing it contained something much stronger than cider. "If it will not be an imposition, the barn loft will prove adequate. If Miss Caroline can sleep there with no more inducement than a kitten, I am certain I will manage."

Mrs. Clapham looked to her daughter's plate of cherries and grimaced. "I will show you the loft after dinner."

WHEN TERESA WAS BUT A CHILD, HER FATHER HAD said, *"It is rare that kindness is repaid, but rarer still that it exacts a price."* He had meant to teach her to do kind things without expecting a reward. That night, as she escorted Mr. Duncan to the barn, a pillow and quilt in her arms, she hoped he had been right about the lack of price.

The man did not act in a way that caused her suspicion or discomfort, though she knew little enough of his story. He had acted as a gentleman throughout the afternoon and evening. She would bolt the doors and shutters of her home and trust God to do the rest.

Mr. Duncan carried the lantern to the foot of the ladder inside the barn. He raised the light upward. "How often do you climb up this rickety thing?" he asked, his free hand giving the ladder a shake. It held firm, thankfully.

"Not often, this time of year. We will hire someone to put the hay up for us at harvest, then I will be up there more often to feed the animals." She handed him the quilt and thin pillow, taking the lantern from him in turn. "There is a large door up there you may wish to open, to let air in. I am sorry our accommodations are not better."

"They will do for tonight." His gaze moved from the shadows of the loft down to meet hers. "Do you often shelter strangers?"

Teresa considered the question a moment. "No. But I would hope someone would do the same for me, or for my child, were either of us in need of a roof above our heads." She gestured to the door leading to the pasture. "I will milk the cow and then leave you to your rest, Mr. Duncan."

He surprised her by executing a very proper bow. Her knees bent out of habit, her curtsy as fine as it ever had been.

"Good evening, Mrs. Clapham." He tossed pillow and quilt upward, where they land upon the loft floor with a thump, then he climbed up without a backward glance. She watched until his shoes disappeared over the edge, then turned her attention to bringing the cow in for the night.

The animal was quick to come in, eager to be milked. "That's my good Abigail," Teresa crooned as she brought the cow into her stall. In a moment, she had the stool in place and worked to fill a clean pail with milk.

She did not hear a sound from above, though she doubted Mr. Duncan had gone to sleep so quickly.

Whatever had caused him to wander about the countryside in dinner clothes, she hoped it would not leave him in poor straits for long.

Teresa hummed as she milked, as was her habit. The tune was one that had been popular the year she came out. The Season she had met Henry Clapham.

When she closed her eyes, leaning her cheek against the warmth of Abigail, she could still remember dancing with Henry to the music. He had charmed her completely, despite his relatively humble standing in Society. He had been so genuine, open, and kind. Perhaps not a great flirt, and that recollection made her smile, but his sincerity had been endearing.

He had not been a gambler or a liar when she married him. At least, she thought he hadn't.

Once the pail was full and Abigail comfortable, Teresa took the milk and lantern with her back inside the house.

Mother sat in the kitchen, a book open before her and a candle on the table. She looked up when Teresa entered. "I think it is time to teach Caroline more about her role as a hostess." Her lips turned upward. "And appropriate dinner conversation."

That earned a chuckle from Teresa. "Valuable skills, for an eleven-year-old girl."

"There is no time like the present." Mother closed her book and regarded Teresa with a more serious expression. "She does not know why a wager is inappropriate, Teresa." It went unsaid that the gambling aspect had hurt Teresa more than the child's secrecy. She could not allow her daughter to make the same mistakes as her father had.

"I know." Teresa lowered herself to the chair. "And we need a kitten, since our last barn cat disappeared for better hunting grounds." She forced herself to smile, though she clasped her hands together tightly in her lap. "Mother, what do I do? I have no wish to tell her about Henry. She still thinks of him as a hero, slaying dragons for her in the fens."

Mother stood and came around the corner of the table to wrap her arm about Teresa's shoulders. "There is no reason to speak ill of the dead, dear one. Even if what they have done leaves us hurting. Let her keep her image of him unspotted, but warn her against poor habits."

"Thank you, Mother." As a woman grown, Teresa rarely referred to her mother by anything except the more formal title. Not out of a lack of love. It was quite the opposite. She adored her mother, respected her, and after taking on the role herself with Caroline's birth, held her mother in the highest esteem. "I will do my best with her, as you did with me."

"Good night, Teresa." Mother kissed Teresa's temple, then lifted her candle and went to the stairs.

Before following, Teresa bolted the doors and shutters. By the time she made it to her daughter's room, Caroline had fallen asleep. The little girl, growing faster than Teresa had ever thought she would, lay curled on her side with one hand beneath her cheek, her hair unbound.

Teresa brushed the dark locks away from her daughter's face, seeing freckles across the child's cheek.

She took herself to her own room, grateful for the tiny amount of privacy it afforded her. She looked out the window, barely able to discern the shape of the barn in the darkness.

Hopefully, Mr. Duncan would sleep well, and go on his way in the morning.

Chapter Five

The night was going about as well as Neil had expected it would. Despite his fatigue, Neil hardly slept. Yet no gentleman ever complained of guest quarters. At least, not directly to the hostess.

Much of the night, he avoided shifting to silence the sound of the crackling straw beneath him. It was clean, and smelled better than the stalls below, but with nothing between him and the straw other than an old quilt, he'd been poked every time he dared move.

His inability to sleep had made it far too easy to think upon his predicament. No friends or family willing to take him in, not enough money to rent rooms for any length of time, and certainly not enough money to live in the state to which he was accustomed. Even if he sold his mother's necklace, it would hardly buy him a new wardrobe, let alone a comfortable room at a fine establishment.

Would the marquess relent in a day or in a year? The uncertainty made it difficult to plan what to do with his funds, even if he attempted modest living.

Wandering about the countryside would not do. The idea of

seeking out anyone who would help him, despite his circumstances, had been a foolish endeavor.

Perhaps he might find work?

The very word made him shudder. He, Lord Neil Duncan,
third son of the Marquess of Alderton, find *work?* Though third
sons were expected to make their own way in law or religion,
Neil had been disinclined to do either.

His allowance was enough for a bachelor to live comfortably,
after all. He had no intention of marrying. Not after a rather
disappointing episode in his youth, when he had been foolish
enough to believe in love and fidelity.

Casting that thought aside before it could trail into memory,
Neil glared at the darkness and tried to form a plan. He had
come no closer to a decision when he finally nodded off, despite
the way some absurd night bird started warbling from the
barn's roof.

A rooster woke him entirely too soon, however, and before
the sun had lightened enough to even be considered *morning.* He
groaned and pulled his coat, which he had removed to use as a
blanket, above his head.

The barn door opened with a groan. Neil sat up.

"There we are, Abigail." He heard Mrs. Clapham's soft voice
with ease in the quiet, and the cow immediately responded with
a noise more moan-like than anything. "I hope you passed a
pleasant night. You did not bother our guest, did you?"

The woman's tone was sweet and soothing as she spoke to
the animal. In another moment, he heard the sound he had realized the night before meant she was milking her cow. Then she
started humming again.

Neil slowly lowered himself back into the hay, staring up at
the beams of the barn. Enough light filtered in through the
walls and door for him to make out the straight slats of the
roof.

The previous evening, Mrs. Clapham had hummed a song he
had not heard in many years. He had been a young man, less

jaded by the world, when it was a popular tune at private balls. That morning, her song was something simpler—a nursery song —yet he found he still enjoyed the sound.

When she finished her chore, he heard her speaking to the cow again. He got out of his temporary bed, slung his coat over his shoulder, and made his way down the ladder.

"Good morning, Mr. Duncan." She stood with pail in hand, a reserved smile upon her face. "I hope you rested."

Wise of her to not assume it was a good night's sleep. "Thank you. I did. Some." He slid the coat over his arm. "And I thank you again for the hospitality."

"You are most welcome." She hesitated a moment, her eyebrows coming together before she spoke again. "Would you like to break your fast with us? There is coffee, hot rolls, and some preserves." A rooster appeared in the barn's doorway and took that moment to crow, with gusto. She laughed, the sound surprisingly light. "We have eggs, too." The heaviness he had seen in her expression dissipated for a moment with her amusement.

What an odd woman.

"While your offer is generous, Mrs. Clapham, I cannot impose upon you any longer. I will take myself to the public house in Dunwich."

She did not press upon him to stay, but nodded her understanding. "Of course, Mr. Duncan. I hope you have a fine day ahead of you." She curtsied, then left him to his preparations.

Neil did not waste time saddling his horse. The creature seemed somewhat resentful of finding himself with bridle and bit in place again. With the unknown stretched before him as the dirt road stretched before his horse, Neil did not blame the animal at all. He rather hated the idea of going about to beg for shelter, too.

Only the girl was outside when he brought the horse out of the barn. She sat on a chair, glaring at an old book in her lap. Chickens were scattered about her, along with several half-grown chicks, scratching and searching the yard for their break-fast. Caroline's expression changed from frustration to disap-pointment when she saw Neil.

"Are you leaving already?" she asked, closing her book. "It is nearly time for breakfast."

"Your mother invited me in. I am afraid I had to decline." Neil led his horse over to where she sat. The girl rose and came to give his horse a pat on its nose. Then she reached into her apron pocket and pulled out an apple. "I was saving this for later. Can I give it to him now?"

"Of course." He watched as she fed the apple to his horse; the animal's ears perked up, as did the rest of him, at the treat. The animal snuffled at her hand, looking for more. Neil had to chuckle. "I think he enjoyed it."

The girl's bright smile appeared. "I like horses. We haven't had one since we came here." She gestured with the hand holding the book, to the barn. "I used to have my own pony." Her shoulders dropped, though her smile remained. "Mama says a horse would be too expensive for us, even if it would be helpful, too."

"I imagine your mother knows best about such things." Neil ran a hand down the horse's neck. Were horses generally expen-sive to keep? He had bought some fine specimens in his time, but once they were in his father's stables, Neil had given little thought to what it might cost to keep an animal fed, watered, and cared for.

Yet another thing his limited funds must somehow cover. He could not give up his only method of transportation.

"I must go, Miss Caroline. It was a pleasure to meet you."

She dipped a curtsy and responded politely. "It was our plea-sure to host you, Mr. Duncan."

He did not chuckle at the charming picture she made, but bowed to her as he would any lady, then mounted his horse. "Good day to you, Miss Caroline."

She waved as he rode out of the yard, back the way he had come the day before.

Neil did not look behind him to see if the girl watched him retreat down the road. He had little energy to spare her another thought. His mind must bend to his own predicament.

When he arrived before the longest building in Dunwich, Neil saw the shingle hanging from it proclaiming it the Lost Mermaid. Strange name for a pub, but it would do.

He tethered his horse outside, then went through the door. A long, dark room with tables scattered about greeted his sight. He looked to an open doorway and caught sight of a trim man, wearing a clean apron and graying hair.

"Good morning to you, sir." The man came out into the main room with a welcoming green, and he made haste to bow. "Welcome to the Lost Mermaid. Need you something to slake your thirst?"

Neil was soon at a table holding a mug of ale, and then a large metal plate full of eggs, sausages, and fried potatoes was placed before him. A few other people ambled inside, some for drinks, some to buy meat pastries. Everyone seemed to know each other, given how casually they spoke to one another.

The owner of the pub, a man who had introduced himself as Mr. Jones, came to check that all was to Neil's liking. Then, with an overly friendly manner, the publican said, "It's a might early for anyone to be on the road, coming from the south. Might you be from the north, sir? Walberswick is not far."

A man with more wrinkles than hair on his head, seated nearer the kitchen, scoffed. "He might've come from Westleton."

"And not had breakfast there?" an equally aged man with white whiskers croaked. "Mrs. Jones is a fair cook, but none would pass up a Westleton breakfast from the Gray Horse."

Neil only raised his eyebrows as the argument continued between the old men.

The wrinkled man huffed. "Who's to say he was at the Gray Horse? Might be he didn't stay there."

"Then how would he have come from Westleton?"

"Look at his clothes. He's a gent. Maybe stayed at a fine house."

"And then rode out come dawn to sit amongst us folk?"

Neil bit the inside of his cheek, irritated with the discussion of his business. "I did not come from Walberswick, nor any other village. I found myself in a barn last night, and here for my breakfast. Does that answer to your curiosity?"

The man with the white whiskers twitched his nose, then folded his arms and sat back in his chair. "Never heard of a gentleman sleeping in a barn. You steal those clothes?"

Neil sat up straighter, but before he could react with offence the more wrinkled of the two gasped out a laugh. "Blind, are you, Billy Higgins? Those clothes fit him better'n your teeth fit in your head. Man's wearing his own clothes."

Having never been subjected to such scrutiny, nor the open curiosity and gossip of men so far beneath his station, it took Neil several moments to determine how best to react. He looked to the owner of the establishment, not for any sort of aid, really, but for direction.

The man shrugged. "Don't pay them any mind, sir." Then he raised his voice to carry to the local men. "They're too old to be of any use to anyone, so they sit about and gossip like old cats all day."

"Old cats? Jones, I've known you since you were in your cradle. Respect your elders." The one called Billy Higgins sniffed, as though he had right to be insulted. "Man comes in here, dressed like that, wrong time of day, slept in a barn, and you aren't the least curious?"

Mr. Jones shrugged. "So long as people pay their bills, I take no interest in their business."

A man came in, shouting about a delivery before disappearing out the door again. Mr. Jones sighed and bowed to Neil. "Pardon me, sir." He followed after the delivery man.

The two old men exchanged a look, then both rose and ambled over to Neil's table. They stood there, looking down at him with twin gleams in their eyes.

"What barn did you sleep in, sir?" the wrinkled man asked.

Neil sat back and folded his arms over his chest. "What business is it of yours?"

The man chuckled, then jabbed at his own chest with his thumb. "I'm Robert Putnam. This here is Billy Higgins. We're old codgers, but we still have our wits. Billy was a butler for Baron Marsham, and I used to be the magistrate's right hand. Your story is—"

"Odd," Billy Higgins put in with a shrug. "Worth noticing."

It would be easier to be amused than irritated at this point, and it would take less energy. Neil sighed and then gestured to the two empty chairs at his table. "Please, sit. I'll buy you both something to drink."

They exchanged a glance, full of a silent conversation only the oldest of friends might have without a word actually spoken, then they sat.

"Tell us," Mr. Putnam said. "What brings you out here? You hoping to find the lost city of Dunwich?"

Neil widened his eyes and looked about. "Isn't this Dunwich? If it is lost, it appears I have already found it."

"This is the village what's left," Billy said. He jerked his head toward the door. "And the ruins of the church, too. But there used to be a whole city here, back before even the Normans invaded. Rivaled London, the stories say. It fell into the sea, with all its riches."

Rubbing at the bridge of his nose, Neil answered with barely concealed impatience. "If it's in the sea, no one is getting to it. No, Mr. Higgins. I am not looking for any lost city."

"Oh." The white-haired man appeared disappointed. "Then what are you doing in these parts?"

"I went too far down the road. I ought to have turned west some time ago, I suppose. I found myself without food or shelter last night, when I was kindly taken in and given both at a farm just north of here."

"Sounds like you came across some good-hearted people." Mr. Putnam's expression went from concern to a knowing smile. He scratched at his whiskered chin. "Was it the ladies up at Bramble Cottage?"

Neil recalled the hedges along the road. Might they have been blackberry bushes? "A grandmother, mother, and daughter?" When the old men nodded, Neil relaxed. "Are they known for sheltering strangers, then?"

"They're hardly known at all," Higgins said, his shoulders drooping. "Good lasses, though, all of them. If I was twenty years younger, I'd marry Mrs. Godwin and take care of the lot. Isn't right for them to be all alone out there."

Putnam sighed and rested his forearms against the table. "How were they after that rain we had a few days back? I told my no-good son-in-law to go up and check on them. The thatch in these parts needs doing up again. We've got a leak in our'n. Are the ladies staying dry?"

"They seemed perfectly dry when I saw them." Neil thought of the thatched cottage roof and could not think how one could tell, merely by glancing at it, that it needed replacing. But these men knew his hostesses well, it would seem. Interesting. "How long have they lived at the cottage? Did they lose their men to some illness or accident?"

"No, nothing like that." Higgins tapped at the table with his fingers, looking to his friend before adding, "They showed up without any men, last year just before winter. Bless them. They were about done in."

"Paid for help, though, right off." Putnam shrugged. "Though I get the sense that was most of their money. They're mighty careful with their pennies on market days."

"Always genteel, though." Higgins met Neil's gaze and

smiled, showing that he had more gums than teeth. "They treat everyone with respect. Kindness. It's a real shame they're out there alone."

"They're close enough to town." Putnam waved off that sentiment. "It's good they took you in, but makes me worry for them."

Neil's mind started turning over the new information he had gleaned. The women had come with enough money to settle, and pay to make the house and land livable, but were no longer spending as much on help. They had a roof that possibly leaked. He had seen the fence in need of repair. They had been willing to feed and shelter him, without asking questions.

A idea formed in his mind, but Neil cast it away. Then drew it out again. No, it was far too ridiculous. Better to forget it and keep trying his luck elsewhere. But he could make his ride about the countryside more pleasant. "Do either of you know where a man might purchase clothing?"

Chapter Six

Never in Neil's life had he found himself in doubt of his path. As the son of a wealthy noblemen, people generally made his way easy with their smiles and willingness to indulge his whims. But no more. He had made it to Saxmundham, to the acquaintance who had somehow already learned of Neil's disgrace. The butler of that house, upon Neil giving his name, had puffed up like a peacock.

"My master bids me tell you that he cannot harbor the disgraced son of Lord Alderton. He wishes you well. Good day." Then the door snapped shut before Neil had said another word.

He went back the way he had come, in search of an inn. The first he passed was an establishment he would not allow one of his favorite dogs to rest in, let alone himself. One could tell merely from looking upon the black thatch and filthy yard that bedbugs and fleas abounded inside the walls.

Neil pressed on. He had some money left in his pocket, even after spending coin for meals that were worth far less than he paid.

A road sign told him Walberswick was but five miles away.

That woman he had met at her cottage, Mrs. Clapham, had suggested the inn of that town to him. Even that slight recommendation was better than wandering about until he settled upon another plan.

A plan. How laughable. He had thought he might sit in a friend's billiard room or library and pass the hours as comfortably as ever. But with each rejection, a cold feeling had grown inside Neil's gut. It was with all the weight of lead that the certainty rested within him that no one he knew would offer him shelter. No one would brave the irritation of a marquess. No one liked Neil well enough to do so.

A strange clatter, clomp, and the horse stumbling jerked Neil out of his thoughts and nearly out of the saddle. Muttering a string of curses to himself, Neil dismounted. The horse pawed at the ground with a foreleg, and the sound of metal against stone grated against Neil's ears.

The cursed horse had lost a shoe.

"You had to make matters worse, didn't you?" Neil gave the horse a pat on the neck despite his displeasure. It was not the animal's fault he was improperly shoed. Neil lifted the horse's foot as he had seen blacksmiths do, holding himself over the hoof to examine the problem. The shoe had vanished. The horse would go lame if Neil continued to ride the gelding. The village was still several miles off.

Neil glared at the hoof, then lowered it back to the ground. As he had not the funds to purchase another animal, Neil walked. The horse seemed to understand the gravity of the situation enough to keep his head low and ears back.

Three miles from the village, Neil found another sign pointing the way. Nearly the same moment his eyes landed upon the wood with *Walberswick* painted upon it in white letters, thunder sounded above him.

"No." Neil looked up at the gray sky. "Absolutely not." The sky paid him no heed. Several fat raindrops landed upon his face.

"Absolutely perfect." Neil kept walking, even as the rainfall sped before him. Trudging through the rain, leading his horse, the man's ill-fitting clothing more suited to a farmer than a lord soaked up the water and mud.

By the time he reached Walberswick, it had grown dark, too. There were no people outside, rushing to and from the little shops of the town. No one to even ask for directions. The sensible people of that village appeared to have all gone home.

Smoke rose from chimneys, and lights glowed in windows. After walking through two streets of shops and houses, Neil found what he searched for. A large wooden sign with a white crown upon it, the word 'Inn' written in large yellow letters.

Neil tied up the horse, then pushed the door open.

The main room was full of tables, and the tables were full of people. Men and women both ate, talked, and some even played cards. The whole place smelled of bread and grease, and wet, unwashed people.

A tall, thin man wearing a white apron hurried through the tables toward Neil. The man's eyes studied Neil's clothes even as he started speaking. "Welcome, friend, to the White Crown, pub and inn. What are you in search of this wet night?"

"A room," Neil said. "Dinner. And someone to take care of my horse, tied up out front. He's thrown a shoe, so I will need a blacksmith or farrier in the morning." The innkeeper's eyes flashed with surprise, most likely due to Neil's educated accent.

"Splendid, splendid. You are in luck, sir." The innkeeper then pulled his lower lip behind his front teeth and whistled, an ear-splitting and unpleasant sound. Neil winced, only then realizing how terribly his head ached.

A boy came through a door, all long-limbed and clumsy. "Yes, Mr. Fletcher?"

"See to this man's horse outside. Get it dry and fed," the innkeeper, Mr. Fletcher, said. "Be quick about it." When the boy scampered away, the innkeeper turned again to Neil. "If you'll find yourself a seat, sir, I'll bring you stew and bread. Ale, too. Just after we discuss the matter of pay."

Neil withdrew several coins and held them out. "Will this do?"

The innkeeper took the coins and pocketed them almost too quickly for Neil to realize it. "Aye, sir. That will do for two days of meals and lodgings for yourself and your horse. We'll get your horse to the blacksmith come morning. Be right back with your dinner, sir."

After a cursory glance about the room, Neil made his way to the only empty table that remained. It was pressed into a dark corner, without windows. The table was wedged too tightly against the walls for more than a single chair to fit. Which suited Neil perfectly. He had no desire to speak to anyone or invite conversation of any kind.

He needed to think. But given the pounding in his head and the noise of the room, even being alone would not be enough to clear his mind. After his belly was full, Neil followed the innkeeper up two narrow flights of stairs and down a long corridor with a low ceiling. The room he had paid for was smaller than the closet he dressed in at his father's townhouse. But he locked the door behind him and fell onto the mattress without complaint.

The noise from the downstairs room did not filter up, but the sound of the rain pounding against the roof above remained steady.

"What am I going to do?" Neil groaned, turning himself over to stare at the rafters. No one would take him in. And there was no telling when his father would allow him back.

Surely, most men of his age had recourse for such inconvenient situations. They had money saved, friends to aid them, or an education to use to their advantage. But Neil had none of those things. He had existed as a creature of leisure nearly all his life. The marquess had at last given Neil a punishment he could not shrug off.

He crossed his arms behind his head. Lord Alderton's punishments for both real and imagined offenses had always been harsh. Most of the time, privileges were removed. Such as the Christmas when Neil had been locked in his room for an entire week, with only gruel for food. But other times, Neil was forced to do labor with a servant as overseer. Cleaning the kennels, chopping wood, and even working with a hammer.

As he had aged, Neil had set himself to the task of attacking the loose nails in the stables when it was that or come to blows with his father.

He hated demeaning himself to the level of a common laborer. Yet when Neil had spent hours at a time, angry at the marquess and the injustice of his punishments, Neil had often grown tired of anger sooner than he grew tired from the chore.

Neil closed his eyes and breathed deeply, trying to order his thoughts despite the pounding of his head and the rain.

Never had he been as angry at the marquess than he was at that moment.

Words spoken by his mother, years before, came back to him. *"He wins when you hate the punishment, Neil."*

She had never lifted a finger to help him, to ask for leniency. His mother was not tender-hearted enough, not brave enough to stand up to the man who had showered her with jewels all their married years. He kept her compliant through wealth, and Neil through threats.

"I suppose he will win this time, too," Neil muttered. The coins in his coat pocket would not last forever. The necklace and earring he still possessed, when sold, might tide him over several weeks. But what was he to do? Sit in an inn all day, eating stew with more fat than lamb floating in the broth?

The last decent meal he had eaten had been at the widow's home. Mrs. Clapham had fed him well, and had never once suggested he give up coin to share her table or sleep in her barn. The house had been clean. The barnyard well-tended and clear. The three women, grandmother, mother, daughter, had been genteel and pleasant company.

"What if I did not hate the punishment?" Neil muttered aloud. "Not *entirely?*" He had thought briefly of returning to Bramble Cottage and offering up work in return for the women's kindness. But he had cast the idea aside as ridiculous and beneath him. But what if it was neither of those things?

What if he could work for his keep, and enjoy gentle manners and delicious meals in the meantime? Perhaps it would not be a terrible fate.

The work might even be good for him.

TERESA STUDIED THE FORMERLY LOOSE BOARD SHE had noticed in Abigail's pen. Despite giving it a shake, the board remained firmly in place. Upon inspecting the place where the board joined the post, she found the nails tightly driven in, though one was somewhat crooked.

After putting away the unnecessary hammer, she went in search of her daughter. Caroline had not completed her schooling for the day. Teresa's mother said it would do no harm for Caroline to enjoy a summer afternoon beneath trees or in the fields, but Teresa would rather her daughter not shirk her duties.

Knowing that Caroline had snuck off to play with Jill Warner, the daughter of a shepherd with more sheep than sense, also made her uneasy. Little Jill might be an acceptable playmate, but she possessed a gaggle of older brothers who were known to brawl with each other and just about anyone they crossed paths with. Not precisely the sort of company the daughter of a gentleman should keep.

Even if they were living a poor life on a farm, Caroline's fortunes might one day change, and she needed to be prepared for it.

She walked the acre of the vegetable field to get to the cherry trees. They needed to harvest that fruit quickly. The local farmers had told her she might make enough on one cherry harvest to cover expenses for her family for many months. But timing was difficult and hauling the cherries to the correct market even more so. She would need to hire someone else to take baskets of her cherries with them—someone with a horse and cart—and that would take some of her income.

At least their garden sustained them with food. But there was little to trade or sell for the other things they needed, such as clothing and medicine.

Why had her great-aunt left Teresa a farm too small to generate an income? How had the old woman lived in the cottage for the last two decades all on her own?

Caroline was not in the gardens or the cherry trees. Walking along the brambles and fence lining the road, Teresa occasionally paused to call her daughter's name. Though she grew increasingly certain Caroline had left the property entirely.

Pausing at the break in the brambles, where she had stood only a few days before to see Mr. Duncan come up the road, Teresa put both elbows on the fence and lifted her hands to cover her face. She took in several deep breaths, more to clear her mind than anything. Though her daughter's disappearances were frustrating at times, she only wished the child had a better understanding of responsibility. Of safety.

Teresa kept her chin in one hand as she gazed down the road. Mr. Duncan had likely made it to his destination by then. Despite his ill-fortune, whatever may have caused it, as a man he had the ability to work through it in any number of ways. Especially given his easy charm.

"When was the last time a man bowed to me?" she murmured aloud. Not since she had come to the farm, escaping her brother-in-law's poisonous critiques and indifferent condolences. He had made certain Teresa knew he found her, Teresa's mother, and his own niece burdensome. When news of the inherited cottage had come, Teresa had known he would be relieved that she would take her family and leave him to the house that had once been hers.

It kept Caroline away from Mr. Clapham's cruel words about her father, too.

Despite the hardship of living by themselves, off a small patch of land in an old cottage, it was better than living beneath the gloom of Frederick Clapham's frowns.

Movement from down the road caught her attention. Teresa turned her head to see who might be coming up the lane.

It was a man on a horse. A familiar horse. And the man—it was Mr. Duncan. His clothing had changed, but his hat remained the same, as did his comfortable posture. Why had he returned? And dressed like a common laborer?

Teresa shaded her eyes and stared harder, but the vision before her did not change. He saw her looking, and the man actually smiled, as though amused. Then he dismounted and walked the final steps to the fence.

"Mrs. Clapham. I trust you are well?"

"Yes." She wished she had put on her bonnet before venturing out of doors. Her dark hair would be a horrid mess after all the work she'd completed. "And you, sir? I confess, I did not think to see you again. I hope nothing is amiss."

"Not at all, though your concern is most kind." Though dressed now in a drab coat, wearing a blue kerchief about his throat instead of a wrinkled cravat, and gray trousers rather than the fawn-colored breeches, he spoke as silkily as ever. He even wore boots, she noted.

He caught her stare, and a slow smile appeared upon his handsome face. He held his arms out, inviting further inspection. "Do you like it? I confess, despite the lack of fashion, I am most comfortable."

"I cannot say I understand the change." Teresa folded her arms. "Nor can I say it suits you, sir."

He touched the scruff upon his chin. "It will take time to

grow accustomed to it, but I have time aplenty. We could exchange remarks all day and never come to the point, but I think it best we are direct with one another. Mrs. Clapham, I sense that you are a practical woman, and I have returned to your home to offer up a proposal."

Teresa's heart clenched. Caution was warranted any time a man used those words. "What sort of proposal?" Hopefully, she sounded indifferent rather than alarmed.

Mr. Duncan's lips curved upward, and he stepped closer to the rail. "You may have gathered that my situation is somewhat unique. I am a man used to the finer things in life, currently reduced to a man without a roof overhead. As I have gathered, you have experience with abrupt reversals in fortune, too."

With a swallow, she nodded once. "That is true. But I fail to see what your misfortunes and mine have in common."

"They have put us both in need of something the other can provide." He swept off his hat and made a show of looking over her land. "You are two women and a child, alone, on a farm that requires more work than you can do on your own. I have heard that you hire out work on occasion, but that cannot be a sustainable way to live. Whatever funds you have, they will not last forever."

Had she misjudged this man, too? Whatever he wished to propose, Teresa prepared herself to give him a thorough set-down. Laying out everything she already knew about her circumstances did not endear him to her in the slightest. He had been so mannerly before, so charming, and kind to Caroline.

"And just what is it, Mr. Duncan, that you think you can provide, as you said before?" She thrust her chin up, her entire body tense and ready for the verbal blow of an inappropriate suggestion.

His eyebrows shot up, and his expression went from calm confidence to confusion. He likely thought she would welcome whatever horrid thing he had planned. Well, she did not and would never be desperate enough to consider—

"I thought I might work for you."

Teresa's bravado hiccoughed. "Pardon?"

The man regarded her a moment as though her head was addled. "I would sleep in your barn. Do odd jobs for you." His eyes narrowed, then just as quickly a look of understanding came upon his face. "Oh. You thought I meant—"

"Never mind what I thought," she said hastily, feeling her cheeks warm. "You want to work for me, after pointing out that my funds are limited? That makes no sense, Mr. Duncan."

"I will not require funds. Only food and a roof overhead." He replaced his hat, a smirk still upon his face. "Until my family situation rights itself."

"I see." Of course, a man of his obvious good breeding would not suggest taking her as a mistress in return for protection or funds. If someone like him wanted a mistress, there were doubtless many willing candidates without calloused hands and sunburned cheeks. She cleared her throat. "I am not certain you understand, Mr. Duncan. We truly cannot hire laborers—"

"Mrs. Clapham, we both know that I am not a laborer. But I am capable of muddling along and offering you an extra set of hands." He opened his hands at that, palm up, revealing a gentleman's fine-boned fingers. "I will give you the use of my horse and do as you bid me. In return, I will only want the loft for my quarters and to take my meals with your family."

He had thought the matter through, had even obtained clothing more suitable to the position he had invented for himself. A hired man who collected no wages. It was a far better proposal than the one Teresa had assumed he was about to make.

"Mr. Duncan," a bright voice called from up the road. Both the gentleman and Teresa turned to see Caroline coming toward them from where the bend concealed the gate. She held a bundle of fur in her arms. "You came back. Look. I have my kitten."

Without hesitation, Mr. Duncan lifted a hand to wave to the girl. She waved back, then disappeared again. It was obvious that Caroline would welcome the man into their lives. Having an extra set of eyes to keep watch over the little girl would be as much of a relief as another set of hands to lift Teresa's load.

"I would like to discuss the matter with my mother," Teresa said, pulling his attention back to her. "But for now, you may stay another night in the barn."

That expression appeared again. A smirk she had thought it, but with how naturally it appeared perhaps that was always how he smiled. She raised a hand to forestall him from saying another word. "We will see, Mr. Duncan. I make you no promises."

He bowed, then took up the horse's lead and started toward the gate.

Watching him go, Teresa's stomach unclenched at last. She felt the blush coming back into her cheeks. He was a handsome gentleman, there was no doubt of that, even with his unshaven face. As a widow, and living with her widowed mother, having an outdoor male servant would not harm her reputation. Much. The meanest of gossips might raise their eyebrows, but she was no Society miss whose life depended upon being seen as a virtuous innocent. The matter of her reputation did not worry her at all.

What did concern her, the thing that made her hesitate the most to accept an offer of what amounted to almost free labor, was what being near such a man might do to her.

Her husband had been gone for eighteen months. For a year, she had lived on their tiny farm and no man for miles had caught her eye or her imagination. But having a man of Mr. Duncan's charm and education occupying the same dinner table as she did—

Teresa shook herself and went to the house to find her

mother. They would make the decision together. And Teresa would remind herself, as many times as necessary, that a handsome man did not at all make for a trustworthy one. She need not be distracted by him if she chose not to be. In fact, if they kept him on, Teresa would see to it he did all the things she could not do, and as far away from her as possible.

Chapter Seven

Neil put his folded arms upon the short wood divider that acted as stall wall for Abigail the cow. Mrs. Clapham sat on a milking stool on the other side, the oil lamp hanging above her the only light in the barn. She milked with her cheek against the cow, her eyes closed as she hummed.

She made a pretty picture as a milkmaid. Neil watched her with a measure of envy. Somehow, she had found enough peace in her situation to be at ease, doing a task she had likely never performed until she came to this place.

Caroline sat in the stall, too, upon another stool. She had the kitten in her lap. The little girl spoke quietly to her kitten. "You will live in the barn at night, and find all our mice. In the mornings, you will keep me company during my lessons."

Mrs. Clapham's eyes opened, meeting his gaze. She lost her rhythm a moment, but Neil said nothing. She frowned at him, but spoke to her daughter. "Cara, darling, your kitten will likely go where he pleases."

"That's what Jill said. She said Tom cats never stay where they ought. But mine will behave, won't you, sweet kitten?"

Caroline nuzzled the top of the kitten's head. The little orange creature answered with a mew.

Though he had dismissed the curiosity over the women's circumstances before, it was easier to think upon Mrs. Clapham's life than his own at the moment. Especially since Mrs. Godwin had enthusiastically accepted his proposal, giving him leave to stop worrying over food, shelter, and how long he could make his funds last.

The milking apparently finished, Mrs. Clapham rose from her stool and gave the cow a pat on its hindquarters. "Thank you, Abigail."

Neil chuckled and opened the stall for the ladies to exit.

The mother looked to her daughter. "Leave the kitten, Cara. He will be safe and warm in the stall."

Though her bottom lip protruded, Caroline put the cat down on the stool and came out, closing the stall door behind her.

"Good night, Mr. Duncan." Caroline curtsied, took the pail from her mother, and walked out of the barn tilted sideways to balance the heavy pail. Neil watched her go, smiling despite himself. He had never spent much time around children. His eldest brother had several little brats, as spoiled as lapdogs, but Caroline amused rather than irritated Neil.

Mrs. Clapham cleared her throat, drawing his attention back to her. "I will have a list of chores for you tomorrow, Mr. Duncan."

Manual labor was a small price to pay for peace of mind, and would serve to distract him from his problems. He had written a letter to his mother, informing her of where he was and how she might contact him. His letters would go to the Lost Mermaid public house and be sent from the same. Not that he anticipated writing with any frequency. He only needed to inform his mother of his good health and where she might send his reprieve, when the time came.

"I look forward to being of assistance, Mrs. Clapham." He bowed, and she hesitated.

"Mr. Duncan, I think we should discuss one matter right away." Her chin came up. "You are under my employment, even though it is unusual, and I require that you treat my family with respect."

The woman had a commanding streak to her, it would seem. Neil knew exactly how to handle her, however. "Madam, have I done anything at all to indicate disrespect?"

She frowned. "No. However, I have noticed a certain air about you. I cannot explain it. I suppose it comes natural to one born to privilege."

Neil had made her wary, despite his attempts to be nothing but charming and forthright. How interesting. Neil stepped closer; though their distance was still respectable it was on the edge of propriety. "I cannot understand what you mean, Mrs. Clapham. I am behaving as a gentleman, am I not?"

To her credit, she did not back away, but he did see her swallow and her cheeks flush in the lantern light.

As understanding crept into his thoughts, Neil chuckled. She found him attractive. *Also* interesting.

"What has amused you, Mr. Duncan?" she asked, her little pointed chin raising higher, her dark eyes flashing with irritation.

"Our situation, Mrs. Clapham."

She scowled at him and thrust the lantern between them. "Here. Do put it out before you fall asleep."

Neil purposefully brushed her fingers with his as he took the lantern by the handle. She shivered, much to his pleasure, and then tightened the shawl around her shoulders.

"Good night, Mr. Duncan."

He bowed. "Mrs. Clapham."

She whirled about on her heel and vanished out of the barn. He walked to the door, closing it only after he watched the door to the kitchen open, a woman's shape slip inside, and close again.

With the woman gone, he allowed his shoulders to fall along

with his pleasant expression. He faced the barn, scowling at his new quarters. Though he had made the choice to return to Bramble Cottage, it did not sit easy with him.

Neil had already put his belongings in the loft above, including a straw-stuffed mattress Mrs. Godwin had provided from some unknown corner of the house. How would a mattress stuffed with the dry hay prove any more comfortable than a pile of the stuff? Neil had the pillow from before, the mattress, two quilts, and his satchel.

He climbed up, somewhat awkwardly with the oil lamp in one hand. He put the lamp on the floor and stripped off his boots, trousers, and the cloth about his neck. The night was warm enough, he laid down on top of the blankets with one arm behind his head.

He put out the lantern, and moments later heard the soft footfalls of a small animal.

"Mew." The cat had found its way up into the loft. It crept over to Neil, and he stretched out a hand where he heard the little one purring.

"Not in the mood to hunt mice yet, Puss?" Neil asked as the creature first sniffed at his fingers, then rubbed against his knuckles. "We both will have to work to earn our keep. I suppose that makes us partners, for now."

The cat came closer and curled against Neil's side, purring all the while. At least the creature did not seem to have fleas. Neil released a sigh and stared above, into the blackness.

Work the next day might well expel the more troubling concerns in his head. If he worked himself into exhaustion, sleep would come more easily than it did at present.

The only pleasant thought he could pick from all that flew through his mind was that Mrs. Clapham found him handsome. While she was not the first, it was certainly gratifying to know he still held some allure, even in his disheveled state. More amusing still, she was upset by whatever attraction he held for her. Why?

It was a pity, really. He had nothing to leverage from the widow. Her interest in him, whether or not she fought it, meant nothing. She had nothing he wanted, other than the shelter she had already given, and he had nothing to offer her. There were no games to play, no politics, nothing to win or lose. She was beneath him, socially, and he had no interest in romantic entanglements.

But watching her blush had been gratifying. Amusing.

Perhaps he might distract himself from his problems through more than the work of a farmhand.

Chapter Eight

Teresa paced the length of the kitchen, waiting for the kettle to boil for coffee. In her hand, she held a precious scrap of paper to write out, in pencil, all that she hoped Mr. Duncan to accomplish. Even if he was unfamiliar with farm work.

Mr. Duncan was tall enough, and appeared healthy enough, to perform physically demanding tasks that would be nearly impossible for her to accomplish on her own.

Her mother's voice startled her. "You are up early."

Teresa turned, hoping she did not appear as tired as she felt. "I suppose it was difficult to sleep, given our change in fortune." Though no money had appeared in their purses overnight, every task Mr. Duncan accomplished was one less for her to worry about, and something she did not have to pay another to do for her.

Mother raised her dark eyebrows, then shrugged and went to retrieve cups for the coffee. She put three upon the table. "Where will you direct Mr. Duncan first?"

Teresa put the paper on the table, smoothing it flat.

"Cleaning out the entirety of the barn, the chicken coop, and chopping wood."

"Ambitious. But they are simple enough, I suppose, even for a man unused to the work." Mother lifted the list. "You wish for him to prune the cherry trees?"

"When I spoke to Mr. Putnam about the trees last month, he said to remove dead limbs as quickly as possible, or we could lose a whole tree. Now that the cherries are all growing, it is easier for me to tell which branches need to be pruned."

Mother nodded and continued reading the list. "Do you think the sheer number of tasks will drive him away, Teresa?"

Teresa adjusted her shawl. "I hope not. Our money is nearly all spent. With Mr. Duncan taking on this much, perhaps we can finally produce an income from the orchard. The cherries Caroline picked two days ago were nearly perfect. We can harvest them and drive them to market ourselves, with Mr. Duncan's horse."

Lifting the pencil, Mother added "drive the cherries to market" to the list. "You will have more time to dry herbs, too. With the nearest apothecary four miles away, we will need to supply ourselves with as much of our own powders as possible."

A creak of the floorboards heralded Caroline's presence. She came into the kitchen blinking and yawning. "Good morning, Grandmama. Mama." She went directly to the door and unlatched it.

"Where are you going?" Mother asked, a knowing smile upon her face.

"To check on my kitten." Caroline smiled, a hint of sleep still in the expression.

Teresa shook her head. "You had better not until you know Mr. Duncan is awake. Here." She lifted a basket from a hook hanging near the window. "Go find eggs for breakfast, but leave the sour, old black hen alone. She's brooding, and any extra chickens will make our Sunday dinners this winter better."

Caroline wrinkled her nose, but accepted the basket and went on her way out the door.

When they had first come to the farm, Caroline had attempted to name the chickens, as though they were pets. Killing one for a meal had left the child dismayed and saddened for some time. But after cleaning up after the irritable animals, and realizing her favorite dinners were those with poultry, Caroline had accepted that chickens on a farm were for eating.

Mother went to the peg where her apron hung, taking down Teresa's to hand it to her. "Do you intend to wait until the gentleman wakes up to see to your chores?"

Teresa looked to the milk pail upon its shelf, where it waited clean and empty. "I suppose I had better not. Abigail should not be made to wait."

She tied her apron on and collected the pail. "Did we do the right thing, Mother? The man is a complete stranger."

"Yet we both feel no threat from him." Mother touched Teresa lightly under her chin, looking her daughter directly in the eye. "We need the help. He may well be an answer to our prayers, or we, an answer to his."

With a chuckle, Teresa stepped to the door. "He does not strike me as the praying sort." Then she left the house, bucket swinging at her side.

When she arrived at the barn door, she hesitated. Ought she to knock, as though the whole of the barn was the man's residence? That would be rather absurd, considering the barn and everything in it belonged to her. He was in her employment, too.

Instead of knocking, Teresa pushed the door open enough to slip inside and called out as she entered. "I am coming in to milk the cow. Are you awake, Mr. Duncan?"

There was a shuffling in the loft, then a muttered word that sounded something like a curse. Teresa had woken him. Guilt made her wince, but a moment later she tipped her chin up.

Their day started early, and he would have to accustom himself to their hours. She came in, humming to herself as was her custom.

In her early days caring for Abigail, it had taken the two of them time to become used to one another. Abigail had been standoffish, and Teresa had been afraid. Humming had soothed them both. As had talking to the cow as though she were a person. Not that Teresa intended to do that in front of someone like Mr. Duncan.

Except for her usual greeting to the cow. "Good morning, Abigail. My sweet cow." She gave the gentle beast a rub of the ear, rather like one would to a favorite hound. The cow always seemed to enjoy it. Teresa settled her milking stool and went to work, humming.

The loft above creaked, then she heard boots on the ladder rungs. With a thump, Mr. Duncan landed upon the barn floor. He came to the stall and leaned over it as he had the night before. He had surprised her then, watching as she milked. This time she was ready for him, eyes open and expression neutral.

"Good morning, Mrs. Clapham. I apologize for oversleeping. I am afraid I ignored your rooster this morning." He spoke with his usual charm and a barely concealed smile. He wore his clothing from the day before, including the blue neckerchief. If it were green instead of blue, it would have made his eyes stand out even in the dim light of the barn.

This time she spoke to him while keeping her milking rhythm. "No apology necessary, Mr. Duncan. Coffee will be ready in the kitchen soon, if you wish, and breakfast too. Toast and eggs this morning."

"Thank you." He gave her a rather cheerful sort of smile, placed his hat on his head, and walked away.

Would he remain cheerful when he saw the list she had prepared for him? Teresa doubted he had ever performed a single task she had written or anything similar in his life. Yet she had never milked a cow before moving to Bramble Cottage. She had been as dainty a gentlewoman as any, with soft white hands, a maid to do up her stays, and the ability to take breakfast in bed.

If Teresa could change her lifestyle so drastically, Mr. Duncan could adapt as well.

When she entered the kitchen a short time later, pail in hand, her mother was laughing and Mr. Duncan sat at the table, smiling over the rim of his coffee cup. Caroline was in her chair, drinking warm milk.

Caroline saw her mother come in and stood to help with the milk. "Mama, Mr. Duncan said my kitten slept with him last night and seemed to be chasing mice in his sleep."

Mother filled a cup and handed it to Teresa. "Mr. Duncan also did an impression of a yowling kitten, and no man ought to attempt such a thing."

"I am sorry I missed the performance. Will there be a matinee later?" Teresa asked, inhaling the soothing and bitter scent of her coffee before attempting the smallest sip.

Mr. Duncan shrugged, tilting his head to one side as though considering. "I suppose it could be arranged. It depends, of course, upon my employer. I understand I have a full day of work ahead of me." He did not speak with distaste. Not at all. He sounded as though he looked forward to his day.

Teresa saw the paper still upon the table, where she usually sat. She lifted it by one edge and slid it across to Mr. Duncan. "Here is what I have thought of thus far. Let me know if you have any questions. Tomorrow, we will all work in the orchard."

He picked up the paper and held it up, sipping coffee as he read. He winced, but whether from the bitterness of the drink or the work ahead of him, she did not know. Mother put a pitcher of milk on the table, then plates of eggs and toast. Caroline served herself, as was her custom. Mother joined the table and did the same.

Mr. Duncan looked over their simple fare with raised eyebrows, but said nothing. Merely waited until the ladies had their food before serving himself. Yet another mark of a well-bred gentleman, Teresa supposed.

He salted his eggs rather liberally before eating. He glanced up as he did, catching Teresa's stare. She hastily averted her gaze to look at Caroline. "Cara, I need your help in the field today. There are caterpillars in the lettuce. If we move them off now, it would be best."

"Why not release the chickens into your fields?" Mr. Duncan asked abruptly. "They would surely eat all your pests."

"And then become pests themselves." Teresa lowered her toast as she spoke, meeting his eyes again. "Chickens love tender greens. They would do harm to the plants, too."

He went back to looking at his list.

"I detest picking bugs off leaves," Caroline muttered over her plate.

Teresa tried to hide her smile. She did not enjoy the chore, either. But what she was about to add would certainly make the prospect even less appealing to her daughter. "We will have your geography lesson while we work."

Caroline groaned, and she looked to her grandmother. "But today is not geography day. Today is poetry, and literature."

Mother raised both hands. "If I am not your tutor today, child, I do not choose the subject. If you wish, you might stay in the house with me and scrub the floors. I also intend to wash the upstairs windows."

"I suppose I can help with the insects." Caroline grimaced, and her lower lip protruded slightly. "I wanted to play with my kitten."

"After your chores are finished." Teresa put her hand out to tuck a strand of hair behind Caroline's ear. The little girl worked as hard as any of them, truth be told. And she would not be little much longer. Teresa might as well have some mercy on her. "If you prefer literature today, you may recite your memorized poems to me instead of geography lessons."

A smile twitched at Caroline's lips, then she sighed. "All our poems are tiring. Isn't there anything we can recite other than Shakespeare and moral verses?"

Her grandmother tutted. "There is nothing wrong with good, moral recitations."

It was then Mr. Duncan spoke again, bringing all eyes to him. "I learned my share of morality poems as a child. Do you know this one, Miss Caroline?" He cleared his throat, then recited with great pomp and ceremony:

> "'A spaniel mightily well bred,
> Ne'er taught to labor for his bread,
> But to play tricks and bear him smart,
> To please his lady's eyes and heart,
> Who never had the whip for mischief,
> But praises from the damsel - his chief.'"

He winked at the girl when she clapped for him. "That was *The Spaniel and the Chameleon,* by a Mr. John Gay, I believe."

"How is a poem about a spoiled dog a morality verse?" Teresa asked, amused despite herself.

Mr. Duncan chuckled and rose from his chair, list in hand. "I confess, I do not remember how the rest of it went. I only liked the first stanza due to the fact it was about a dog. Now a man grown, I rather wish I remembered it. I find I have a great deal in common with the spaniel."

Teresa considered that, then waved him away from touching his plate. "We will care for the kitchen things, Mr. Duncan. You had better start on your list."

"Or else finally get the whip for mischief." He sighed dramatically, making Caroline giggle again. "I will begin with the barn, if that suits you, Mrs. Clapham."

"It does. Thank you." Teresa forced away her own smile. The

chore ahead of him was not pleasant and would likely take him the day. "The entire floor must be cleaned, tools organized to your liking since you will be the one using them, and supplies checked. The stalls must be cleared, and your horse may have one for himself."

There were only three stalls in the barn. Abigail's was the only one prepared for any sort of animal habitation.

Mr. Duncan took his leave with a bow. "I am off to earn my keep. Good luck with your poems today, Miss Caroline."

He went out the door, and Teresa heard him start to whistle a familiar tune. The same she had hummed his first night in their barn. One of her favorites. She gathered his dishes and her own.

"Do you think he knows what he is about?" Mother asked, still sipping at her cooling coffee.

Teresa glanced out the open kitchen window in time to see Mr. Duncan step into the barn. "I hope so."

THE ORGANIZATION OF A BUILDING SET APART FOR the keeping of animals and tools ought not be difficult. Yet Neil was three hours into the task and felt as though he had made no progress.

After he released Abigail into the paddock with his horse, he started his work in the stalls. He ought to name the gelding. It seemed the two of them would be companions for a while yet.

Mucking stalls was similar enough to cleaning out kennels. Old straw in a wheelbarrow, hauled outside to the corner of one of the fields. As long as he found no rot. Not that he entirely knew what rot looked like, but he had been warned against it by his father's gardener strongly enough to have an idea of what it looked and smelled like.

Everything else he raked and swept with a broad broom. Then he went about organizing the tools. He drove nails into the wood boards of the barn to hang things that had laid on a shelf without much order. His only company was the horse, on occasion, hanging its head in through the split barn door, and Caroline's cat.

Flies came and attempted to distract him, earning more than one remark no lady ought to overhear. By noon Neil felt he had done enough to merit a rest.

He exited the barn, the cat on his heels, and stretched. He had his coat over one arm, but as he had seen many a farmer working in fields without that restrictive piece of clothing it could not be too wrong to go without it for a time. Did the working class have rules about when to appear in shirtsleeves and when not to?

The list with chores was in his coat pocket. Neil drew it out and studied the neatly written task that came next. The fine handwriting did little to make the list less loathsome.

Cleaning out the chicken coop. He wrinkled his nose and turned to the side of the barn, where he had seen the feathery pests that morning. The coop was smaller than the barn. It could not be nearly as difficult or time consuming.

An hour into the work, with a full wheelbarrow and sweat making his shirt stick to him in ways he was certain it never had before, Neil went to the fields in search of Mrs. Clapham. He dumped his wheelbarrow load at the corner of the field, then went striding through the green of growing things to the corner of the field nearest the orchard. He could hear Caroline's voice, chattering away, but did not stop long enough to decipher what she said. As soon as he was within shouting distance, he called out.

"Mrs. Clapham?"

Both figures started, and Mrs. Clapham rose from her place on the ground. She picked up a bucket at her side and walked toward him, until they met with a row of cabbage growing between them.

"Mr. Duncan. How goes your work?"

Neil drew in a deep breath, but the twinkle in the woman's eye said she could well enough guess the answer to her question. "Splendidly." He tried not to grit his teeth too much as he answered. "I am ready for the chicken house."

"Yes." She glanced over him, likely taking in the grime he knew he would never be free of again, no matter how many times he bathed. "It is rather filthy work. I am afraid I have put it off. It ought to be done at least once a season." Then she leaned to one side to peer around him. "I am glad you knew to bring everything out for the fields. But how did you know?"

"I guessed." A trickle of sweat made its way down his temple. If his sleeves were in better condition, he would use one of those to wipe it away. "Is there more required for that chore than ridding the coop of their leavings?"

"Oh, yes. You must clean out their boxes with vinegar. And be careful with the brooding hen. It's probably best you move her eggs into a basket with straw. She won't like it, but she likes being off them even less."

"Vinegar." It wasn't enough he smelled like the lowest of stable hands, but now he had to smell of pickled herrings? "Where might I find it?" he asked, not bothering to hide the distaste in his voice this time.

"In the kitchen. My mother will have some. Mix it with equal parts water and give everything a good scrub with a brush." She held the pail out to him. "You can take these and dump them in the yard for the birds."

He looked down into the bucket. Slugs of various sizes, and some kind of horrifying looking beetles, squirmed about in the bottom of the wooden container. His stomach turned. He better understood Caroline's reluctance to perform the chore. He took the rope handle of the bucket most reluctantly. "Yes, madam." He started to turn away.

"Mr. Duncan?" Her voice, low and soft, halted him. He turned, waiting for a reprieve, for some word that might allow him to put off the chore. Instead, she looked at him with that same twinkle in her eye, as though she enjoyed his discomfort. "Thank you."

Neil nodded curtly and went on his way, biting his tongue.

This day of chores alone had more than earned him a place in her barn.

Chapter Nine

It was nearing the dinner hour when Teresa went in search of Mr. Duncan. The hen house had been cleaned, she saw with relief, and he had done a fine job of it from what she could tell. She stepped into the barn, leaving the door open behind her. It was clean, too, but she saw no sign of her hired hand.

"Mr. Duncan?" she called, her eyes going up to the loft. He could not have retired already. She had not seen him for hours, and there was yet much to do. She came further into the barn. "Are you here?"

A quiet mew made her look up. The orange kitten sat at the edge of the loft, peering at her. "There *you* are. Caroline will want to see you." She tried to coax the kitten down with a snap of her fingers, then by patting her knee. But the kitten merely tilted its head to one side and flicked his tail.

"Cats." Teresa shook her head. If only dogs were mousers. She had always preferred dogs. One knew whether or not a dog liked them, whereas a cat's temperament seemed to change by the hour.

Since the barn appeared empty, and Caroline would certainly

ask after her favorite new animal, Teresa started climbing the ladder up to the loft. As soon as her head came above the boards making up the floor, her eyes caught a sight that made her go still.

Mr. Duncan, stretched out upon his pallet, had one arm thrown over his eyes as he breathed deeply enough for her to realize he was sleeping. On the verge of snoring.

The man had not even put in a full day's work, and he was abed again?

She glared at his prone form and came up the rest of the way. There was plenty upon his list he might yet accomplish. And she needed the work done soon. She had spent the entirety of her day in the fields, tending plants, touching insects, distributing the manure he had delivered. Her mother had spent the day working in the house. Cleaning, baking bread, preparing their food, putting up eggs, preparing to make cherry preserves.

And the man *slept*.

She took two steps toward him, then stopped.

He slept without a shirt on.

She glanced around, trying to determine what had happened to the covering, but only found his coat. She picked it up, then clomped as loudly as she could to stand by his side. Mr. Duncan did not even stir in his sleep.

Teresa's temper flared. Cheap though his labor may be, they still had an agreement. They would feed him and provide him shelter. He would help them in return. She did not raise her voice above a normal speaking level at first. "Mr. Duncan?" He did not flicker so much as an eyelash. "Mr. Duncan, wake up."

He shifted, lowering his arm, but his eyes remained closed. Teresa frowned and bent down closer to him, staring at his face, willing him to wake.

His cheeks were sunburnt. There was dirt along his jaw and neck. The neckerchief was missing. His hair was mussed and the man really needed a shave. That made him no less attractive. Before she could go down the path where that thought led, she acted.

Teresa threw his coat on his chest, and his eyes finally opened. But he also flew up, nearly crashing his head into hers. Teresa stumbled back a step, and his hand came up and caught her arm somewhat roughly. He glared at her, his coat on the floor between them. She stared, too alarmed by his quick reaction to demand an explanation or pull her arm away from him.

Taking in a deep breath, Mr. Duncan's sudden hostility seemed to evaporate. "Mrs. Clapham." He relaxed his hold on her, then slowly lowered his hand. "What are you doing up here?"

Although she had been prepared to take him to task, Teresa's mind stuttered and whirled. Her eyes flicked from the intensity in his green-brown gaze to his bare chest. Her cheeks warmed and she hastily stepped back. "Where is your shirt, sir?"

Mr. Duncan looked down at himself, then slowly folded his arms over his chest. "Soaking in a bucket of vinegar and water." His nose wrinkled. "I thought to attempt cleaning it rather than burn it, as I was first inclined to do."

Her shoulders dropped. "Burn it? If we went about burning clothing every time it became soiled we would all walk around naked." Heat flared in her cheeks again, all the hotter when he raised both eyebrows at her. What was the matter with her? She was a widow. His appearance ought not to fluster her. It had not been too long ago that she had seen a bare chested man—her husband. She turned away from him, going to the ladder.

"I will bring your dinner to you, Mr. Duncan. You are not fit to join us this evening."

He sounded much less than amused as he answered. "I completely agree with you." When she looked up, he stood at the edge of the loft, coat in hand. "I will make certain to come to breakfast appropriately clothed."

"And smelling of vinegar," she muttered.

"Mew." The cat stood innocently in the doorway of the barn, as though the whole awkward exchange had not been his fault. She spared the traitorous feline a glare.

Teresa marched back to the house. When she entered, she noted that Caroline was not yet in the kitchen. She must be putting on her best gown for their meal. Good. That would make her conversation with Mother easier.

"Did you find Mr. Duncan?" Mother asked, a wooden spoon near her lips as though she had just tasted the gravy made for dinner.

"I did. In a rather abominable state of undress." Teresa made certain she sounded horrified. "Mother, the man only owns one shirt and he apparently made it filthy enough—"

"He is soaking it in vinegar. I know. I suggested it." Mother smiled innocently. "Though I had rather hoped it would be dry by now."

Teresa gaped at her mother for a moment before asking, somewhat accusingly, "And did you know he did not work the rest of the afternoon?"

"I am not surprised. He is not accustomed to hard labor, after all. I imagine he will become used to it, or he will leave." Mother picked up a tin plate and filled it with cooked beans, mash, and then the gravy on top. She added a roll. "Will you take him dinner?"

Although Teresa had planned on that course, she quickly changed her mind. "I think you had better take it to him." Thinking on his lack of proper dress had addled her. She knew nothing of the man. That he was handsome and charming had flustered her, that was all. Obviously, she needed to set her mind to rights.

There was one thing she could do. She still had some of Henry's things, hidden away in a trunk. Though, the very thought of going through the things from her old life made her stomach twist.

Teresa lowered herself to a chair at the table, noticing her mother's concerned expression.

"Teresa. You are distressed." Mother put down the food and came to sit at the table with her, putting her hand to Teresa's cheek as she had done since Teresa's childhood. "Did Mr. Duncan say something? Did he behave inappropriately?"

She shook her head. "No. But I do see the potential for future difficulties." Teresa rubbed at her forehead. "I am sorry, Mother. You need not worry."

"I am a mother. That is what all of us do." She brushed Teresa's dark hair back from her face, her maternal care softening the edges of Teresa's worries. "We are doing a kindness for him, and he for us. But if it is too difficult, we can send the man on his way."

A kindness. Looking at things from that perspective would help. Teresa closed her eyes. "I am going to look in one of our trunks. I think I have a few of Henry's old things. The man needs at least another shirt. We cannot have him doing half a day's work merely because he is particular about the cleanliness of his clothes."

Mother stilled, then she leaned forward. "Henry's things? I did not know you'd kept any."

Teresa opened her eyes and forced a smile. "Nothing special. Not really. I kept a few things for Caroline to have, someday, and when we were packing to come here, I did not know what to expect. I brought along some of his shirts and cravats. I think— even though I was angry—I missed him." The admission made her heart heavy. All her years with her husband, nearly a decade of loving him, could not be erased by the betrayal of his gambling.

"Do you need my help?" Mother asked. When Teresa only shook her head, her mother gave her hand a gentle squeeze. "Wait until Caroline is asleep, if you want privacy. I will take Mr. Duncan his dinner."

"Thank you."

Hours later, after the kitchen had been put to rights and Caroline slept peacefully in her corner room, Teresa took a lamp up the narrow flight of stairs to the attic.

It was a very spare attic. Caroline could not even stand perfectly straight beneath the roof. It did not cover the entirety of the house, either. Only Teresa's room was below it. With the light placed on the floor, Teresa went to the corner above her room, looking at the wood and where the thatch needed to be replaced. It was too dark for her to see the damage that would soon cause greater issues. If the wood became too wet, would it rot?

Tucking that worry aside, she went back to one of the small trunks she had brought to the farm. It did not contain much of use, nor much of value, and she had ignored it for nearly a year.

Teresa undid the latches and pushed the lid open, staring inside at the things she had saved for Caroline. Except Caroline would not care about the shirts that used to smell like her father's soap. When Teresa took out the cravats, she laid them aside. There was no use for those cloths at present. But the two shirts she had kept, those would be useful.

She took the first out, hesitated, then held it up to her nose and took in a deep breath.

Henry's scent was gone.

With the cloth covering her face, Teresa took in a slow breath. Of course it would not smell like him. It smelled like the lavender sachet she had put in with the trunk, and that was all. There was no reason to cry. She tucked away her feelings, focusing instead upon the moment.

She put the shirt aside, took out the other, and stared at what was beneath it. A small locket, in which she had drawn nothing more than a picture of Henry's bright blue eye and a piece of paper on which he had signed the 'H' for his Christian name. Teresa nearly laughed at the silly lover's token. When he had begun courting, he had slipped her a note and asked her for a ribbon, then tied it to his pocket watch so whenever he checked the time he would think of when he might next see her.

Their courtship had been sweet, romantic even.

How had it all gone wrong?

Teresa covered the locket with the cravats. She took out a small box. Henry's shaving things. Then she closed the trunk, leaving the past to the past.

Chapter Ten

The rooster did not do its job in waking Neil up, and the cat seemed to take it as his duty when Neil failed to rise. The kitten pounced on his bare chest and began to knead Neil's chest with the tips of his tiny claws. Neil woke with a yelp and reflexively grabbed the cat by the scruff of its neck.

He immediately remembered the previous afternoon, when he'd woken up already springing at Mrs. Clapham. The woman had not come back that evening. Not even to milk the cow. Mrs. Godwin had brought his food and milked Abigail.

Perhaps Neil had frightened Mrs. Clapham, or offended her. She certainly had not liked seeing him without a shirt on. He had misjudged her before, when he'd thought she found him attractive. Likely, she merely thought him a curiosity. As he thought her a curiosity. Nothing more.

Even if she had that lovely black hair and cool gray eyes that spoke of both tragedy and triumph.

Never had Neil met a woman like her. He had to admire her strength of character and her resolve to create a new life for her family.

Neil brought the cat back down to his chest, where the animal started purring at once, butting its head up against Neil's chin. He scratched the cat's head and released a deep sigh.

"Admiration is all well and good. From afar." He stared at the rafters of the barn, his thoughts whirling about like children dancing 'round a maypole. "But I am only biding my time, and offending the sensibilities of my hostess—my employer, I should say—will only see me wandering about England again. At least here, I retain some dignity."

The cat meowed directly into Neil's ear, making him cringe. "Or at least as much dignity as one can have while conversing with a feline."

He sat up, the kitten jumping from his shoulder to the floor. His shirt hung on the top rail of the ladder where he had placed it after pulling it out of the vinegar bucket. The cloth had reeked terribly. Burning it certainly held an increased appeal. But he had nothing else to wear.

He stopped before he made it to the ladder. White cloth in folded rectangles waited for him on the floorboards. He picked one up and shook out a shirt. Not exactly his size, were he to go to a tailor, but close enough to be comfortable.

Neil pulled the shirt over his head, then tucked it into his trousers. He adjusted the sleeves, looked down at the open neck, and smiled to himself as the faint smell of lavender reached his nose.

A practical gift, but still a gift. Perhaps he had not offended Mrs. Clapham too terribly after all.

Neil pulled on his boots, contemplating the change in his station. Would anyone from his former life even recognize him, dressed as he was? Certainly, none of his acquaintances would expect him to go about a farm doing chores. Most would scoff at the very idea of Lord Neil Duncan stepping foot inside a chicken pen.

Except, perhaps, for Lady Fox. Before she had wed, as Miss

Wedgewood, she had admitted to understanding people who did what they must to achieve their desires. And she had made a point of looking him in the eye and telling him he could be more than what people thought him.

Though Neil highly doubted even she would have thought him capable of lowering himself to farm labor.

After tying the blue cloth in place about his neck, to protect from sun, sweat, and immodesty, Neil made his way down the ladder. Abigail was already out of her stall, which meant she had been milked. Neil released his horse into the paddock as well, then went on his way to find breakfast.

Caroline was at the table with a slate, chewing on toast while she did sums with chalk. She looked up when he entered and smiled brightly at him. "Good morning, Mr. Duncan. We get to pick cherries today."

"That sounds like delightful work." Neil did not have to force himself to sound cheerful, given the alternative chores waiting for him. He took the chair he had used before, across from the little girl. "Much more fun than mucking out stables."

She wrinkled her freckled nose at him. "It smells a lot better out there, too."

Neil chuckled and then leaned back as Mrs. Godwin put a plate before him, along with a cup of coffee. "There you are, Mr. Duncan."

"Thank you, Mrs. Godwin." He glanced around the kitchen. "Is Mrs. Clapham not having breakfast?"

"Mama ate early," Caroline answered, bending her head to her sums again. "She went to ask Mr. Finley about the price of cherries at market."

Mrs. Godwin saw the confused expression on his face, given the explanation Caroline had provided. "We need to determine what we will sell fresh and what we should preserve in jars."

"Ah, I see." Then she hadn't been avoiding him. Neil gave his attention to his toast, which had been spread liberally with preserves. He took a large bite, then hummed in satisfaction. "This is delicious, Mrs. Godwin."

When Neil finished eating, Caroline put on her apron and a bonnet. Under her direction, Neil fetched baskets from the barn and carried them out to the orchard. It was not a large grove; his father had a pear orchard easily four times the size of the cherry tree lot. But the fruit certainly appeared ripe enough to go to market.

Caroline started on the lower branches, while Neil returned to the barn for a ladder to get into the trees. When he arrived at the barn, he saw Mrs. Clapham leaving the house, more baskets in her arms. She immediately smiled at him.

"Mr. Duncan, good morning. Are the shirts to your liking?"

Neil looked down at the cream-colored cloth. "They are. I thank you for not forcing me back into the pickled clothing." He ran a hand over the front of the shirt. "Though your mother assures me that a few hours in the sun will do wonders for the shirt's smell."

She gave him the barest of smiles. "I am pleased to find a use for the shirts." Then she pressed her lips together, as though to hold something back. Her eyes darkened and she looked toward the orchard. "Is Caroline already harvesting cherries?"

"Yes, she is. I am come for the ladder." Though he did not care, he told himself it would do no harm to satisfy his curiosity and confirm his suspicions. "Am I wearing a shirt that belonged to your late husband?"

The color disappeared from her cheeks. Mrs. Clapham's gaze fell to the ground between them. "Yes. I had a few of his things, and the size seemed close. I hope you do not mind."

"Not at all." He took a step backward, then another. "I will get the ladder and walk out to the trees with you." He turned on his heel and went into the barn, in search of one of the shorter ladders he had hung against the wall opposite the stalls. He pulled it from its hooks, tipped it parallel to the ground, and tucked it under his arm. When he walked outside again, he suspected Mrs. Clapham would have gone ahead rather than wait.

But she remained standing there, holding her baskets to her side. She fell into step next to him as they crossed the field toward the trees.

"Will the cherries fetch a good price?" Neil asked after a few moments of silence.

She answered without looking at him. "A very good price, sold by the pound. My neighbor has said we might borrow his scales. Market day in Southwold is the day after tomorrow. There are closer villages, but the market is larger and fresh fruit more dear in Southwold. It is only about six miles north of here, by road."

"It sounds as though we have a journey ahead of us. You will want my horse to pull the wagon?" Neil thought that sounded a great deal better than anything she might ask him to do on her farm. Perhaps he could go another day without mucking out anything.

"Yes. If you do not mind, and if you will accompany me." She cast him a quick glance from the corner of her eye, but Neil kept his expression purposely pleasant. "I think it makes the most sense for you and me to go alone. Caroline will not like being left behind, but I cannot possibly keep watch over her and tend to any who might offer us custom."

Neil observed her with interest. "Have you sold your cherries at this market before?"

Mrs. Clapham shook her head, a black lock of hair falling across her forehead as she did. "I am afraid not. This is the first time I have taken my cherries to market. Last year, when we arrived toward the end of summer, there were not many bushels left to sell. I hired Mr. Putnam and his son-in-law to take the cherries to Westfold. They received a portion of the profit for their trouble."

The woman had ambition. Never having sold the cherries

herself, she was willing to not only attempt the task but had chosen a place where she might maximize her profit. That kind of common sense intelligence seemed rare in someone of their birth. Especially a female someone, likely raised to do no more than look after a household and let a husband manage finances.

"It sounds as though you have given our excursion ample thought. Of course, I am at your command, Mrs. Clapham." That she went to a town north of the farm meant he was unlikely to meet anyone who might know him or his family. That made the decision an easy one.

They had arrived at the trees. She gave him a fleeting smile, then went to join her daughter. "We work on one tree at a time. Leave the unripe and overripe. We will pick them all after the rest have sold and make jams and preserves."

"As you say, madam." Neil put the ladder against the trunk, took up a basket with a large loop that would go over his shoulder, and climbed up into the tree.

It did not surprise him in the least when Mrs. Clapham took up singing, and her daughter joined in with her sweet, clear voice. Whether Miss Caroline knew it or not, her mother was likely overseeing her singing lessons at that very moment.

The thought made him smile as he used the small pruning knife to cut the cherry stems from the branches. Caroline had explained to him that plucking the cherries or pulling them from the tree would hurt the overall health of the tree limbs. The child ought to be a horticulturalist.

They sang music he had heard in church, and then a folksong, and all the songs had a joyful sound. Despite the growing heat of the morning, Neil found himself quietly humming along. If the Clapham ladies could enjoy themselves while harvesting cherries in the August sun, he certainly could. They moved from one tree to the next, and time passed without Neil noticing.

Until Mrs. Godwin came out to them, carrying a hamper.

Neil climbed down the tree, hitting the ground at the same

moment Caroline let out a delighted squeal. "We are having a picnic," she said, dropping basket and pruning knife at once. "Thank you, Grandmama."

"'Twas your mother's idea." The grandmother accepted her kiss, then put the hamper down. "Look at all those baskets. Have we a good harvest?"

Teresa came up behind him and answered. "We do. The fruits are perfect. We will need the rest of the baskets tomorrow."

Neil folded his arms and looked over the half dozen baskets already nearly full. "You have *more* baskets?"

"Lots, in the pantry," Caroline chirped while the two grown women smiled. They did so without looking at him, though they had to have heard the dismay in his voice. They had spread a small cloth on the ground to put out plates of sandwiches and a jar of cider, then several cups.

There would be another day spent with the pruning tools. He looked down at his left hand, which had done most of the work. He held the fruit in his right, gently so as not to bruise it, and cut with his left. The skin where he gripped the handle of the knife was already turning red. He had thought himself lucky when raking and shoveling the day before had not given him blisters. It seemed the luck would not hold.

Neil tucked away his first irritable thought. If the women could continue on, he would as well.

He took the sandwiches offered him. It surprised him, the moment he took his first bite, how delicious they tasted. Though he had sat at many a fine table, presided over by the most influential men and women of England, he had never tasted anything quite so good. Likely because he had rarely worked up an appetite in his past. But the thick slices of bread, cheese, and boiled chicken disappeared quickly, and the cider— liberally mixed with more of their dandelion tea—refreshed him.

Mrs. Clapham refilled his cup when he drained it, a sparkle

in her dark gray eyes. "I do hope this is enough to keep up your strength, Mr. Duncan."

He nearly replied, a quip upon his tongue, but he took another drink of cider instead. Miss Wedgewood had also told him he had the ability to be kind, if he so chose. Perhaps he ought to put in the effort to prove her right.

He could think of no one more deserving of kindness than his present company.

Chapter Eleven

The second day of cherry picking started off well enough. Teresa only spoke French to Caroline, and though her daughter grumbled at first, when Mr. Duncan joined in, Caroline cheered up a great deal.

The man had a beautiful accent. Teresa had not heard French spoken so well since they had left Society. Mr. Duncan was kind enough to keep his vocabulary simple, allowing Caroline to follow his conversation with ease.

He told them a story about his sister, younger than him, attempting to coax a deer close enough to capture it and turn it into a pet. Caroline's giggles were highly contagious, and Teresa had to bite her lip to keep from laughing as he described his sister getting a leash around a young doe, only to end up being dragged through the trees.

The story brought back her curiosity about his situation. He had claimed his lack of finances was the fault of his family. Was there not one of his kin willing to take him in? Her thoughts lingered upon Mr. Duncan as she attempted to imagine what he might have looked like as a child. He had likely been a little imp, with his honey-blond hair and dancing green eyes.

Someone shouted Teresa's name, startling her into nearly slicing her finger with her pruning knife. She jerked around to face the direction of the house.

A man with a familiar build, and an accompanying frown, strode across her field toward her. Teresa saw her mother coming behind the man as fast as she could without stepping on any of their plants.

The man, Teresa's former brother-in-law, took no such care for their growing food.

"Teresa." He said her name in such a way as to make her flinch. He had never been an especially temperate man. His character and mannerisms were in large part the reason for her leaving the family home in favor of her poor, inherited farm.

She glanced up into the tree, where Mr. Duncan had stopped working to stare at the oncoming gentleman. He glanced down at her, his eyebrows furrowed. From the corner of her eye, Teresa glimpsed Caroline putting down her basket and slinking away, to hide behind a tree before her uncle caught sight of her.

Teresa put down her pruning knife on top of her cherries and brushed her hands on her apron. "Frederick. I was not aware you were coming to visit."

"He only just arrived," Mother said, hand on her chest as she recovered from the near-run across the field. "I offered him refreshment, but Mr. Clapham said he must speak to you at once."

He glowered at Mother, taking another step so only a pace separated him from Teresa. "I was traveling down to Ipswich and thought I had better pay my respects. But Mother Godwin informs me that you are harvesting your cherries to take them to market."

Widening her eyes, Teresa nodded slowly. "Why, yes, Frederick, that is true." She hated that he called Mother the same term Henry had chosen to use. Likely Mother disliked it, too. Frederick had never shown her much respect or consideration. "Would you like to try some of our cherries?"

"No." Frederick's nose wrinkled and he glared at the baskets. "How have you sunk so low, Teresa? Henry would be appalled that you are living like a farmer."

Her temper flared, but Teresa kept her tone overly sweet. "I am living how I must in order to feed my daughter, Frederick. You know the pittance I was left after Henry died. As you are unable to assist us with funds due to the difficulties with the estate, I thought it best to provide for myself and my family."

Frederick scoffed and gestured with one hand to the baskets. "By going to market and standing about, hawking cherries, like some sort of peasant?"

"Lady farmer, I should think," Mother corrected quietly.

"Can you not send someone else?" Frederick suddenly looked up into the tree. "Like whoever that is? Is that a servant? If you can pay a servant to pluck cherries, he can certainly take them to market for you."

The next sound Teresa heard was Neil's boots scraping each rung as he climbed down the ladder. She did not turn to look, though she heard him step up behind her. Rather closer than necessary. "This is Mr. Duncan. He has agreed to helping on the farm. He isn't a servant."

Frederick stared at Mr. Duncan, eyes narrowed, and face pale. "He doesn't look like a farmer, either."

Before Teresa could respond, Mr. Duncan spoke in his usual smooth, soft tones. "That is because he is not a farmer, but a gentleman." A tiny knot formed in her stomach at his pronouncement. "A gentleman who has agreed to come to a lady's aid, rather than take her to task for making difficult decisions."

Oh, Teresa would treasure for some time the way her brother-in-law's face paled and mouth gaped open. She would have to find a way to thank Mr. Duncan for that satisfying sight later. No one had ever put Frederick in his place like that. By establishing himself as a gentleman, Mr. Duncan had raised himself to a station equal with Frederick. That would make it difficult for Frederick to say much more on the subject.

Frederick finally spoke, his words strangled. "Mr. Duncan, that is most kind of you." He swallowed and turned a simpering expression upon Teresa. "My dearest sister-in-law knows I would help her if I could."

"Would you?" Mr. Duncan managed to sound bored when he asked that question. "I notice you are wearing the new cut from London. I had my own man inquire into a tailor capable of reproducing those lines. The drawings appeared in my magazines only three weeks ago."

With a start, Teresa observed her brother-in-law's complexion turn splotchy, and she realized the cut of the coat was not one she had seen before. Men's fashions changed so subtly, she never would have noticed, but the coat did appear new. And of high quality.

"In my position, I could hardly dress like a pauper," her brother-in-law muttered.

Mr. Duncan made a sound of disinterest. "Of course not. A gentleman's image is important." Given that Mr. Duncan wore clothing more suitable to a laborer than a gentleman put a twist to the words which further mocked Frederick. Mr. Duncan was certainly clever with his tongue.

Frederick's purchase of a new coat did not mark him as heartless. Teresa knew that. But it was interesting that he would deny her the ability to make even simple purchases and tell her the estate could not afford to give her more than fifty pounds per annum.

"Teresa, might we speak in private?" Frederick asked, casting Neil a suspicious look.

Without a reason to deny him that simple request, Teresa nodded. "Come, this way." She took him toward the open field, devoid of vegetables. She looked once over her shoulder to see Mr. Duncan and her mother in conversation, and Mr. Duncan's eyes upon her.

"Where did that man come from?" Frederick asked, tone harsh.

Teresa tried not to wince. "Perhaps you ought to ask him, as it is not my business to tell you of him." That would keep her from having to confess she knew nothing about him, save that he claimed to be a gentleman.

That remark made a vein in Frederick's forehead appear. "Henry would not wish for you to gain a reputation for having strange men about."

Her heart squeezed, but not as painfully as it once had when he tossed veiled accusations at her. "Then it is a good thing Henry is gone, where my reputation cannot matter to him anymore."

Frederick stopped walking and threw his hands in the air. "I am trying to help you, Teresa. You are as a sister to me—"

She held her hand up. "Stop, Mr. Clapham. We both know that is not true. From the moment Henry died, you made certain I knew exactly how you felt about my presence in the house. You did everything you could to drive me away, and it was a relief to both of us that I inherited this farm. You have no authority over me anymore. If you have only come to lecture me about propriety, you ought to leave. I have no time for this today. I must get my cherries harvested."

He lifted his chin, glaring at her from beneath the brim of his hat. "You are acting like a child, speaking to me in such a way. I took care of you as best I could, given what Henry did to all of us by gambling away everything not entailed to the estate."

Teresa turned back to look at the trees, seeing her mother had started back to the house. Mr. Duncan continued to watch her exchange with Frederick, his arms folded over his chest. "I have work to do, Frederick. Tell me what you came here to tell me."

He spluttered. "I only came to check on you, and then I found out you are ruining the family name."

"Henry did that for us." She gave her brother-in-law a hard glare. "My concern is not at all for our name, but for my daughter's upbringing and my family's health. The money I earn from those cherries will see us through the winter. Please excuse me from seeing *you* off my property. Next time you wish to visit, send word first. I am far too busy to entertain callers at present." She strode away from him, her chest tight with worry even though she kept her nose in the air.

She hadn't played Society's games in a very long time, and she was not about to start playing them when her family relied upon her. If Frederick truly worried over the family's reputation, he would have done more to help her. Or at least not have driven her from the family home with his caustic remarks and complaints about everything from Caroline's piano playing to Mother's enjoyment of reading by the fire at night.

He had made certain Teresa knew she burdened him with her existence. There was no inclination, on her part, to bend to his will anymore.

Chapter Twelve

D riving a wagon, Neil discovered, was not so different
from a curricle. Though it was not nearly so comfortable, given the lack of spring on the bench where he
and Mrs. Clapham sat. She had woken him early, when she
came to milk Abigail, and they had hitched his horse to the
wagon and been on the road before dawn.

It would take two hours to make it to Southwold, and she
wanted a good place to park their wagon and sell her harvest.
"Not everyone will have had cherries yet," she said, in the
middle of explaining to him how markets worked. "Though I'm
told some varieties are ready in June, others are not until
August. I think ours, coming ready right toward the end, will do
quite well. People will wish to secure their last taste before the
fall, and any they wish to put up."

They bumped along the road in silence for a time. Neil had
turned over in his mind the visit from Mr. Clapham the
previous day. At first, he had accepted the man's dismay over
his sister-in-law going to market. What man would wish such a
thing on a female relative? Yet all his concern had been for
himself. Or so Teresa had said.

It was easier to think of her as Teresa, though it might not be proper. Linking her to the irritating specimen of a man from the day before, even if only through their shared surname, did not sit well with Neil. Teresa was a woman apart, unlike anyone he had met before. She had lost her husband, her station, her fortune, and yet had turned into a woman of strength rather than someone to be pitied.

Not that he wished for such a life. The blister on his left thumb reminded him every time the reins brushed against it that he must purchase gloves while in town. Sturdy working gloves. Something he had never owned in his life.

"Mrs. Clapham," he said after a stretch of silence passed. "Your brother-in-law. He said he does not have the funds to support your family. Do you believe him?"

She tipped her head to the side, the better to see him from beneath her bonnet's brim. "I am certain you know how inappropriate that question is, Mr. Duncan." One corner of her mouth curled upward. "But I suppose it cannot hurt to tell you of it, now that he has made you a part of the situation by speaking so openly before you. You must understand, my husband died unexpectedly. He was thrown from his horse while riding." She shivered and pulled her light blue shawl tighter around her shoulders.

"He fell into a coma and died. We sent for Frederick right away. He did not live far from us. He was studying to be a solicitor. Frederick took care of everything. He saw everyone who came to settle debts, to pay their respect. I existed in a sort of— a sort of fog." She shrugged. "I stayed in my rooms with Caroline. My mother lived in Bath at the time. She came to me as soon as she received word of what had happened."

Neil tried to keep his eyes on the road, though a pang of sympathy made him wish to reach out to her. Yet he doubted she would appreciate any physical gesture from him. Honorable women tended to withdraw if he offered so much as a hand to hold.

"The solicitor came and read the will, then told Frederick and me the state of my husband's accounts. Everything was gone, he said. Frederick was greatly distressed. Only our family house in the country remained, as it was tied up in an entail. We left Ipswich for the country, where my mother met us, and Frederick shut himself away in my husband's office to go through the accounts."

She paused in the telling, and when Neil glanced at Teresa, he saw that she had closed her eyes, lifting her face to the morning sunlight. The soft lighting colored her cheeks a lovely shade of pink and glinted off the tips of her dark eyelashes.

The woman's natural beauty made him swallow and turn before she could see how he stared. If she caught him admiring her, it would only cause her discomfort. He spoke as normally as possible, ignoring the stirring in his chest. "What did he find in your husband's books?"

Teresa opened her eyes, looking up at Neil with a pained smile. "Frederick refused to tell me at first. He grew more and more irritable by the day. When I finally came out of my grief enough to ask what had happened—I thought Henry had been swindled, and we might take his robber to court—Frederick told me that Henry had gambled all the money away. Including the ten-thousand pound fortune my father left specifically for my use, for any of my daughters, should I find myself without a husband."

That explained her reaction to Caroline's attempts to win a kitten. She would not look upon any sort of gambling with tolerance.

Something about the story did not sit right with him. "You saw no evidence of your husband's difficulty prior to his death?"

Her gaze fell to her lap, where she laced her fingers together. She wore no gloves. "I saw nothing that would even make me suspect he gambled. Not like that. But some people are good at hiding such things, I suppose."

As Neil's family had expertly hidden any number of indiscretions over the years, even from him though he was apparently a product of such a thing, he believed her. And yet. A decade of marriage was a long time to hide such a thing from someone as intelligent as Teresa.

"I try not to think on it," she said. The wagon went over a bump that made the baskets of cherries clatter, and Teresa shifted to look into the bed of the wagon, her movement bringing her closer to him, her shoulder brushing his. Apparently satisfied, she turned forward again, still near enough her skirt brushed the side of his boot.

Teresa continued the conversation, sounding contemplative. "It is better to remember the good years with Henry rather than the lie. He was a very good husband. I loved him, and Caroline adored him. She does not know about his gambling. I hope she never will."

"I will not speak of this to anyone," Neil promised, watching her from the corner of his eye. How could any man betray her trust? The woman had the bearing of a duchess, even if she had never been more than a gentleman's wife. And this was her figure, her manner, at thirty years of age and after hard toil. As a younger woman, her debut had likely set many a bachelor on the idea of marriage.

"Thank you." Then she nudged his shoulder with hers, telling him she had known all along how near they sat, and she did not mind it. He almost smiled. "Do you intend to tell me any of your history now, Mr. Duncan?"

His pleasant mood sank away, and he bent to rest his elbows upon his knees. The posture would horrify his mother. He spoke with disinterest. "What do you want to know?"

Rather than being put off, she seemed amused. "Oh, do not grouse so. I have no wish to pry into anything. I only thought it would be nice to get to know you better."

Neil bit the inside of his cheek and cocked his head to the side. "Nice?" he repeated, the trivial word somehow insulting in any context.

She raised her dark eyebrows at him. "Yes. Nice. Pleasant. Perhaps even enjoyable. I know nothing about you except your name, and that you were brought up to be a gentleman. How old are you?"

He chuckled and rubbed at his chin, wishing again for a razor. It would not be long until he had a full beard. "I am five and thirty."

"Such an advanced age," she said, eyes overly large. "I can claim five years less experience than you, sir."

"I thought women did not reveal their ages, on principle." He knew his own mother never admitted hers, and Olivia had taken to forgetting which birthday she celebrated after her twenty-fifth.

"I suppose some do not. I have never seen harm in it. We all age the same, do we not?" Teresa had her hands folded in her lap again. "Do you enjoy the theater?"

Neil answered her questions, benign as they were, for the remainder of the drive. She asked nothing more personal than his age, did not delve into his history at all, and merely asked for his opinions. They spoke of the arts, music, and she tested him on his French. The woman had an excellent grasp of the language, and apparently knew more Spanish than he did, but no Greek. They compared experiences in London, where she had only been once, but found they were both familiar with Ipswich.

And once, he made her laugh. A sound so light and joyous, as lovely as her singing, that he immediately held it close and committed it to his memory.

It had been ages since Teresa's thoughts had bordered on optimistic. All her plans until Mr. Duncan arrived had centered on surviving through the winter. But with a wagon at her disposal, cherries to sell, and a box with packets of her herbs as another possible source of income, the day was bright with hope.

All because a man had appeared, however unlikely, needing shelter as much as she needed his help.

Her training as a gentlewoman had not let her down on their long ride to Southwold. With pleasantries, she passed the time, and somehow kept herself busy enough talking that she forgot how nervous she ought to be.

They arrived at market near eight o'clock. Southwold's streets were lined with farmers and carts, and a kind farmer directed them to where most of the fruit sellers had set up their wares. The crowds of horses and people made for enough noise that Teresa knew she would have a headache before long.

Mr. Duncan helped her arrange the wagon and a stool. Then he bowed. "If you do not mind, Mrs. Clapham, I would excuse myself for a short time. I have a purchase or two to make, but I will return to assist you shortly."

Shopping. What a lovely thought. Teresa nodded at once. "Of course, Mr. Duncan."

"Have you need of anything I might find for you?" He took a step backward toward the crowded road.

"I cannot think of a single thing." It was a bit of a stretch of the truth. Teresa could not think of only one thing, but knew of dozens of items that might help her family—things they needed and even more they might want. But she did not have the coin in her hand yet.

"'Scuse me, missus, what's yer price for the cherries?" The inquiry pulled her attention from Mr. Duncan, and she saw him slip away.

The next hour passed quickly, and with a great deal of success. Her first customer was an innkeeper, but after that came a cook's assistant from one of the larger houses and she bought a whole basket of cherries, and then an apothecary proclaimed loudly that hers was the best fruit he had seen all day, which brought other customers closer. Some bought only a few for a treat, others enough to preserve. By the end of the second hour, her cherries were nearly gone, and Teresa had a tidy sum of money in the pouch concealed behind her apron.

Mr. Duncan returned, clean shaven and with a crooked smile on his face as though he had been up to some mischief. "Mrs. Clapham, it seems you are nearly out of product."

"I know." She bounced on her toes once, unable to hide her cheer. "It has been wonderful. But what happened to you?" she teased. "You have lost something."

He raised his hand to his chin, turning to grant her a view of his rather dashing profile. "What do you think? I contemplated keeping the whiskers, but I find I am more fond of being without."

The pleasant mood made her tongue looser than normal. Teresa did not stop herself from laughing and saying exactly what she thought. "You know well enough how handsome you are. You do not need me to confirm it."

His eyes, more green than brown in the sunlight, widened and shifted to stare at her. "Do you think me vain, Mrs. Clapham?"

At that moment, a young woman sidled up to the cart, peering into it with interest. Mr. Duncan quirked an eyebrow at Teresa. Rather than answer his question, she turned to the prospective customer. "Would you like some cherries, madam?"

The woman peeked at Mr. Duncan from the corner of her eye. "I had in mind a tart recipe. These would be perfect. What's your price?"

Teresa named the price, but the young woman smiled and shook her head.

"That is too dear for me just now, missus. But I thank you." She started to back away, casting one last appraising glance at Mr. Duncan, who merely stood with arms folded and a disinterested expression.

"There, you see," Teresa said, coming to stand next to him,

their arms almost brushing. "She did not come to look at cherries, but at you."

"How many male customers have you had today? I imagine most of them came this direction for a similar reason." He leaned one shoulder against the back of the wagon, that almost rakish smile reappearing.

She laughed and waved at the air between them, brushing his compliment away. "I am a widow with an eleven-year-old daughter nearly as tall as I am."

Though he opened his mouth to answer, another person appeared. A servant, seeking cherries for her mistress. Then came another, and another, until the cherries were gone. Teresa climbed into the wagon and stacked her empty baskets. She had sold a few, along with the cherries inside, which would mean a making purchases of baskets closer to home. But she had enough to purchase shoes for Caroline, the fabric for warm winter coats, and money to put by in case of any emergencies.

Mr. Duncan prepared the horse, then took them out of town the way they had come in. "Do you feel the day went in your favor?" he asked.

"I feel many things are in my favor of late." Teresa watched the people they passed, smiling to herself. "And what of your day? You were gone for some time."

"So I was." He offered her the reins. "Would you mind taking hold of these a moment?"

Amused, Teresa accepted, and he reached into his coat to pull out a pair of thick leather gloves. "It took me some time to find these." He slipped them on, then took out a slim book. "And here, a small collection of Shakespeare's Sonnets, for you and Miss Caroline."

"Oh, you did not have to—"

"Of course not. But I wanted to. I also have a bag of sweets for the ladies to enjoy." He tucked the book back inside his coat and reached for the reins again, which she gave up to him freely. He faced forward, his attention on the road.

"Mr. Duncan, you are too kind."

"Not really. I left you to yourself all morning." He shrugged his shoulders, almost as more of a stretch than a gesture. "I knew you could take care of things on your own, though. Apart from being an attractive woman, you are highly capable."

Teresa should not have spoken so openly to him about his looks. It invited such comments to be returned in kind. "I think we had better leave our opinions about such things unsaid, Mr. Duncan."

"That would likely be wise. The last time I complimented a lady, her husband threatened to call me out." He sighed deeply, and Teresa almost laughed.

"That is a jest, surely."

He turned just enough in her direction to offer a wink. "Perhaps."

Teresa bit her lip, trying not to grin. The man's behavior was never exactly inappropriate, but she sensed a great deal of playfulness hiding beneath the surface of his polite veneer. If she had not adapted to the working class life, if she had met him in a ballroom or at a card party, perhaps she would glimpse even more of his wit and charm.

The drive home was more pleasant than the one to town, and they stopped to eat a simple repast of bread, fruit, and cider while the horse watered himself at a stream. Teresa nibbled at an apple while reading through the book of sonnets, already planning on which she would ask Caroline to memorize first.

Some were likely inappropriate for such a young girl, given how passionately themes of love were proclaimed within them. But Shakespeare was an essential part of any English child's studies.

Mr. Duncan sat with his legs stretched before him, leaning back upon his elbows, watching the horse at the stream. The road was within an easy distance, and more than one person had passed since they had stopped for a rest.

"I have been thinking," Mr. Duncan said abruptly, "about your late husband."

Teresa lowered the book, keeping her place with her thumb. "I beg your pardon? Thinking of Henry? Whatever for?"

"You were married to him for ten years. I come from a family full of secrets. Even if I could not tell what someone was hiding from me, there were always signs of secrets. Was there truly nothing that made you wary of your husband's behavior?"

Her throat tightened on her last swallow of apple, and Teresa had to drink more cider to rid herself of the unpleasant sensation before she could answer. "There was nothing. I have thought on it again and again, but perhaps he was a very good actor. Or he did not think it wrong, so he did not behave as though there was anything amiss."

That answer did not seem to convince Mr. Duncan. He leaned all the way back, tucking his hands behind his head. The man was long, from head to toe, and he certainly filled his clothes out well, though she would never call him a broad man. He had an elegant, trim and masculine stature.

Did men object to being called elegant?

Teresa pushed that wayward thought aside and brought her focus back to the topic at hand. "The solicitor and Frederick were very clear on the matter. Henry lost everything he could lose. And then some."

"My brother is a gambler," Mr. Duncan said, his eyes still on the clouds drifting overhead. "It is not something one can hide, when they feel the call to cards. It becomes something of an obsession, the way others rely upon drink or laudanum. They find any excuse to sneak away to tables. They constantly think of getting away from company to feed the hunger."

With a sick twist in her stomach, Teresa closed the book. "I never saw Henry behave in such a way." Her words sounded defensive, even to her. But she had no wish to continue the conversation. None at all. To distract herself from the topic, she began tidying away their food back into the basket her mother had packed. Mr. Duncan did not move to help her, but he did turn his head to watch.

"Teresa—"

She dropped their tin cups into the basket with a loud clatter. "*Mrs. Clapham.*"

He sat up then, bringing up his knees and resting his forearms upon them. "I beg your pardon. That was a slip of the tongue."

"That, I do not believe. You were testing me. Come. I need to return home. There is work to be done." She lifted the hamper and went to the wagon. She heard him sigh, and then he called to the horse. Teresa climbed atop the wagon without assistance and took her seat.

She told herself she had grown upset because Mr. Duncan had become too familiar, had asked too many personal questions. But he had not. Not really. Yet the turn in conversation to Henry's gambling had unsettled her.

Nothing about Henry gambling had ever made sense to Teresa. It had been easier to put aside thoughts of those circumstances once she, her mother, and Caroline came to the farm. To think on it again, to try to understand what she could not, merely to soothe Mr. Duncan's curiosity, would only prove a frustration to her.

Never mind that her pride had been hurt, too. The man had dared to compliment her looks, not once but twice that day. Seeing him as anything other than a laborer would not be wise. Even if he was a gentleman, and witty, and charming. Nothing could ever come from a flirtation with such a man, especially given her current state.

Teresa looked down at her hands, brown and calloused, her nails short and her knuckles rough from work. They were not the hands of a lady. They never would be again.

She was a farmer. And he was a temporary hireling, likely to return to his family once their problems were resolved, leaving her behind upon her patch of dirt.

Chapter Thirteen

Neil stood beneath one of the cherry trees, now stripped of fruit by birds as well as the people on the farm. Mr. Putnam, leaning heavily on a rough-hewn cane, stood next to him. "You see that branch, there? It's not got a leaf or stem upon it. You need to get it down, before it hurts the rest of the tree."

"It is only a dead branch." Neil folded his arms over his chest and peered up into the shadows of the tree. "Surely it can stay where it is until the wind brings it down."

But the old man shook his head. "Nay, lad. The branch may be blighted. Cherry trees, they are forgiving if the bad branches are removed right away. But if it's left, the whole tree could be sick by next spring. You need to go through the orchard and cut off every limb not bearing leaves."

Neil looked from the tree above him to the others, his heart sinking. There were a lot of trees. He had been sick of them, fully, when they harvested the last of the cherries the week before. Teresa had stopped working near him and only addressed him when she needed to give him the next chore upon the growing list.

He had mucked out the stables every other day, chopped wood, fetched and carried grain from the nearest town, fixed the fence on the property, and tilled up more dirt for an expansion of Teresa's herb garden. He had been gathering deadfall from around the property and bringing it to the house to break into kindling, when Mr. Putnam had appeared and informed him of Teresa's new chore.

Lopping off tree branches.

Neil looked back over his shoulder at the house, glaring at the back door. Though their relationship had started unusually, he had thought a friendship had begun to grow between Teresa and himself. Until he opened his mouth to talk about her husband's gambling. Or had it been his use of her Christian name that drove a wedge between them?

It seemed he would forever attempt friendly relationships with the wrong people.

He sighed and turned to the tree again.

"Mr. Duncan?" The old man studied him, his bushy gray eyebrows drawn together. "Is there something on your mind, lad?"

With a forced smile, Neil shook his head. "Not at all. Thank you for showing me what must be done. I will begin at once." Even if the ache in his left arm was enough to make him wince. It hurt nearly precisely where he had broken it the year before.

"Best get a move on, then. Rain is coming. I feel it." The old man patted his wrist.

"In your bones, hm?" Neil asked, amused.

"Aye. Where I broke this one, thirty years ago. I was about your age. Fell off the back of a wagon and snapped my wrist." Mr. Putnam tucked his hand into his coat pocket. "It never fails to warn me of a change in the weather. The rest of me just aches about all the time." He chuckled and started on his way.

A break in the bone. Interesting. Neil's arm, broken in a

carriage accident, might serve him the same way. How unfortunate.

He went along to the barn to fetch a ladder and a saw he had seen with a long handle. Once inside, Neil shed his coat, too. The work would go faster, and likely be safer, with more freedom of movement.

He returned to the orchard, grateful when he saw clouds moving in to block the sun.

His skin had turned darker with each day spent outside. His hat and neckcloth could only protect so much of him. The gloves helped a great deal. The blisters had stopped appearing, but his hands were rougher than they had ever been.

Yet he did not utter a single word of complaint. Not to Mrs. Godwin, Caroline, Teresa, or even in private to any of the animals. The women worked as hard as he did, and had been at it longer, though even less prepared for such a way of life than he. If Teresa could sing and hum as she performed the labor of a peasant, he could bite his tongue.

Though he said several choice words over the lack of any word from his mother and sister. Every other day, he rode to Dunwich to check for any post. Nothing had come, though it had been nearly a fortnight since his arrival at Bramble Cottage.

His mother might have at least written to him and revealed who his true father had been. He could think of no one in their lives that he resembled and doubted the affair had continued for too many years. Though he and Olivia looked a great deal alike, and seven years separated them in age.

Going down that path with his thoughts would lead nowhere. But all his thoughts seemed to take him that direction of late. Trying to determine why his father had leaped upon the opportunity to banish Neil had no explanation he could turn up. He could write to his brothers, but neither of *them* were ever interested in anyone outside of themselves. They would likely take his father's part. Whatever it was. Maybe he ought to write some of his acquaintances in London, though they might spurn him as those in the country had done. Leaving him, again, nowhere.

The saw seemed to laugh at him as he pushed it through each branch. The push made a shush sound, the pull a harsher growl, and when the movement was fast enough he heard the word in the work: *nowherenowherenowhere*.

The branch fell, and Neil climbed down the ladder and went to the next tree. He looked up and found a branch devoid of leaves, far above the reach of the ladder. That meant he would need to climb into the branches as he had when picking cherries. But the work would be more difficult, moving the saw.

With a shrug, Neil reconciled himself to the climb. Up he went, thoughts still circling.

His birth, the marquess, his heartless family, were all better forgotten.

That left him to think on Teresa and her situation. Despite what she believed, he doubted her husband had been a true gambler. And one or two nights of bad luck would not have left the family in such financial straits. There was more to that story than Teresa knew, and the appearance of her brother-in-law the previous week only made Neil's suspicions grow.

But he doubted Teresa would speak to him of any of it.

Stubborn woman.

And since his last conversation with her on the subject had led to her cool temperament, he had no wish to revisit the matter.

It was all a mess.

He pushed the saw into the branch, pulled back on it roughly, and at the same moment—

"Mr. Duncan?"

He slipped. The saw stayed in the branch, but Neil slid downward. He whacked his knee into a branch below and grabbed at another, but slid once more so that his elbow smacked into the trunk of the tree. He caught a branch at last, wrapping his arm about it, and looked down.

The accident should not have happened. Yet there he was, hanging several feet in the air.

"Mrs. Clapham," he growled, then released the branch. His feet hit the ground, and he bent his knees to take some impact out of the fall. But she rushed forward, reaching for him, and Neil stumbled back, his tailbone hitting the earth with an unso-phisticated thump.

He groaned.

"Oh, I am terribly sorry." Teresa appeared before him and kneeled, heedless of her dress in the dirt. "Are you hurt?" Her hand went to his cheek.

Neil's irritation with the entire situation made him act rashly. At least, that was what he told himself when he took the hand from his cheek and pulled her forward into his arms.

THOUGH TERESA'S HEART HAD ALREADY STUTTERED and then sped up watching Mr. Duncan fall through the tree—Heavens, what if he were killed?—it positively galloped when he pulled her down beside him, his arms going around her.

She ought to protest immediately. But when she attempted to reprimand him, her words came out breathy rather than stern. "Mr. Duncan. Stop this." She cleared her throat and leaned away from him. "Has the fall addled your head?"

He groaned, kept one arm about her shoulder while rubbing at the back of his head with the opposite hand. "It may have."

She peered more closely at him, then wriggled out from under his arm. "I am not some green girl barely out in Society, Mr. Duncan. I know a trick when I see one, and if you think for one moment I would encourage such attentions—"

"I would never dare to presume such a thing, Mrs. Clapham." His sigh came out with exasperation. "Though I will admit freely that you are quite lovely, even when you are flustered."

Teresa narrowed her eyes at him. She refused to be taken in by pretty words and compliments. She drew a folded paper out of her apron. "I came out here to give you this." She thrust it toward him, trying not to study the beautiful penmanship directing the letter to *Mister Neil Duncan, Lost Mermaid Public House, Dunwich, Suffolk.*

Mr. Duncan took the paper from her almost hesitantly, his eyes running over the handwriting. "Olivia," he muttered before breaking the seal. Teresa averted her eyes, even though it would be a simple matter to read along with him.

"I will leave you to it." She made as if to stand, but his hand closed around her wrist. Teresa stiffened and prepared to give him another dressing down.

The soft look in his eyes made her hesitate. "Please, do not rush off so quickly. It is a short letter. My sister writes only to tell me that the situation has not yet changed, and to stay where I am." He dropped the letter into the grass beside him, then lowered himself all the way back to the ground, staring up at the branches of the tree.

Teresa had no business staying. She knew she ought to leave him to his thoughts, however complicated they might be. And she certainly had no reason to silently rejoice that *Olivia* was a relation and not a *paramour*. Mr. Duncan's sister.

"I did not know you had gone to town," Mr. Duncan said, before she made up her mind whether to stay or go.

"I have not been. Mr. Jones came to ask if we had more cherries to sell, and he brought the letter with him." Teresa shifted next to Mr. Duncan, then allowed herself to look down at his handsome face. His whiskers were grown out again. Not to the point that they made him any less enjoyable to look at, of course. His hat had come off in his fall, leaving his blond hair to curl just above his forehead.

Mr. Duncan's eyes flicked to hers, catching her staring. She forced a smile.

"I am sorry you did not receive better news, Mr. Duncan."

"As am I. It means I must trespass upon your hospitality longer yet."

"You mean that you must work to earn your keep a while yet," she countered, trying to tease a smile back upon his face. He looked far too dignified when he frowned.

It worked, at least a little. One corner of his mouth turned upward. "I suppose that is good news to you, Mrs. Clapham."

"Of course it is. I appreciate having a pair of hands to fetch and carry for me." She poked his arm with one finger, and he chuckled. Why had she been avoiding him of late? It felt good, to sit beside him. "I would far rather see you climbing about on ladders and mucking out stables than perform the tasks myself."

To Teresa's surprise, his expression softened at those words. His smile gentled, the light in his eyes brightening as he spoke. "Even though you have done an admirable job for months, without my help? You are a marvel, Mrs. Clapham. Every time I think on what you have done all this time, just you, Caroline, and Mrs. Godwin..." His voice trailed away, though his gaze remained persistent.

Why could she not look away?

"We have managed, but it has been a near thing at times." He need not know how she struggled, especially in the beginning. And yet. Telling someone might relieve the burden upon her weary shoulders. "When we first came, we had a little money my mother had put by from her own marriage settlement. It was enough to repair a few things, and hire men to plow a field and get the barn ready for a cow. We bought Abigail, and the chickens, and saw to the most pressing household needs. But the money will not last forever, so we save it now." The repairs needed for the house and barn to be livable had been extensive and needed with immediacy. Animals had cost a pretty sum as well.

"You bear up well." Mr. Duncan sounded almost admiring.

Teresa scoffed and folded her hands in her lap, looking away from him at last, staring through the orchard trees to the field, and beyond that to the barn and house. "No. I hide my difficulties well. The truth is, before you came, I was quite terrified of what winter would mean for us. So thank you, Mr. Duncan, for doing so much for us."

He sat up again, shifting to face her. "I have never worked so hard in my life." He drew off first one leather glove and then the other, dropping them on the ground. "And if you knew me better, you would not be so quick to praise me. You have taken on the welfare of your family. I am not even worthy of your time."

Had Teresa not been staring directly at him, had she not glimpsed the pain in his eyes, she could have shrugged off his words as mere flirting. "You cannot believe that, Mr. Duncan." She leaned closer, her words earnest. "I may not know much of your past. You have left me only guesses at your history. But I can see who you are in all that you do. You are kind to my daughter and take the time to answer all her ridiculous questions. You are respectful to my mother, never forgetting to ask if she has need of your help. And you have never once looked down upon us or our circumstances."

He leaned closer, his eyebrows drawn together. "I would be a fool to do so, my dear." The endearment made her heart leap, but he did not leave her time to think on it. "I am not nearly so noble as you believe me to be. Because if I was, I would not dare do this."

The remaining distance between them vanished in an instant, and his lips were upon hers. It was not a passionate lover's embrace, but it was not the gentle press of lips from an innocent, either. His lips slanted over hers perfectly, giving rather than taking. He did not touch her otherwise. No hand to her cheek or waist. Only his mouth, inviting her to partake if she wished.

Teresa leaned into the kiss, returning the token with hesitancy. It was heavenly, to breathe him in, to know that a man she admired found her attractive and even desirable. The temptation to give in further, to deepen the kiss, nearly overtook her. But—

Teresa pulled away, and he remained still, not chasing after her. Not demanding more than she would give.

Her eyes fluttered open.

Neil looked away, gathering up his gloves and the letter. "Forgive me, Mrs. Clapham. I do not know what came over me." He stepped away, turning to scoop up his hat.

Mortification filled her. Had she done something wrong? Other than kiss him back, of course. Oh, she had behaved foolishly. Teresa struggled up to her feet and glared at his back. "Mr. Duncan."

He put his hat on, then his gloves, and turned slowly to look at her. "Yes, madam?"

His bearing was noble as ever. Shoulders straight, chin up, and as tall and athletic in appearance as any Adonis from her days in Society. But the confidence was gone from his eyes. The smugness had disappeared from the twist of his smile.

It was impossible to understand him. And she should *not* have returned his kiss. She had a responsibility to her mother and daughter, and to herself, to avoid dalliances and distractions. That was what she had been thinking in the instant she pulled away.

"Tomorrow, I need you to speak to Mr. Putnam about thatching roofs. Ours is in terrible need of repair."

Thunder rumbled in the distance. Teresa wrapped her arms about herself. More rain meant more damage to her roof, attic, and house. It also meant she could not go for her walk to the cliffs that day. Which she sorely needed, to clear her mind.

"Yes, madam." He gathered his ladder. "I will see to it first thing."

Teresa nodded. "And do not speak of what happened a moment ago to anyone."

He paused and quirked an eyebrow at her. "Do you think I would?"

She blushed. No. He seemed too kind to humiliate her that way. But there was no use admitting as much. "Just see to it you do not." Then she strode by him, making her way to the house as quickly as possible. Trying not to think of the way her lips tingled and her whole body went warm and soft beneath his attentive kiss.

Chapter Fourteen

Muttering to himself as he tromped through the wet, drippy trees, Neil roundly cursed every aspect of his homeland's weather. The mud sucked at his boots, too, and there would be no valet to clean them. If Neil wanted them restored, he'd be the one to work out how to scrape off the dirt clods without damaging the leather.

The worst thing was, of course, that he had brought the entire situation upon himself by leaving the long-handled saw out in the weather rather than bringing it in with him.

Why had he even attempted the chore? What did he know about pruning trees? The only associations he had ever had with that particular bit of flora had been when he climbed them as a boy or lounged beneath them as an indolent youth.

The mistake certainly had not been made due to distraction. Not at all. Kissing the enchanting Teresa Clapham had not addled his wits. He was too sophisticated. Too worldly—

And obviously too starved of companionship, to go about kissing a woman who did not want to be kissed.

It was like what had happened with Lady Inglewood all over

again. Except Teresa's loyalty was to her home and family, not an absent husband.

Or maybe it was. Lack of mourning attire after a year did not mean anything.

Neil found the spot where he'd fallen from the cursed cherry tree, easily recognizable by the man-sized dent in the soft earth. But he didn't see the saw upon the ground. He muttered to himself and looked upward. There the instrument waited for him, still halfway through the branch, and now perilously out of reach given the damp branches.

Would one night in the rain ruin the tool?

Neil debated whether the tool or his safety might be of more importance to Mrs. Clapham.

Most certainly, it would be the saw.

He would need to go all the way back to the barn to get the ladder if he hoped to reach the saw without breaking his head open. Defeat pulled him downward. He dropped his head and relaxed his shoulders, feeling the raindrops hit him upon the back of his neck. Without a fine collar and cravat, without a stylish hat or warm greatcoat, the elements could further testify as to how low he had fallen.

A soft whine reached his ears. A pathetic, hopeless sound. The very sound his soul would make, were he to lose the last shred of pride. But the noise had not come from him. Not yet.

Then where—?

Neil turned toward the hedgerow. On the other side of it was a lane, commonly used by the farmers in the area. He went that way, eyes searching through the brush for whatever creature might be concealed inside.

Another whine, softer and longer, made him hasten his steps.

A dog. It had to be a dog.

Neil came to the hedges and bent, trying to peer closer to the ground. But an overcast sky and overgrown bushes made it difficult to see anything. He gave one glance to the heavens, wondering when he might be showed any mercy at all, before dropping to his knees upon a pile of wet, dead leaves. Then he crouched lower, on all fours, searching deep in the branches.

A pair of eyes stared back, from above a long snout and in a fur-covered face. The animal had blue eyes, gray tufts of fur, and the thinnest belly Neil had ever seen on a dog.

"Oh, you poor devil." Neil kept his voice soft, unwilling to cause the animal further distress. The bedraggled creature was likely frightened. He whistled quietly and held his hand out in invitation. The dog pushed itself deeper into the hedge and turned its head away from him.

An animal trained as a guard dog would react defensively. Most of the hunters he'd raised would've wagged a tail and come out, head ducked down. But this creature behaved as though it hoped to be ignored and forgotten. A gentle animal, then, likely with reason to distrust a man.

Neil considered the animal. If he pretended he had never seen the dog, walked away, it would likely be gone as soon as the rain let up. Which might occur sooner rather than later.

Neil slowly backed away from the blackberry brambles, rose to his feet, and walked calmly back toward the house. When he was several yards away from the dog, he picked up the pace, almost running toward the cottage. When he arrived at the back door, he nearly ran directly through, but remembered his boots before stepping on the kitchen floor.

That likely saved him from a rebuke from Mrs. Godwin. He cleared his throat and looked inside.

Caroline sat at the worktable, holding a biscuit. Her eyebrows went clear up to her black curls.

"Caroline," he said, grinning widely at her. "I need a few of those biscuits. Would you get them for me?"

The sweet child did not even ask a question. She beamed back at him, likely pleased because he finally needed something from her. She slid off the bench and ran to the pantry. When she came out again, both hands were full of ginger and shortbread biscuits. She held them out to him, her grin wide. "Here you are, Mr. Duncan."

"Thank you." He bowed deeply as he accepted the abundance of treats. "I'll have a story to tell you later." He winked, then hurried back into the rain.

It didn't take him long to return to the bushes, pockets full of sweets. He found where he had kneeled before and resumed the position. The dog was still there. It made eye contact with him a moment and then tried to ignore him again.

"That's hardly friendly," Neil said, soft and coaxing. "I've gone to get you something. A real treat." He took a shortbread biscuit from one of his pockets and held it out to the animal, still too far away from him for him to touch it. The dog's eyes moved and froze upon seeing his hand. Hunger shone in the pitiful animal's eyes.

Good.

Neil tossed the biscuit directly beneath the dog's snout.

Cautiously, the animal bent and sniffed the biscuit once before gulping it down. Neil grinned at his success and tossed another biscuit, this one ginger. The dog snapped it up even faster. Neil tossed the next one a few inches closer to himself.

"There's a good dog. Try another bite of biscuit." He soothed with his voice, bringing the dog closer with each treat, and backing away from the bush. The dog stopped just shy of leaving cover, watching Neil carefully. Slowly the gray head raised, the dog's blue eyes wide and afraid. Its tail wagged, hesitantly.

"You can trust me," Neil said, still low to the ground. He held out his hand with another biscuit as far from himself as he could reach. "I promise. I've never hurt any creature, and dogs are my favorite of all four-legged sorts."

The animal sniffed the biscuit, then carefully took it from him and chewed it to bits before swallowing. Neil held out only his hand next. The dog sniffed at it, then licked at his fingertips, likely tasting all the leftover bits of sugar and ginger. The tail wagged again, with somewhat more enthusiasm than before.

Slowly, Neil moved his hand to scratch behind the dog's floppy gray and black ears. He'd never seen a dog bred to look the way this one did. The gray, wavy coat was reminiscent of a Spaniel, but the structure of the animal's head was all wrong, the snout too long. Its tail hadn't been cropped, had no curl to the bone, and the fur grew long enough to make a banner of the tail when it wagged.

A mongrel, then. The dog was likely the product of an unwanted mix of parents. But it wasn't a puppy. It hadn't been killed at birth, as most unwanted litters suffered that fate from kennel masters. Where had the poor bedraggled thing come from?

He offered the animal another ginger biscuit.

"Wherever you came from, and whatever your lineage, I will not turn you away now." Neil scratched the dog behind its ears, pleased when the animal leaned into his touch. "Wary beast that you are, I can't imagine you've been treated well in the past." He carefully wrapped his arms around the dog's legs before standing, lifting the animal with him.

The dog did not fight him, but relaxed against his chest. It seemed he'd won the animal's trust. Or perhaps the creature was too hungry, tired, and wet to care what became of it.

But Neil cared, much to his own surprise, and the dog would soon find itself warm and dry. And fed on more than biscuits.

Chapter Fifteen

Teresa fretted at the kitchen window, looking out repeatedly across the barnyard to where the lantern light glowed from the open doorway. Her mother sat behind her at the table, reading by another lamp the book of sonnets Mr. Duncan had gifted them.

"What is taking Caroline so long?" Teresa asked.

She had decided it would be best to let her daughter practice milking Abigail at night. Not because Teresa wished to avoid the barn that evening. Of course not. It was merely time for the girl to take on greater responsibility, and Caroline always wanted to check on her kitten anyway. The arrangement made sense.

The only sound in the kitchen was when Mother turned the page in the book. Until she spoke. "You will bite a hole through your lip if you keep that up."

Immediately, Teresa let her lip out of her teeth. She pulled her shawl closer. "Old habit."

"Very old." Mother put a ribbon between the pages of the book and closed it. "You used to do that when you were a child, working yourself up to ask for something you were certain your father or I would deny you."

Teresa relaxed, letting out a strained laugh. "Was I a vexatious child?"

"No more so than our sweet Cara." Mother looked at the door, then pointedly at Teresa. "You may as well go and see what is keeping her. Mothers often must go looking for wandering daughters. At least until they're old enough to know best when to come home."

"I am certain Caroline is well enough out there." Teresa looked out the window again and pulled her bottom lip between her teeth before catching herself.

"Teresa." Her mother pointed to the door. "Out with you."

"You do not understand, Mother." Teresa went to the door, going so far as to rest her hand on the latch. "I have complicated things between Mr. Duncan and myself."

Mother sniffed and turned her back on Teresa. "Oh, dear child, I understand quite well. Never doubt that."

"And you would still send me out there?" Teresa asked, hesitantly. Her mother could not truly know and certainly never guess that her only daughter had kissed a man that very day. The man currently residing in their barn.

"I would." Mother rose and took her book up. "Good night, Teresa."

"Good night, Mother." Teresa watched her mother go through the kitchen into the main room of the house, then turned back to the door. Strengthening her resolve, Teresa undid the latch and walked out into the night, toward the barn.

When she entered, her lamp in hand, she did not immediately spy her daughter or Mr. Duncan. She heard him speaking, though.

"We cannot always tell what a creature has been through by looking at them, be it man or beast. But people certainly hide things better. This poor creature, you can see she is afraid, though she wants to trust me."

Teresa paused, waiting for her daughter to answer.

"It is a good thing you found her, Mr. Duncan. She is so sweet and gentle." One could hear compassion in Caroline's voice. Her heart was always quick to love and care for people and animals alike. It would be hard on her the day Mr. Duncan left.

Likely hard on all of them. The man had stirred up their lives with his company, his quick wit. And now, for Teresa, with his kisses.

She called out from the entrance to the barn. "Cara, dear, have you finished milking Abigail?"

The straw in the empty stall between Abigail's and the horse shifted, then Caroline peeped over the wall. "Mama, come and see what Mr. Duncan found."

Given that Abigail did not complain and moan at the sound of Teresa's voice, the cow had likely been seen to. Teresa held her lantern up and approached the middle stall, where Caroline's head disappeared again.

When she came close enough to look over, the sight that met her gaze warmed her heart. Caroline sat in one corner with her lantern and kitten; in the opposite corner sat Mr. Duncan, his lantern out of his reach. In his lap, he held a dog. The dog's head was upon Mr. Duncan's knee, its eyes nearly closed, and Mr. Duncan was carefully combing through the matts of the dog's hindquarters.

He looked up at Teresa, and he shared no more than a tip of the head before focusing on the animal again. The dog trembled but did not resist his ministrations.

She kept her voice low as she spoke. "Where did that poor thing come from?"

Mr. Duncan's tone was gentle, soothing even. "I found her beneath the brambles, in the rain. I fed her some of my dinner, and she trusts me enough now to let me get her clean." The dog shuddered and turned its head into his side as though hiding, then it huffed.

Caroline giggled. "I think she likes Mr. Duncan. He saved her."

"That he did." Teresa smiled at her daughter. "And it's kind of you to look in on them both, but if you have milked Abigail you had better take the milk inside and go on to bed."

"Yes, Mama." Caroline stood, kissed her kitten on the head, and came out of the stall. The dog's ears twitched when the latch clicked shut again. Caroline grinned at her mother, took up the pail where she had left it on a barrel, and Teresa followed her inside. The child was likely already planning how to play with the dog the next day and win its affection.

Once the milk was seen to, Teresa kissed her daughter's forehead and sent her to bed. But Teresa hesitated to make her own way up the stairs. She stood still, in the main room of the house, and looked to the basket upon the shelf full of her sewing things. Her best scissors were in that basket. It would be simple enough to have them sharpened again, and that dog's fur had been in rather terrible shape.

She went to the basket and found what she needed. Then, after another moment of hesitation, she fetched Henry's shaving kit where she had left it in a cupboard. She hadn't given it to Neil before, as it had seemed too personal a gift.

"I might as well see them both trimmed," she said. Leather pouch and scissors in one hand, lantern in the other, Teresa went back outside.

She had only been away from the barn for ten minutes, perhaps. Yet she was relieved to find that Mr. Duncan had not moved from where she had seen him before. Teresa hung her lantern from a hook above the stalls, then entered. The dog in Mr. Duncan's lap trembled again.

"Poor little thing," she whispered.

Mr. Duncan did not glance up at her. "Wherever she came from, she was treated poorly. I cannot think why. This dog has not barked, and she's not even once tried to bite. If she was not kept as a guard dog, why mistreat her?"

"Some people are cruel for cruelty's sake." Teresa lowered herself to the straw next to Mr. Duncan, on the side near the dog's tail, where most of the tangles were. She put the shaving pouch aside and kept the scissors in hand. "I brought some shears. If you wish to keep her calm, I can trim out the worst of the knots. It does not look as though you can do much more with your comb."

He looked down at the tool in his hand. "You are right, of course. Thank you." He looped one arm gently beneath the dog's body and used the other hand to keep stroking her gray and brown fur. "She seems to do better when I'm talking. That is why Caroline stayed. My conversation kept her outside. I apologize."

He still had not looked at her.

"Caroline's little heart would break if she saw a creature like this be neglected. I imagine sitting here with you did her a great deal of good." Teresa used the comb herself to lift the matted fur away from the rest, keeping her hand gentle. When the shears opened, the dog cringed and whined. "Poor dear girl. We best keep talking."

"I hope your afternoon was pleasant, Mrs. Clapham."

Teresa's eyes narrowed, and she looked at him, finally catching him looking at her. His smile was weak at best.

Had her rejection of his kiss actually hurt him? That would put the situation in a new light entirely. If Mr. Duncan had been hurt, perhaps there had been more to the kiss than an impulsive gesture.

She turned her attention back to her work. "It was pleasant enough. There was a great deal of work to do, but we have put up all the cherries in the jars I bought with the market money. Now we can trade or sell the jars."

"A wise investment." Mr. Duncan rubbed the dog's ears, and the animal's shaking slowed. "It is admirable, how careful you are with your funds."

Teresa lifted one shoulder in a shrug. "Saving pennies here

and there has kept us fed and clothed. Some years ago, I never thought much about it. I have had to learn."

There was a bit of his old teasing back in his voice as he spoke. "As I have had to learn any number of things these past days. Tomorrow, I will have been here three weeks. Have I come along enough, do you think?"

"Certainly." She snipped off a particularly awful knot, then immediately gave the dog a gentle pat. "Especially when it comes to mucking out the stalls. One would think you had previous practice."

"Some. My specialty was actually in dog kennels." He smirked, and then leaned his head back against the stall wall. "It was a regular form of discipline, for me to clean my father's kennels."

"Dear me. Regular." Teresa kept combing, looking for more places where the teeth of the comb could not pass. "Were you a very ill-behaved boy?"

"I must have been." Mr. Duncan's eyes closed, but he kept comforting the dog. "But the punishment hardly mattered to me. I was never happier than when I was with the dogs. They are good creatures, when they are not half-starved before a hunt. They are loyal. Affectionate without reserve."

Teresa heard something in his voice, something sad and lonely. She worked on the animal's tail a moment before deciding to pursue her thought. "Not like people. People hold back their affection, they love conditionally."

Mr. Duncan lowered his head again, his eyes green in the lantern light. "Especially the people that I know. Yes."

"Even your sister?" Teresa asked, remembering his letter, and the odd relief that had come to her when she realized the lady was his relative. Only—she told herself—because that meant no one was calling him home right away.

Mr. Duncan shrugged, adjusted his hold on the dog, who nuzzled her nose back into his coat to hide. "Even my sister. I thought she was different. Growing up, the two of us were quite close. But Livvy—" He swallowed. "Olivia changed after she entered Society. She liked the games too much. Playing with people's reputations, their hearts, and flaunting her popularity. I suppose she only did as our mother trained her to do."

Teresa nodded a little. She had met women like that in the past. "Can we turn your dog to her other side, please?"

Neil carefully rolled the dog, putting her back to his stomach. She did not seem to like it, but as soon as his hand resumed his gentle attentions, she stilled again.

"Why do you suppose you are different? That you do not behave as your family does?" Teresa asked, taking him back to their conversation. When he did not immediately answer, she glanced up at him, wincing. "I have overstepped."

"No." His lips quirked upward, but his eyebrows had drawn together tightly. "I suppose I ought to confess to you that I am *not* different."

"Your sister does not sound like someone who would bother herself to help a poor woman on her farm," Teresa said lightly, working gently through the dog's fur.

"I suppose not. But I am getting something out of our arrangement, do not forget."

"A roof overhead, and peasant food." Teresa kept her words light, amused. She accepted the truth of her situation well enough. "And you have never once complained."

"Not out loud," he corrected, though his smile had widened. "I have never heard you complain, either."

"That is different. This is my life. What would complaining do, except place more weight and drudgery upon my shoulders?"

Mr. Duncan's eyes softened, and he moved his arm to gently nudge her shoulder. "Come now, Mrs. Clapham. We both know there are people who complain about every facet of their lives. Even if there is no more wrong than a cushion misplaced upon their couch."

A giggle escaped her, as she had known several ladies who

would bemoan such a small thing as though their worlds were ending. "Mr. Duncan, we cannot judge others so harshly. Perhaps a misplaced cushion is the only tragedy they have ever known. They have nothing greater to measure it against."

He raised his eyebrows and shook his head with a dramatic sigh. "There. You have proven again that you are a woman like none I have met before. Compassionate and merciful."

Teresa lowered her gaze to the dog again, her fingers having found another knot. Never mind that she also wished to hide a pleased smile. "I can attribute those same qualities to you, sir, in this very moment."

He spoke dismissively. "I am fond of dogs."

"And kind to kittens, talkative children, stubborn cattle—I saw the chase Abigail led you on yesterday, you know—and respectful to women who have fallen from Society's rungs. You cannot fool me. Perhaps you know how to play Society's games, as your sister does, but I believe you are more the man who lives in my loft than whomever you were in a ballroom." Teresa's hands stilled. She bit her lip. Somehow, her little speech had gotten away from her. She had not meant to sound so admiring.

She cleared her throat when he said nothing, then snipped the last of the knots from the animal's leg. "There. She ought to be fine now, if she stays out of brambles."

Mr. Duncan took the dog from his lap and tucked her into the straw. "I need to find her a box. Dogs prefer smaller spaces to curl up."

"I likely have a few. Or a basket, if we find a shallow one." Teresa put her scissors in her apron pocket and stood, brushing off the dog hairs.

Mr. Duncan picked up the leather pouch she had brought and held it out to her.

"Oh. No. That is actually for you." Teresa tucked her hands behind her back. Despite the heat burning in her cheeks, she met his steady gaze. "A shaving kit. I thought you could use it. There is even some soap inside. Powdered, I think."

"Where did you get it?" he asked, lowering his hand. There was an intensity in his eyes that made her swallow, nervously.

"It was my husband's. I have no use for it now. But you said you preferred being shaved to bearded."

He shook his head. "I cannot take it, Mrs. Clapham." He lifted the pouch to her again. "I will see to my own needs."

Teresa stared at the pouch, and tears pricked at her eyes most unexpectedly. "I wish you would use it. You may not understand, but I only want to show my gratitude for all you have done. At least borrow it, while you are here. When you leave, I will take it back."

He lowered his hand. "Is that why you disliked my kiss so much? The beard?" he asked, his tone too low and sorrowful to truly count the comment as teasing.

Teresa's gaze shot up to his, seeing the curiosity in his eyes, the wrinkle in his forehead. Speaking of that moment would do neither of them any good. But she would be lying to herself if she pretended it had not happened, for she had thought on nothing else all day. At the memory of his touch, her lips tingled, and her heart twisted.

"I—" She started, then stopped. Then tried again. "I did not dislike it. But I cannot repeat it. Or allow my thoughts to linger upon it. I am a poor widow, Mr. Duncan."

Teresa wrapped her arms about herself, trying to hold herself together. Did she owe him an explanation? The man had admitted to a flirtation with a married woman in the past. How many women had there been in his life? Women who would see nothing in a token so small as a kiss, women who might well go to greater lengths to experience pleasure without consequence.

He brushed his free hand through his hair, averting his eyes. "I thought, with the way you have looked at me at times…"

Mortification made her cheeks burn. "You know well enough what I think about your looks. But this is my fault. I am certain

I must have encouraged you. I loved my husband, very much. His memory is precious to me, despite what his decisions have done to our family." She squeezed her eyes shut. "And I am lonely. I miss what it meant to belong to someone that way." Teresa's fingers flexed against her shoulders, hating the pain she heard in the admission. "But I cannot allow myself to give way to such feelings. I have a reputation to maintain, a daughter to raise, and my own self-respect to look after. Do you understand?"

His voice was softer than before. "I believe I do."

Teresa relaxed, finally opening her eyes. His expression had closed, and it gave away nothing of his feelings. "As I have said, I know you are a compassionate man. I hope we can continue on, as friends."

"As friends." He nodded, then opened the stall door, standing aside for her to exit. "Thank you for your help with the dog."

As Teresa left the barn, having said all she wished, she wondered why she did not feel better than when she had entered the building.

Mr. Duncan understood her feelings at last. He had treated her with respect and understanding and would continue to do so.

"Then why," she whispered to her empty bedroom upon entering it, "do I feel that I have lost something?"

Chapter Sixteen

nother branch fell with a crack, causing Neil to wince. He looked down and over, to where Caroline sat in the sunshine with the dog in her lap, and the kitten pouncing on small insects nearby. The little girl was reading her sonnets out loud to the dog in an attempt to keep the animal calm.

She looked up, saw Neil watching, and waved. Her bright smile made his shoulders relax. He had tried to leave the dog in the stall, but the animal had whined and yipped until he let her out to follow him. But she did not like the crack of the tree branches falling. Thankfully, Caroline's arrival had soothed the agitated animal.

"What should we name her?" Caroline asked from where she sat, one arm full of gray dog and the other holding her book. "We can't keep calling her 'dog.'"

They certainly could. "Pick something you like," Neil called back, then turned to the next branch.

He had beaten back his disappointment over Teresa's rejection for the better part of the night, and most of the morning.

Teresa had no intention of allowing anything more affectionate than friendship between them. That sounded about right for Neil. Not that he had been offering a great deal more than flirtation. Or the mutual enjoyment of each other's company. He had not, he told himself firmly, dreamed up any plans of becoming emotionally or physically entangled with Teresa Clapham.

Merely looking at her, with her high-necked work dresses, spotless aprons, and kind eyes, was enough for a man to know she would countenance nothing but the sincerest of courtships. Neil had only attempted to court a woman once in his life, and she had happily strung him along until an heir to an earldom showed interest.

Another branch fell, and it was time to move on to the next tree.

Neil went down the ladder, saw in hand, and walked to the next cherry tree in need of attention. He climbed back up, his memory turning back to that horrid courtship. He had been twenty-three years old. Twelve long years had passed since that rejection, and his family's subsequent mockery.

His elder brothers had thought it a great joke that Neil had considered himself any kind of catch. Without their father's funds, he had nothing of his own. Lord Brunfield and then-Lieutenant Duncan had made it quite clear no woman would want him unless she already had a well-feathered nest.

Neil finished off another limb of the tree, wiped the sweat from his brow, and went back down to the ground. That task done, he started gathering branches into a heap. As they were dead or diseased, burning them in the house would not be a good idea until they were well dried. He needed to cut them into smaller pieces, stack them beneath the shelter of an eave, and find his next task.

Caroline stood and followed him, the dog on her heels, and cat pouncing along behind.

Despite his foul mood, Neil smiled when he saw the merry

parade. Despite the circumstances of Caroline's childhood, she was a cheerful girl.

If he had found a woman to marry, back when he still thought someone might have him, he might have a child Caroline's age. Of course, that child would be at school most of the year. Not following him about, even during holidays, because he would be in a study or elsewhere managing a wife's estate.

When Caroline stood close enough to where he would strip the wood using an old stump and handsaw on the dead cherry branches, she chirped, "I think we ought to call her Muse."

"Muse?" Neil stripped off his leather gloves and sat on the tall stump. "Why is that?"

"Because the muses used to help people with ideas, and people wanted them around. I think that name will make her feel useful and wanted." She bent to scratch the dog behind the ears.

"It sounds perfect, then. What about your cat? Have you named him yet?" Neil asked.

"I don't know if I should. Dogs will stay close by, if you feed them, but cats just disappear sometimes. The last one did." Caroline frowned and looked to where the cat had stopped pouncing in order to sun himself, all stretched out on his back with tail twitching.

Neil considered the cat, and her words, carefully. "Perhaps that is true. He may find another barn he likes better someday. Cats are wanderers at heart, I suppose. What was your other cat's name?"

Caroline sat, fluffing her dress as she did. Muse, the dog now bearing the title of Greek goddesses, crept closer until she could put her head in the child's lap.

"The last cat was Ginger. She was yellow and white."

"And do you hope she is well-treated, wherever she may have gone?"

Caroline nodded without hesitation. "She was a very good

cat. Sweet." But her shoulders fell more. "I wish she would have stayed."

Neil gave her an understanding smile. "I know. We cannot always control who comes into our life, or who leaves it. But I am certain most would tell you to make what you can out of the time you have. Name your kitten, Cara. Love him while he is here and wish him well when he goes."

To Neil's surprise, the little girl ducked her head and started to cry.

That had not been his intention, nor had he seen it coming. He came off the log and went to sit beside her. At his approach, Muse's tail started to thump happily against the ground. The dog lifted its head from her lap, appearing equally distressed by the child's change in temperament.

"Caroline. Did I say something unkind?" He had a handkerchief, clean, and in his coat pocket. But he had left the coat behind in the orchard. How did one comfort a crying child without a handkerchief to offer?

"N-n-no." Caroline made a handkerchief appear from her apron. She started dabbing at her eyes, but it seemed ineffectual. "But I do not want anyone else to leave."

"Anyone else?"

"Like my papa." She sniffled and wrapped her arms around Muse's neck. The dog snuggled into the girl's chest, as any self-respecting dog would. "I hated that he left. That he died. And then we had to leave our house. I like it here. But it was d-d-difficult." Tears glistened in her eyes as she turned her head toward Neil, putting her cheek atop Muse's head.

How had talk of a cat brought her to mourning her father? While Neil well knew fully grown women to be emotional creatures, he had not expected to find one so young susceptible to the same.

"That must have been very difficult for you." Neil pulled one knee up and rested his elbow upon it, looking out over the vegetable patch toward the road. "You miss your father still?"

She nodded and swiped at her eyes again. "Mama said he did not want to die and leave us. And I know that. But that doesn't stop it from hurting. Sometimes, it's hard to even remember him. I know he was tall, like you. But he had black hair, like me and Mama. And he laughed, all the time."

The poor mite. And yet, how fortunate she had been, to have a father that obviously adored her. Not all children were so lucky. Neil had not been. He sighed and took his hat off, scratching at his head. "Would you want to forget your father, if you could? If you could forget all about him and stop missing him, would you?"

Caroline shook her head, ruffling the dog's fur. "I would never want to forget him. Ever. That would be worse."

The cat chose that moment to come closer, batting at Neil's dangling fingers. He obliged the animal by stroking its back. "It hurts when someone leaves us, it hurts all the more if we cared for them. You loved your father a great deal. But forgetting him would be worse; it would leave a different pain and hole behind. There is nothing wrong with loving someone, or caring for a cat. It makes our lives better, I should think. Richer."

Caroline released a sigh and said, most reluctantly, "I know."

"Good. Because I happen to know the opposite is also true. There are very few people who care for me as your mother and grandmother do for you, Cara. I am the poorer for it. Everyone who loves you, and everyone you love, will give your life greater depth and joy. If you go about withholding your affection, simply because of what *might* happen, you will be lonely."

Much as he was. There was no one upon whom Neil could depend upon or call upon for aid. His sister's letter the day before had been terse, impatient with him. His mother had not written at all. He did not know if he expected her to do so until there was real news.

What had become of his life that it was so empty?

Neil rose and brushed off his trousers. Then he offered his

hand to Caroline and pulled her to her feet. "I need to go to the village, Caroline. Will you look after Muse for me?"

"Yes, Mr. Duncan." Then she offered him a wobbly smile, her eyes drier. "Thank you for speaking with me. I think you must be right." She looked down at the kitten, and the light of determination sparked in her eyes. "I want to name my kitten. What do you think of the name Cider?"

"A perfect name." Neil's chest grew heavy, though the girl smiled brightly at him before leaving, walking toward her house.

Muse looked up at Neil and whined. He sighed and pointed to Caroline. "Go on with the girl." The dog lowered her head and followed after Caroline. No doubt the child would shower Muse with love and more biscuits, if there were any.

Neil went to the barn and took up his saddle. Perhaps there would be a letter for him that day. Perhaps not. But he could use a drink of something other than cider, and some time to himself.

WHEN NEIL ARRIVED IN DUNWICH, THERE WERE NO letters waiting for him. Only two old men in the pub, Putnam and Higgins. The proprietor, Mr. Jones, served Neil a bowl of stew, a thick slice of bread, and a large mug of ale. Not precisely better than what he had consumed of late, but different. Different would need to be good enough.

Putnam and Higgins moved from their table at the front of the public dining room to his, against the wall, without his invitation. They brought their drinks with them.

"How are you enjoying working for our Mrs. Clapham?" Putnam asked. "She's a good sort, isn't she?"

"A fine gentlewoman," Neil agreed shortly, keeping his eyes upon his food. He had not come seeking out company.

"Too fine for that farm," Higgins said with a sigh. "I keep hoping that vicar will do something about them out there."

This was the first Neil had heard of a vicar. The women had gone to church after his arrival, but he had not attended with them. "What vicar?"

"Our vicar, at the church." Putnam chuckled before taking a long pull of his ale. "He's a widower."

Neil had to work to loosen his jaw enough to chew his bread. Once that was cleared, he tried to ask with disinterest, "Has he shown an interest in Mrs. Clapham?"

If a man of such standing as a vicar was interested in a woman, he ought not to wait around and let her continue the burden of caring for her family alone.

"Not Mrs. Clapham." Higgins chortled. "Mrs. Godwin. The man's sixty if he's a day, and he always makes a point of speakin' to Mrs. Godwin at length. My own missus has noticed and said he better get to courting if that's what he wants."

Relief made everything from the back of Neil's neck to his hands around his spoon relax. Apparently, Putnam noticed, given the way his eyes started twinkling.

"Courting is serious business," Putnam said. "Man has to be sure the woman is worth it."

Higgins settled back in his chair, cradling his drink in both hands. "One look at a woman can be enough for that," the old man said. He scratched at the whiskers on his chin. "Take Mrs. Clapham for example. Strong, handsome woman, even though she looks as though a strong wind might blow her over. Like as not could run a big house as well as she runs that farm."

"Aye. A woman of many talents." Putnam grinned most impudently at Neil.

Neil put more stew in his mouth to avoid talking. Perhaps the old men would take the hint and change the subject. But before they could, the door to the pub opened again. All three men glanced that way, though Neil could not say why he cared who had entered. He knew no one in the area, so he would not recognize the newcomer.

Except he did.

Mr. Frederick Clapham entered the public house, sweeping off his tall and fashionable hat. "Refreshment at once," he demanded, turning to the room. He stopped when his gaze fell upon Neil. Then he smiled, slowly. A predatory smile, if Neil had ever seen one.

"Gentlemen," Neil said quietly to Putnam and Higgins. "I think you had better change tables."

Higgins muttered something that sounded resentful, but he and Putnam stood and went back to their original table across the room. Mr. Clapham approached and bowed.

"Mr. Duncan, I believe? The gentleman farmer?"

Neil had no intention of revealing his true status, not to this man. Having practiced deceit himself, his first instinct about Clapham stayed with him. Something about the man made Neil uneasy and suspicious.

"Mr. Clapham." Neil did not stand, though he nodded once.

"May I join you?"

Neil gestured to the recently vacated chairs across the small table from him. "You may."

Mr. Jones returned with a tray. He hastily set tea, a plate of sandwiches, and a bowl of stew before the new arrival. It seemed he was familiar enough with Clapham to give him a specific sort of refreshment.

After Mr. Jones withdrew, Clapham took up his teacup. "When we met, I thought you only dressed as you did for the day's work. Now that I see you again, I wonder if you have a preference for such attire." He sipped at his cup.

With as smooth a tone and perfect elocution as ever he had used, Neil responded coldly. "I fail to see why my decisions regarding fashion would be worth any speculation. It is not as though we move in the same circles, Mr. Clapham." Disinterest was the way to act with this man. Clapham thought too highly of himself. Feeding into that might make the man lower his defenses, but Neil preferred to maintain his own dignity.

Clapham cleared his throat, lowering his eyes. Perhaps he had forgotten that Neil's accent marked him as someone perhaps even above himself.

"Quite true. But I do believe we understand one another when it comes to matters of honor, and of a woman's place in a family."

"Do we?" Neil affected a bored expression. "Mr. Clapham, if there is something you wish to say, I do wish you would spit it out. I am not an idle conversant."

Twin spots of red appeared on Clapham's cheeks, but he cleared his throat and leaned closer. "I have wondered, Mr. Duncan, where you are from. I have asked here and there after your name, and no one knows a Mr. Duncan. You can see then, I am merely concerned for my dear sister-in-law's reputation."

Neil chuckled, somewhat darkly. "Mrs. Clapham has nothing to fear from me, sir. I am nothing if not her humble servant." He did not lower his voice, did not lean closer, but spoke as though the topic were free for all to hear. "Mrs. Clapham is a fine lady. I honestly doubt you are truly concerned about her wellbeing. It is more likely, to my way of thinking, that you are concerned about your own. I gathered from our first meeting, and from what has been said of you by others, that you were all too happy to see her gone from your house. One must ask oneself, why? Why make her feel unwelcome, bid her farewell most happily, only to come back and insist she is not behaving as she ought? It is most curious behavior, Mr. Clapham."

Clapham paled. Then took a big gulp of his tea. He grabbed a sandwich. "There is nothing curious about my interest. My departed brother would expect no less."

That rubbed at Neil's temper. How could the man claim to honor his late brother's memory by turning out his widow? "I rather think any man would expect a great deal more of the person who is supposed to look after his wife."

The other man snapped his mouth shut upon the sandwich, then choked. After a moment of gasping, during which Neil only raised his eyebrows and waited, Clapham took hold of himself. "I beg your pardon."

"I do not give it."

People thought Neil was conniving. This man was hiding something, and it involved Teresa.

"Mr. Duncan, I have done what is right for Mrs. Clapham. It is she who decided to leave my protection, to take up her pitiful inheritance." Clapham squared his shoulders. "I am trying to keep my eye upon her, to make certain no one takes advantage of her innocence and *naïveté*. You are a man practically living at her property, from what I understand of the matter."

"You understand very little." Neil tapped his fingers on the table impatiently.

"What if I asked you to leave her alone?" Clapham asked at last. He attempted to sound sly and knowing. "To go your own way? Perhaps all that is keeping you here is the hope of funds. My sister-in-law has no money, as you must know." The man reached into his coat and pulled forth a small bag, full and heavy with coins given the sound it made when it hit the table. "I can give you the means to get beyond this place and strike out elsewhere."

Neil chuckled, thinking of his mother's necklace, his own coins, the earring he had not even sold yet. "I have no need of such a paltry sum."

Expression hardening, Mr. Clapham swiped the money up and tucked it back in his coat. "Then what will it take to be rid of you?"

Slowly, Neil rose to his feet. "I come and go at my will, Mr. Clapham. Before this meeting, I might have forgotten all about you. But now, you have made me curious." Neil bared his teeth in a grin he knew would make Clapham shake in his boots. It was all a ploy, of course. He had no power on his own. No one who owed him favors. But Clapham did not know that.

"I can see we are not friends, Mr. Duncan." The horrible excuse of a gentleman stood and offered an abbreviated bow. "I hope we will not become enemies." He took his sandwich with him out the door.

Neil remained standing still, thinking.

"What was that about, lad?" Putnam asked from his chair across the room.

Higgins looked out the front window. "He's headed south. Back to where he came from."

Uncertain, Neil tapped his fist against his thigh. He had no one who owed him favors. But there were people in his life who were unfailingly *good*. At least two such men, who happened to be married to the only two women of Neil's acquaintance who might actually like him the smallest bit. Those men also had a penchant for justice.

Even if it was Neil who presented them with the issue, they might help for no other reason than for their enjoyment of righting wrongs.

The chance was worth it, in this instance, if he could help Teresa.

Neil went to the kitchen, pushing through the door without preamble.

"Mr. Jones." The startled proprietor jumped to his feet at the unexpected address. "I need paper and pen, sir." Neil took several coins out of his pocket. "And the use of a quiet room to write a few letters."

"Of course, Mr. Duncan." Jones showed Neil to a staircase. "The family parlor is just upstairs. Follow me, sir."

Chapter Seventeen

At first, Teresa had feared her candid conversation with Mr. Duncan would lead to unpleasantness between them. Instead, he behaved as he had from the first. He was cordial, a gentleman in every way, with his occasional witty turn of phrase.

Caroline had taken to following him about as he worked. The dog, christened Muse, followed them both. That made it easy enough to find where they were.

One afternoon, a few days after Teresa and Mr. Duncan's conversation, she went in search of her daughter to insist upon a geography lesson. Mr. Duncan, with a wheelbarrow full of stone, was going about the irrigation trenches in the farm. The rain had abated, but water still stood in areas where it should not. At breakfast, he had informed everyone at the table of his intent to discover the reason for the blockages and get the water moving as it should.

Teresa suspected that Mr. Putnam had come by to point out what must be done, and how to do it. While she had thought to ask the old farmer to advise Mr. Duncan, she had hesitated.

Would a man used to prestige and position listen to a poor, old farmer?

It seemed Mr. Duncan was not too proud to do so, a thing which intrigued her.

Teresa went down the line of fence where the brambles grew, spotting the gentleman, girl, and dog. Rather than call out, she approached slowly and listened to their voices drifting up to her.

"Avez-vous déjà rencontré un Français?" Caroline asked, stopping Teresa where she stood.

Mr. Duncan removed a large clump of weeds with his shovel, then went to the wheelbarrow to lift a flat stone. He answered her daughter in French. *"I have met any number of French people. During their revolution, hundreds of Frenchmen and their families came to England to escape Madame Guillotine. Their families still speak French."*

Caroline picked up a smaller stone and followed him. He appeared to be lining the place where the invasive plants had grown with rocks.

As a headache had begun to build behind Teresa's eyes, she had no wish to shout to draw their attention. Coming all the way toward them, Teresa spoke in French, too. *"I see you are having a French lesson today, ma petite chérie."*

When Mr. Duncan looked up at her from where he crouched, wrist-deep in muddy water, he dared to wink at her. "I told her she could only follow me about today if she agreed to speak French."

"Mr. Duncan says my accent is charming," Caroline added with a grin.

Though amused, Teresa tempered her reaction to a tight-lipped smile. Then she pointed up the hill. "Let us hope your geography lesson will be just as charming. Your grandmama is ready to bake, so you ought to join her. I believe you are discussing Spain today."

"Yes, Mama." Caroline curtsied to Mr. Duncan. She went up

the hill, plucking a wildflower as she went. Teresa watched her daughter, and contentment settled in her heart. Caroline grew more kind and loving every day, and she had a gentle soul. If Teresa accomplished nothing else, as long as her daughter grew into a happy and generous woman, any trouble would be worth it.

"Your daughter does you credit, Mrs. Clapham."

Teresa turned to see Mr. Duncan, out of the mud with dripping wet hands, watching her.

"I think her sweet nature came with her, Mr. Duncan. It has been my privilege to watch her grow." She felt a cough tickle her throat and hastily turned to cover her mouth with her handkerchief. "Pardon me."

He gave her a momentarily concerned expression but continued the conversation. "I have often wondered about the nature of children." Mr. Duncan stepped over the rivulet of water, now rapidly disappearing through the irrigation canal. "If we are all a product of our family, why does one see so much divergence in childhood temperaments?"

With a raised eyebrow, Teresa tucked her handkerchief away. "Any woman will tell you, Mr. Duncan, that their children come into this life with personalities. We only mold the medium we are given, as parents. I know a woman with six children, each of them different in temperament and talent, though all raised by the same good lady."

He made a thoughtful hum of sound, then placed his shovel over the double handles of the wheelbarrow, pushing it further down the hill. Teresa followed, somewhat curiously.

They had come to another place with standing water, overflowing from the narrow ditch. Mr. Duncan stopped there, lifted his shovel, and went to work on a patch of long, wild grass. He dug around the plant, ignoring the water and mud that flecked his boots.

"Thank you for doing this," Teresa said. "It was not even on your list."

"No, it was not." He sounded pleasant, despite the labor he undertook. The shovel came up, filled with mud. He tossed it aside, stuck the shovel in the ground, and leaned upon it as he regarded her. His hat was tipped at a rakish angle. "Mr. Putnam must make his own repairs and replace some thatch upon his roof this afternoon, weather permitting, and he has said he will show me the way of things if I will assist him."

"That is kind of him." Teresa tucked a loose strand of black hair back behind her ear. "Mr. Duncan." She swallowed, wondering why her voice sounded rather tight. "I am terribly sorry that you have not yet received word about—about whatever it is that keeps you here." She had not exactly meant to say such a thing.

Mr. Duncan ducked his head, and she saw a muscle in his jaw tighten. "Do not trouble yourself, Mrs. Clapham. Things will resolve themselves, sooner or later. I have written to other acquaintances. Perhaps they will help me sort matters out." He stepped around the shovel and went to the wheelbarrow, taking up another large, flat stone.

"What are you doing, precisely?" Teresa asked, watching with fascination and perhaps a bit of admiration, too, as his forearms flexed beneath the stone's weight. He knelt in the large puddle that had begun to recede and put the rock into the middle of the ditch. They were at a place where the flow of water seemed to turn in order to make it through the middle of the field before running downhill, and eventually to sea.

"Whoever dug the irrigation ditches originally did a fair job, according to our Mr. Putnam, but it has been two years or more since any work to maintain the integrity of the ditches was performed." He stayed crouched there, resting wrists on knees and looking up at her. "If the larger growths of greenery are cleared, and stones put in place to keep them from coming back, it will all flow downhill as it ought."

The pounding in Teresa's head increased abruptly, enough to

make her forget herself and put her hand above her brow where it most hurt.

The gentleman stood, green eyes wide, and approached. "Mrs. Clapham, are you unwell? You have turned terribly pale. Except..." He wiped his dirty hand on his trousers. "Forgive me, madam." He put the back of his cool hand against her forehead, and she leaned into it with some relief. The touch felt quite wonderful, not only due to the difference in temperature.

"You are burning with fever," he said, his eyes darkening.

"It is nothing. I am merely overtired." Yet even as she spoke the excuse, Teresa could not think of a thing she had done to wear her body out. Her chores that day had been light.

Mr. Duncan's frown deepened. "Come, let me walk you back to the house."

Teresa took a step back. "I am perfectly capable of walking back up this little hill, Mr. Duncan. Though I do thank you for your concern." She cleared her throat again. It hurt to swallow. Botheration. Teresa did not have the time to fall ill.

"Then go up the hill, madam." Mr. Duncan's smile seemed sad, somehow. "You are perfectly capable, as you said, of doing things without my assistance. Please drink some of your marvelous herbal concoctions and rest."

The sincerity with which he spoke touched her heart. And reminded her of how gently he had pressed his lips to hers in the kiss that never ought to have occurred. She went hot all over, then shivered with cold.

"Yes. Yes, I must be ill," she said aloud. "Good afternoon, Mr. Duncan." She turned about and started up the hill. The hill she had climbed hundreds of times, and come down with ease less than a quarter of an hour before. By the time she made it to the top, the house within view, her state had changed drastically.

Forehead and back of the neck wet with sweat, her heart pounding, and her head as thick with fog as a marsh on a summer morning, Teresa stumbled the last few steps to the kitchen door.

REPAIRING A LEAK IN A THATCHED ROOF WAS NOT nearly so complex as re-thatching an entire roof. Neil stood on a ladder over the corner of Mr. Putnam's cottage.

"The truth of the matter," Putnam said as he worked new straw into place, "is that the last time we had thatchers to work here was thirty years past. The very tops of the houses and the corners are seeing problems. We just need to send for a thatcher that's worth his salt."

"I cannot say that I have ever seen a thatcher at work." Neil used bent sticks, shoving them into place, to hold the straw where Mr. Putnam put it. "If you know how to do the repairs, could you not do the entire rooftop yourself?"

Putnam leaned his elbow on the roof, atop his own ladder, and fixed Neil with a narrow-eyed gaze. "Thatching is an art, Mr. Duncan. 'Tis no easy thing to do a good, quality job when you aren't bred to it. I can fix this leak, here, and it will be set for a year or two. But a true thatcher can lay an entire roof that will last the length of a man's lifetime."

Neil looked over the roof, gray everywhere except where he and Putnam had fixed the leak. "This straw has been up here for thirty years?" Nearly as long as he had been alive.

"Aye." Putnam started down the ladder. "And it's time to do it over, I'm thinking."

"Are thatchers difficult to find? Is it an expensive undertaking?" Neil climbed down as well, his mind already on Teresa's roof. She had said the only leak was in her bedroom. He now knew how to remove the thatch, replace the wood, and recover it with straw. His work likely would not be even so good as Putnam's, but if it held long enough to have a real thatcher come recover the roof—

"It's a dear cost, and one we must pay if we are not tenants. I've heard it's a year's worth of rents and more to have a roof recovered. My father won our land through his hard labor to our baron. I believe Mrs. Clapham's land came through a family trust, and so there is no landowner other than she." He shrugged his wiry shoulders. "Most of us know to start putting a bit of money by before it's needed." Putnam stared up at his patch job with a deep frown. "I could pay before winter comes."

Teresa would not have money put by for such a thing. Especially considering how worried she had been over making enough merely to get through winter.

Neil immediately remembered his mother's second ruby earring. It might not fetch enough. The job sounded as though it would cost well over one-hundred pounds. If the earring did not suit, the necklace would be at least worth two-hundred pounds.

"What are you thinking, lad?" Putnam asked, his clear blue eyes serious. "Will your Mrs. Clapham have the wherewithal to replace her thatch?"

Neil cleared his throat. "It's not really my business, is it?" He took the ladder off the roof and slowly laid it down, allowing Putnam to pick up one side. There was no use discussing the subject with the old farmer.

Teresa would not allow him to pay for her rooftop's replacement. Not outright. "Is fire a concern for a roof such as yours? I would think clay tiles or tin might be a better material."

The old man snorted. "The whole building is made of wood. It's all likely to catch fire. But think on this. Clay is hard and brittle, and we'd have to find a way to get it here. Same with tin. And can you imagine the noise of rain on a tin roof?" He scoffed. "Thatching has been part of our homes and our lives for hundreds of years. I cannot see people changing such an important thing any time soon."

Neil returned to Bramble Cottage with less than two hours of sunlight left. He would have to wait to make the necessary repair. A new board, a bit of hammer and nail work, and then carefully dried straw roped back into place would take more time than the sun would allow.

Muse appeared the moment Neil's foot stepped onto the property. She approached him cautiously, as though uncertain as to what sort of greeting to give. Neil whistled and bent down, and she hurried toward him with her tail between her legs. Poor girl would need more time to learn she was wanted. He rubbed at her ears, praising her quietly until her tail started to wave back and forth.

She followed him with more energy after that.

He went to wash himself for dinner. He pumped the water from the underground well into a pail, then took that pail with him to the back of the barn where he had created something of a washroom for himself. A tall table held a basin, chipped pitcher, and a bar of soap. On a nail just above, he had hung the shaving pouch provided by Teresa.

After a few minutes, Neil was clean enough for keeping the women company. His alternate white shirt was on the line, and he took it into the barn to pull it overhead.

Muse followed him all the way to the kitchen door, then sat politely. Such an intelligent creature. He gave her a smile and determined to bring her out a portion of his dinner when he had finished.

He entered the kitchen with a ready smile for Caroline, but he immediately saw the girl sitting with slumped shoulders at the table. Her grandmother and mother were not in the room, despite the hour.

"Is something wrong?" Neil looked to the stove, but nothing but a stew pot and kettle were upon it.

Caroline sat up, and when he met her gaze, he could see the worry in her eyes. Her lower lip protruded slightly. "Mama is ill. Grandmama is looking in on her with tea and broth."

Neil's stomach twisted. "How ill is she?"

A creak on the stairs alerted him to Mrs. Godwin's return,

and she had apparently heard his inquiry. The first thing she said upon entering the kitchen, looking directly at him, was: "Teresa is quite poorly, Mr. Duncan. We are not certain yet what the illness is, only that it came on suddenly. She has caught a chill only, perhaps, though it is somewhat unusual a time of year for it. She has a fever, headache, and cough."

"What can I do?" Neil closed his hands into fists, though he was helpless to fight an illness. His mind running through tasks he might attempt. "There is no apothecary in Dunwich, though I know there is one in Westfold. I could start on my way there now. On horseback, I could return soon."

He stopped talking when Mrs. Godwin, who had appeared rather tired at first, started to laugh.

"You are a darling, Mr. Duncan, but that is not necessary. We know precisely the powders and potions an apothecary would advise us to use. We already have everything we need, thanks to Teresa's herbal garden."

His shoulders slumped. "Oh. That is…very good news." He cleared his throat and took a step back, clearing the way for Mrs. Godwin to step around him to the stove. "Mrs. Godwin, are you sure there is not anything I might do?"

"You already do so much for us, Mr. Duncan." The woman looked over her shoulder at him, her eyes flashing in a manner similar to her daughter's. Mrs. Godwin apparently found his concern amusing.

Neil went to the table and took his usual chair across from Caroline. The girl sighed.

"I suppose you will milk the cow tonight, Miss Caroline?" he said, bending his head in an effort to catch her eye.

She lifted one shoulder. "Yes."

"Good. Muse and Cider will be happy to see you."

Her gaze came up, one corner of her mouth lifting. "I do enjoy playing with them."

Mrs. Godwin brought two bowls of stew to the table. "Our

meal is simple tonight, as I have been looking after Teresa the last few hours. I hope you do not mind, Mr. Duncan."

"I eat like a king at this table every night, Mrs. Godwin. The food is always delicious and filling. What more does a man need?" Even as the words left his lips, it startled him how much he meant them.

What more did he need? Countless courses had passed before him throughout the years of his life. He had eaten at tables filled with the richest dishes. Stuffed swan, gold-leafed and sugared fruits, puddings, cakes, pastries as light as a feather, with all manner of spices to delight the palate.

But with spoon in hand and the stew before him, consisting of more vegetables than meat and only salt, garlic, and onion to enhance the flavors, he found himself content. The one thing he had missed was tea. Real, dark, soothing tea. The coffee was almost an acceptable replacement, but the ladies drank it on rare occasions.

Mrs. Godwin sat and began asking questions about the roof repair, pulling Neil from his thoughts. They spoke for some time, then he escorted Caroline to the barn to milk Abigail. The little girl's spirits brightened when she successfully sent an arc of milk into her kitten's open mouth. Muse did not understand how to take part in the trick and ended up with milk dripping from one ear.

Neil carried the pail for Caroline, while she carried the lantern, back into the house. When he left, he looked up at the windows. He knew Teresa's room by the worn-out corner of the roof directly above it. There was no light inside. It seemed she had already gone to sleep.

Though Neil had not uttered a prayer since childhood, and seldom turned his thoughts heavenward, he thought a plea that night. A plea that nothing would be seriously wrong with Teresa, and her health would return as strong as ever.

Chapter Eighteen

Teresa woke late, her head pounding less than it had the previous evening. She groaned and rolled over in bed, pulling her quilt up to her chin. The sun already streamed through the window on one side of the house.

A knock on the door reminded her what had woken her. She tried to call out, but had to clear her throat and make a second attempt. "Come in."

The door opened and Caroline came in, her curls in disarray and a brush in hand. "Good morning, Mama. Are you feeling better? Grandmama sent me upstairs to fetch my school things. She told me to check and see if you were ready for breakfast." The words flew from her daughter with speed.

Teresa smiled and pushed herself up in her bed. "I am a touch better. Here, let me brush your hair. Then you can bring me breakfast."

Caroline did not argue. Though she was certainly old enough to brush her own hair, and she usually did, Teresa still enjoyed giving her daughter the attention. It gave them time to sit quietly and talk, without worrying over lessons or chores.

"Did you milk Abigail last night?" Teresa asked as her daughter perched on the edge of the bed, back to her mother.

"I did. And I played with Cider and Muse. Mr. Duncan laughed when I showed him how to squeeze milk into a cat's mouth. He laughed even more when Muse didn't know the trick."

The mention of their gentleman-hireling made Teresa smile more than the story did. "I imagine Mr. Duncan did not know the trick either."

"He said he had never seen it before." Caroline fidgeted. Something in the way Caroline spoke made Teresa curious. The girl sounded as though she attempted to speak well of Mr. Duncan for a purpose. "I hadn't either, before we came here. Mr. Duncan said that I know a lot more about living on a farm than he does. I think he is learning rather quickly."

She pulled the brush gently through Caroline's black locks, so like her own. "I agree. He has accomplished more in this last month than I thought he would. He did not seem like a man used to physical labor when we met."

The girl's nod was slight, then she shifted just enough to look over her shoulder at Teresa. "He was anxious about your illness. Last night, he even offered to ride to the apothecary in Westfold." The girl's eyes were comically wide, her words spoken with an air of innocence. Yes, she was certainly trying to hint at something.

As her mother, Teresa refused to rise to the bait. She kept her own tone disinterested. "Did he? How kind of him."

"Mr. Duncan asked if I would tell him when you woke, so he can begin the roof repair. He said the hammering would wake you up. Should I go tell him that he can start working? After I tell Grandmama, of course." She faced forward, shoulders squared. "He is looking for weeds in the garden today, since you cannot."

"You may tell him I am awake."

Though she would not allow her pleasure to show to her

fanciful daughter, her gratitude for Mr. Duncan grew at his thoughtfulness. She finished brushing Caroline's hair, tying it back from her daughter's face with a ribbon.

"Thank you, Mama." Caroline kissed Teresa on the cheek. "Would you like me to come read to you?"

"After you have done your chores and helped your grandmother." Teresa leaned back against her pillows, surprised that she already felt tired again. Perhaps she had not recovered as much as she had thought upon waking.

Caroline disappeared out the door as quickly as she had entered.

Mother appeared moments later with a tray made weighty by tea, ginger biscuits, and a bowl of hot cereal. She put everything on the small table near Teresa's bed. "How are you, dearest?"

"I think better." Teresa leaned forward when her mother put out her hand. Her mother's frown was not at all reassuring.

"Your fever seems to be gone, but your voice would indicate you still have a sore throat. The tea will help, and there is honey in your porridge." Her mother sat on the end of the bed, hands folded in her lap. "You know, Mr. Duncan was most concerned for you last evening."

"Yes, so Caroline said." Teresa attempted to keep her voice light, but apparently that trick worked no better on her mother than it did when Caroline tried it on Teresa.

"He asked again at breakfast if he might do anything to help. I suggested he take on some of your usual tasks." Mother's eyebrows raised. "He is such a good sort. I often wonder about his history; if his family has truly cut him off, what will become of him?"

"I do not suppose it's our business." Teresa found a thread loose at the edge of the quilt. She tugged it gently and told herself to mend it as soon as she felt better.

Mother stood and smoothed the blanket. Her tone became

far too innocent. "That might be true. But if he has nowhere else to go, perhaps he could stay here."

Teresa groaned and slid down onto her pillow, pulling her quilt up over her head. "Whether he stays or goes, I do not care." She had absolutely no intention of discussing Mr. Duncan's future with her mother.

At that, her mother laughed. "Oh, I very much doubt that, daughter. Now, eat your breakfast before it turns cold. I will come and look in on you in a little while."

When her mother left, Teresa took the blanket off her head. Her mother did not fool Teresa at all. She wanted to determine if Teresa had any intention of trying to keep Mr. Duncan with them. Well, the answer was a resounding "no." For one thing, the man could hardly spend the rest of his life in their barn. And Teresa absolutely would not imagine any circumstance which might allow him to live inside her house. How could she?

The very idea was preposterous, really. She had told him no flirting, and she meant it. No kisses beneath trees, or in the dark of night. No affections or tokens traded. It made no sense for her to open her heart to him when he had plans to leave.

No matter how easy it would be for her to care for him.

Teresa drank her tea, hoping it would soothe her throat enough to make the porridge easier to eat. She was nearly finished with her breakfast when a loud thump against the wall of her room made her jump.

She stared at the window, then rose and went to look out. A ladder was propped against the house. Mr. Duncan climbed it.

Teresa hastily stepped away from the window and took up her shawl, wrapping it about her shoulders. Then she went back, just as he prepared to pass her on his way to the top of the house.

He paused, right there, looking straight through the glass at her. His hat was on at its usual jaunty angle, his coat was nowhere in sight, and his shirtsleeves were pushed up and secured above his elbows.

She swallowed, then winced. Mr. Duncan's expression changed from one of surprise to concern.

"Are you feeling any better?" he asked through the glass.

Shouting through even the thin pane would prove too much for her. Teresa unlatched the window and swung it open, allowing the room to immediately fill with fresh air. Her face, when she leaned out, was less than a foot away from his.

"I am somewhat improved, sir. Thank you for asking." She looked down, and when she did not see her daughter or mother upon the ground, decided she might continue the conversation. "And thank you for all your assistance. My mother and Caroline told me that you have been most attentive."

His smile returned, broader than before. "I wish there was more I might do. I intend to have your roof patched up in short order, then I am to go to Dunwich. Might I fetch anything back for you?" The incongruity of his fine mannerisms and rough style of dress still amused her, and all the more when he made such a dashing figure on a ladder offering her assistance.

"I cannot think of anything I might require. Thank you." She looked upward, at the protruding corner of the roof. "Are you quite safe? Do you need someone out there with you to hold the ladder, or anything at all?"

Mr. Duncan shook his head, still looking at her. "The ladder has a hook at the top, to keep it in place in the thatch. I had wondered about it when I saw this ladder in the barn. It is made especially for your house and outbuildings. It is sturdy enough, and I will be careful."

"Good. It would distress me if you came to any harm." She had meant to say those words lightly, but they came out far too serious, too honest and earnest. Teresa felt her cheeks warm when his eyes darkened.

When he spoke, it was also without levity. "I feel much the same about you, Mrs. Clapham. Please, tuck yourself back up in bed and try to rest." His smile returned. "As much as you can with me at work."

Hesitantly, she reached out to grasp the latch and pulled the window closed again. Only after it was shut did he continue on his way upward. Teresa went back to bed, as ordered, her shawl pulled tightly around her.

What if Mr. Duncan never left? The question her mother had put to her, that she had avoided until that moment, seized her imagination fully, and her lips tingled when her daydreams led her back to his kiss.

Teresa had come to the cottage with no other options. She had to support her mother and daughter and needed to get far away from the poisonous fumes of her brother-in-law's home. But nothing would keep someone like Mr. Duncan on a tiny farm. There was no fortune to be made, no opportunities to turn the dirt into gold. Even she had not found full contentment in her new station, though she had happiness with her family.

There was a noise above her head. The clatter of wood. Before long, the pounding of a hammer. She released a sigh and snuggled deeper into her blankets. Her bed creaked again. It was time to tighten the ropes with a bed wrench. She could put it off no longer.

Despite the noise of Mr. Duncan's repair, she drifted back to sleep and into troubled dreams.

AFTER SOME TRIAL AND ERROR WITH THE THATCH, Neil took himself to Dunwich. He rode the horse, and went straight to the Lost Mermaid to inquire after the post.

"Aye, sir. You have two letters." Mr. Jones went to his sorting boxes. "And one for Mrs. Clapham, if you would be so kind as to take it to her."

"Of course. Thank you." Neil accepted the folded papers and went outside, tearing the seal off one addressed to him. He recognized the handwriting, though he had seen it only once before. It was from Lady Inglewood, which somewhat surprised him. True, he had written to her, but he had not held much hope for an answer, let alone one that had to have been penned and sent the same day she received his letter.

To Mister Neil Duncan,

How strange to address you thus. I have heard of your father's actions. He wasted no time in spreading the news throughout all our acquaintances. The whole county must know of your dismissal. One does wonder why. My husband believes the marquess intends to make a bid for a more important role within their political party. All that is supposition, however.

I gave your letter to Lord Inglewood, and he has promised to forward your inquiries to his solicitor. They will look into Mrs. Clapham's circumstances. I will write as soon as we have news.

Nothing else in her letter was of interest. There were only a few lines asking him about his circumstances. He had to smile over that. Lady Inglewood had a kind and forgiving nature. Much unlike her husband. Flirt with the man's wife and he never forgave you, it would seem.

Neil smirked and leaned back against the sun-warmed wall of the public house. A year ago, he had sought out a woman he had thought as lonely as he. The fact that he could humble the self-righteous and morally strict Lord Inglewood with that flirtation had made the idea even sweeter. But Lady Inglewood was loyal to her husband. Loved him, even. Which meant Neil envied Silas Riley, Lord Inglewood, all the more.

It had been foolish, of course, to attempt such a flirtation and affair. But Neil had never claimed any sort of wisdom beyond what was necessary to survive in the British peerage.

He opened the other letter, from his sister.

The first portion of her letter detailed her plans for the coming fall. Nothing of note. The latter assured him that the marquess had not relented, though their mother had started a domestic war with his lordship. She had dismissed his favorite servants, sold a prized hunter without his knowledge, invited several guests to their home whom he detested, and served nothing but the foods to which he had a personal aversion.

Neil smirked. They might seem like little things, but some wars were won with subtle tactics rather than sweeping battles.

Then he read the last lines of his sister's letter.

"Mother has told me our secret. I hope you have not let it bother you, Neil. No one need know outside the three of us. At least you and I are fully brother and sister. But this explains why we have far better taste than our elder brothers."

His smiled faded, as did his mood. He tucked the letters, along with the unopened letter for Teresa, into his coat pocket. Then he strode down the road to the dry good store that sold most things a person needed in a pinch.

He bought chalk for Caroline. He had noticed her supply running low. Honey for Mrs. Godwin. Coffee measured out into a tin, for all of them. He stared at the other wares. There were pencils, bottled fruits, but nothing that seemed necessary. The store clerk let Neil look, with complete patience.

"Have you anything a lady might like," Neil asked at last, hardly believing himself. "Something pretty to look at, or use."

The clerk, a Mr. Lane, considered the question. "There are some ribbons, just here." He walked down his side of the counter and pulled a box of ribbons from beneath. They were brightly colored, on spools. He chose two lengths of the silvery-blue ribbon that reminded him of the shawl Teresa wore most often.

Purchases in hand, wrapped up in brown paper and string, Neil returned to the farm. He took the coffee and honey to Mrs. Godwin immediately. She showered him with praise. He left the chalk on the table next to Caroline, who smiled up at him before returning to her sums. He gave her the letter to deliver to her mother, too. But the ribbon stayed in his pocket.

How would he give it to Teresa without seeming to overstep his relationship with her?

The moment the question crossed his mind, Neil kicked a

stone across the barnyard. A chicken nearly hit by the stone let loose an awful screech, hurrying away as though under attack. Neil almost smiled at the fretful bird, then sighed.

Muse's head appeared beneath his hand. Neil looked down into the dog's large, soulful blue eyes. "It does not matter how I give it to her. It will look like a gift from a lovesick youth."

The dog appeared sympathetic, then it licked his hand and trotted away to the water trough for a drink. Neil looked back at the house, to Teresa's window. The ladder was still in place. He needed to put it back in the barn where it belonged.

But he turned and made his way into the orchard instead. He would read Olivia's note again. And Lady Inglewood's. They both had said things about the marquess. If he thought on it enough, he might learn the man's plan behind cutting him out of the family without warning.

Chapter Nineteen

The sun had set, and Teresa lay awake. She had rested throughout the day, and now that the rest of the world slept, she had no inclination to do so herself. The letter from her brother-in-law lay on her table, folded up after she had read through it twice. He had shared information about Neil Duncan. Information that Frederick likely thought would upset her. Yet she found herself almost relieved.

The man who had appeared on the road, wearing clothing more suited to a dinner party than a ride through the country-side, was not a mere gentleman. He was Lord Neil, son of the Marquess of Alderton. Obviously, her brother-in-law informed her, Lord Neil had lied to her to gain her trust.

Lord Neil had not lied about his family situation. Frederick had taken great delight in detailing how the marquess had made it public knowledge that his youngest son had caused "irreparable harm" to the family, and Lord Neil had therefore been cut off. After outlining the importance of the marquess, Frederick urged her to turn Lord Neil out.

Strange, but that made her more determined than ever to keep him.

Teresa rose and lit her lamp. She had half a mind to write Frederick back immediately and profess to have known all along who and what Neil Duncan was, and that she did not care. But it would likely cause her brother-in-law distress, and he may well appear at her door again. She would need to take some time to think on her response.

With her small room glowing with light, Teresa found the book of Shakespeare's sonnets. Caroline had recited three from memory that afternoon, with Teresa following along in the book to make certain each word was correct. She turned the pages and started to read, the words soothing her as well as music once had.

How she missed music.

> Some glory in their birth, some in their skill,
> Some in their wealth, some in their bodies' force,
> Some in their garments, though new-fangled ill,
> Some in their hawks and hounds, some in their
>   horse;
> And every humor hath his adjunct pleasure,
> Wherein it finds a joy above the rest:
> But these particulars are not my measure;
> All these I better in one general best.
> Thy love is better than high birth to me...

The words of the Bard touched her. She had none of those things in which people gloried. She put her finger beneath her favorite line and repeated it aloud, "'Thy love is better than high birth to me'." She sighed, and went on reading the rest of the sonnet. To have such a love, richer than any wealth and worth the cost of giving all such things up, would be a miracle. Especially for her. Given what she now knew of Lord Neil.

A small tap against her window made Teresa pause. She looked up at the glass, considering if she had imagined the sound. Then there was another tap.

She put her book down and went to the window, a bubble of excitement growing in her chest. There was only one person she could think of who would attempt to gain her attention at her window.

Of course, she ought to open her window and tell the man to leave her alone. Remind him of the appropriate boundaries they must keep to, but her brother-in-law's attempt to turn her against Lord Neil and the poem running through her thoughts made her feel rather bold and young.

Teresa opened the window and leaned out, looking down at Lord Neil in the moonlight. He smiled up at her, the flash of his grin easily seen in the blue shadows.

"Mrs. Clapham. I saw your light," he said, voice barely loud enough to carry to her. "May I come up and chat with you a moment?" He pointed to the ladder still against the side of the house.

Though she initially hesitated, Teresa gave him permission with a nod. "Yes, but you must be quick. It is late."

It was not late. Not really. Especially given the fact that she was not tired, having rested the whole day.

Teresa fetched her shawl to wrap about her for modesty, then went back to the window. He had made his way up the ladder to draw even with her. Once there, he relaxed against the ladder, one arm draped through the rungs and the other at his side. Meeting in such a way, allowing him so close when she knew what others would think if someone saw, made the moment more thrilling. When was the last time she had taken such a risk?

Something of her delight must have shown on her face, because Lord Neil wore a secretive smile of his own.

"I take it you are feeling better?" he said, voice soft now that he was near.

"Yes, much better. Whatever it was that plagued me seems to have gone for now."

"That is good news. But I have no wish to hinder your recovery, so I will not keep you long." He reached into his coat. "I have something for you. When I went to Dunwich today, I did not want to return empty handed. I brought something back for everyone. I could not think what you would like. I hope this will do." He withdrew a length of ribbon that appeared like silver in the moonlight.

Teresa leaned out a little more, though her feet remained safely on the floor of her room, and accepted the ribbon from his hand. Their fingers brushed, and she smiled at the bit of satin. "It is lovely. Thank you. I will wear it in my hair on Sunday." The gift, though simple, reminded her of the lover's tokens she and her husband had once exchanged. Surely, Lord Neil did not mean for her to see the gift in such a light.

Though he had said he would not stay long, he did not immediately appear ready to leave her, either. "You had a letter today. I hope it was good news."

That made her sigh. She laced the ribbon through her fingers, looking at her hand rather than at him. Perhaps she would not reveal that she knew his secret. It might change things between them. That ridiculous thought brought a laugh, small and without much humor, from her. Nothing would change. She knew better now than ever that there could be nothing more than friendship between them, for more reasons than she had supposed.

"It was news. I am not sure if it is good or bad. But it is interesting."

"Are you attempting to keep me in suspense?" he asked, and when she looked up, she saw a light in his eyes. He did not flirt. He teased. Perhaps he always had been playful rather than amorous.

"It is news you already know," she said lightly. "My brother-in-law wrote to me. I suspect he meant to shock me, but I must confess that I am only relieved."

His expression changed, darkening and becoming cautious.

"Relieved? I cannot think what he might tell you that I already know."

Teresa shifted, resting her elbows on the window, her wrists crossed. If he leaned closer, she would easily be able to touch him. "He has told me who you are. Who you really are, my lord." The man outside her window stilled, though she felt his stare upon her. "I think he hoped the revelation would cause me to send you away. But the man he describes in his letter, I have seen no evidence of during your time here with us."

Lord Neil sounded almost hoarse. "What do you mean? You do not think I am a lord?"

"I know you must be. It explains so much about you, and your education. And Frederick's letter confirms that you have been cut off from your rather powerful family." Teresa lifted her gaze to meet his at last, that familiar warmth stirring in her chest. "But he describes a selfish man. A lord so wrapped up in himself that his own family had grown to despise him. Yet every moment that you have been here, with us, you have conducted yourself with honor and generosity. Lord Neil."

He winced at the title and averted his eyes. "I wish you would not call me that."

"It is truer to who you are than Mr. Duncan, though I have grown rather fond of that name."

The man looked sideways at her, cautiously. "You have?"

Teresa nodded. "You have been kind to us, my lord—"

"Please," he interrupted, his eyebrows drawn together. He swallowed. "Do not call me that. Not here. I am not a lord here. And if Mr. Duncan will no longer do, would you consider calling me only Neil? We are friends enough for that, are we not?"

Her heart skipped a beat. "You have called me Teresa once before. I took you to task for it."

His shoulders dropped. "So you did."

"Perhaps you ought to try it again." Was it her recovery from illness that made her bold? The fever had likely addled her brain for her to suggest such a thing. Yet she had been told of the gifts he brought back from the village. She had seen him work in her fields, orchards, and in her barn. Caroline adored him. Mother had made it clear that she thought highly of him, too. And Teresa had found him handsome from the first moment they met.

Knowing his true identity did not scare her. It soothed her. Not because it changed anything between them. They were as unlikely friends as ever. Yet it confirmed the good opinion of him that had already formed.

"Teresa," he said, his silky tone making her name a caress.

She closed her eyes and released a sigh. "That was not terrible."

He chuckled. The ladder creaked as he adjusted his hold upon it. "Not at all. It is a lovely name, so it suits you."

"No one else can hear you use it," she said quickly, rushing to cover her delight. "They will form the wrong impression."

"And what is the right impression?" His grin turned sly as he watched her. "We are naught but friends."

"I am well aware of that." And disappointed by it, though she knew it was all that could be between them. The son of a marquess could never be more to a poor widow such as she. The nobility of England did as they wished, but rarely turned upon one of their own. His father would reinstate him, she had no doubt, and Neil would leave her behind for good.

The knowledge that he would take a piece of her heart with him when he did made her ache. But she would keep that secret from him. He need not know that every moment of her waking hours she must remind herself not to care for him. Not to see the tenderness with which he spoke to the animals, or the gentleness with her daughter. She had tried to ignore him. To pretend there was nothing for her to admire, that he was the same as any other man.

But he was not. He had lowered himself to the position of a farm worker. He had done every task she presented him, and others she had not, to the best of his ability, with humility.

"Teresa," he said when the silence stretched long between them. "You are not upset with who I am?"

She shook her head, feeling tears burn at her eyes. She swallowed them away, her sore throat aching. "I am not. Truly. It did not even surprise me as much as you might think. It matters little to me who you are, Neil. All that I have cared about is how you have behaved while here."

"Ah, so you will always think of me as an inept laborer who falls from trees and cleans out chicken houses." He tipped his head back, sighing dramatically. "I suppose that is not an intimidating or frightful person to have about."

Teresa laughed unexpectedly, then hastily covered her mouth. She had no wish to wake her mother or daughter with their conversation. That might cause questions later. "You are a good man, Neil. That is all that matters."

His eyes focused on hers and he leaned closer, nearly to her window. "Is that all that matters, Teresa?"

She swallowed back the emotion again. "Of course. A person's actions are more important than their birthright."

"That is not what I meant." He somehow came closer.

If she leaned forward, just a touch, she could kiss him. And oh, how she wanted to. But her heart already ached, knowing she must lose him eventually. Teresa withdrew, clutching the ribbon between her fingers. "I had better turn in. I am afraid I am not fully recovered yet, and I need my rest."

He considered her a moment, not withdrawing. "What keeps you from me, Teresa?" Her name was a purr, a gentle touch upon her heart.

Her lips parted in her surprise, but she hastily closed her mouth. This was the moment she should close the window, blow out the lamp, and go to sleep. Or tell him to leave. Perhaps feign offence.

Yet his expression was open and curious. Not hurt or sly. Neil's honesty was plainly written upon his face. How could he not know, not understand, all that separated them?

"Neil." She savored his name a moment before she continued, hearing the disappointment in her voice and not bothering to hide it. "I am an honorable woman. I cannot pretend, not even for a moment, that more than friendship could ever grow between us. I am a poor widow, reduced to circumstances so beneath my station that none who knew me in the past would admit to knowing me now. You are a lord, the son of a powerful nobleman. The time you have had here, with us, has been a blessing. But it has also been something of a dream."

Neil averted his eyes, his expression closing. She saw the denial of her words in the way he tightened his jaw, and heard it as he spoke. "A dream? To work alongside you in your fields, to clean up after animals? That is not a dream. It is more real, of more substance, than any other part of my life. I feel as though I have been an actor on a stage until now. I have played my part to the best of my ability. I have been the nobleman's son, the arrogant lord, as shallow in my feelings as in my relationships."

"This has been the act, Neil," she told him firmly. "You are not a farmer. You could not live this way forever."

"Perhaps I could." He faced her again, nothing wavering in the strength of his gaze. "If I am with you."

It was the closest he had come to a declaration, and Teresa wondered if he had ever laid himself so bare before another in his life. She saw it all. His determination, of course. His earnestness. But she saw something else that made her heart hurt for him, something in his eyes that revealed how easily she might damage him should she turn him away. Yet it would be the right thing to do, to give pain where he had looked for hope.

Teresa put her hand to her forehead. "Neil. I am tired, and overwhelmed, and—and ill. I know you mean the things you say, but I cannot let myself believe them. I have nothing to offer. If you tried to stay here, your family would not allow it. Please. I am asking you to speak no more of this. It will only hurt us both."

He withdrew, standing straight upon the ladder again. "If that is truly what you wish," he murmured, "I will not say anything more. For now."

It would be easy to let him in, not just into her heart but into her home. Her loneliness, her longing to be held and cared for, had not abated. But it would hurt all the worse when he left, because she knew she could not stop herself from falling in love with him.

But her life was not his. He would leave, and return to the world of ballrooms and perfumed ladies. Wealth and prestige were his birthright.

"Good night, Neil."

"Good night, Teresa." He went down the ladder, and she watched him stand at the bottom and lift it free of the roof. She leaned out and took hold of the window latch, pulling it closed.

Going to her lamp on the table, she put the ribbon upon its surface. She glanced at the slim volume of sonnets. "*Thy love is better than high birth to me.*" Teresa blew out her lamp and crawled into bed.

Though the poem was beautiful, the sentiments perhaps real enough, there was nothing to be done about her situation. Nothing to be done about her growing love for Neil Duncan.

Chapter Twenty

Another week passed, and Neil received a letter from Lady Fox. The woman had formerly been one Miss Millicent Wedgewood, a guest in his family's home. It was while visiting with them earlier that summer that she had met and fallen in love with Sir Isaac Fox, a baronet. They had wed recently. Lady Fox had received his letter, and promised as Lady Inglewood had to look into the matter with her husband's assistance. She also assured him that he was welcome, whenever he wished, in her home.

Fox Hall, as the baronet's home had recently been renamed, sat far too near his father's country estate for Neil to even consider staying there. But the offer was kind, as was the lady who made it.

Neil kept his hands busy, and his mind with them, and avoided more than brief conversations with Teresa. She was the same as ever, once recovered from her brief illness. No one watching the two of them could possibly suspect how much his arms had begun to ache for want of holding her, nor how his heart leaped for joy every time she came within sight. He was a lovesick fool, of the very worst sort, and could do nothing about it.

Not once since that single Season when he had tried to open his heart to another had Neil felt such things. And those feelings in his youth were nothing compared to the transformation his heart underwent now. At five and thirty, he had seen enough of life's pain, misery, and foolishness to give him a greater depth for more tender feelings.

Teresa's perspective of their situation, though accurate, did not put an end to his feelings.

Caroline followed him about when her own chores were complete, speaking in French with more ease than before. Despite wearing a bonnet when the sun was out, she had more freckles across her cheeks than when he had met her. The little girl was endearing, speaking to him of her thoughts with innocence and honesty. When she discovered he had been to the menagerie in London, the Tower animals were a favorite subject for days.

They were in the barn, Neil in Abigail's stall and Caroline sitting on one of the stall walls, discussing the exotic animals kept by the Crown.

"Will you draw a picture of the lion for me?" she pleaded. "And the elephant?"

"I am not a great artist, Cara." He raised his eyebrows at her and grinned, mixing together oats for Abigail. The cow had seemed agitated, and Mr. Putnam told Neil that Abigail likely had eaten something that disagreed with her. A treat of oats and grain mixed and warmed would likely set her to rights.

"But you have seen them, which means your pictures will be better than nothing." She made her bottom lip protrude, fixing him in place with her large, pleading eyes. "Please, Mr. Duncan?"

Teresa had not told her mother or daughter about his identity, so their address to him had not changed.

Neil pretended to heave a sigh. "Very well. If you bring me your slate, I will do my best."

Caroline's grin burst through her pretended pout. Neil gave the bucket to Abigail, then put his hands out to help Caroline down from her perch.

The girl's arms went briefly around his neck and she placed a kiss on his cheek. "Thank you, Mr. Duncan." She rushed out of the barn, unaware of what her simple gesture had meant to him.

Neil walked out slowly into the sunlight. He watched Caroline run into the house, and his stomach twisted. Yes, he was in love with Teresa. He had also come to care for her daughter. The girl was a delight. She was happiness and sunshine, and as kind as her mother. He would do anything for either of them.

A clatter near the gate drew Neil's attention. He turned, curious as to who might have come for a visit. Teresa's former status seemed to keep her from having many friends among the farmer's wives, but he had seen a few women come and go.

But it was not a wagon or farm cart that entered the yard. It was a carriage, with a familiar crest.

Neil froze where he stood, staring at the emblazoned yellow shield with three red birds upon it.

The Earl of Inglewood had arrived.

The carriage went to the front of the house, up a pebble and dirt path Neil had not seen anyone use in his whole time at Bramble Cottage. Rather than wind its way behind the house to the yard between cottage and barn, it went to the front door.

Brought out of his stupor by that fact, Neil ran across the yard to the kitchen door. Teresa would be confused to have such guests descend upon her. He entered the kitchen at the same moment the knock sounded at the front door.

Mrs. Godwin looked first at him, then toward the passage to the front room.

"Guests." Neil spared her a quick smile before going to answer the door himself.

Teresa had been in the front room, sewing a new dress for Caroline. She was already at the door, hand on the latch, when he arrived at her side. Caroline was on the steps, coming down with her slate and chalk.

When the door swung open, Neil had a perfect view of an Inglewood liveried servant standing at the door. "If you please, is this Bramble Cottage, the current residence of Mrs. Clapham?"

Teresa put her hand to her throat. "Yes, I am Mrs. Clapham."

"Madam." The servant bowed, not conveying any surprise to find his master and mistress calling upon someone in such humble circumstances. "My master, his lordship the Earl of Inglewood, and his lady, have come to call upon you." He turned and made a gesture. A servant similarly dressed, standing by the carriage, now held open the door.

Teresa looked over her shoulder at Neil with alarm in her eyes, then stepped outside to greet her guests properly. Neil followed, and Caroline remained behind.

Silas Riley, Lord Inglewood, came out of the carriage first. He was dressed in fine traveling clothes. As tall as Neil, but broader in the shoulders, he only spared the scene before him a brief glance before reaching inside to take his wife's hand.

Lady Inglewood stepped out one dainty shoe at a time. Her eyes fell immediately on Neil, and her lips parted in surprise. Her husband looked to see what had her attention, then his stare remained upon Neil, his own shock evident by the slow enlargement of his eyes.

"It cannot be—is that you, Lord Neil?" Lady Inglewood came forward, step light and smile large. "I did not recognize you."

With a stiff bow, Neil acknowledged them both. "Whereas I could never fail to identify you, my lady, as one of the most extraordinary women of my acquaintance."

That put the frown back on Lord Inglewood's face, even

though his wife laughed away the compliment. "That is quite enough of that, Lord Neil. I understand there is another lady here who holds such a distinction, and I should very much like to meet her."

Neil put his hand out for Teresa to take, which she did, a shaky smile upon her face. He presented her as he would have done at a ball or court function.

"May I introduce to you, Lord and Lady Inglewood, Mrs. Teresa Clapham. She is a true friend, and a woman of honor and distinction."

The earl bowed, and his lady curtsied, returning Teresa's bend of the knee.

Inglewood spoke next. "It is a pleasure to know you, Mrs. Clapham. Please, forgive our intrusion, but we come upon a matter of some urgency."

Teresa looked to Neil, then back to the earl and his wife. "Of course. If you need to speak to Lord Neil in private—"

"You mistake the matter, Mrs. Clapham." The countess's tone was quite gentle. "We have come to speak to you."

Though obviously somewhat confused, Teresa invited them inside. She introduced Caroline, who had lingered near the stairs, and her mother, who hurried away to prepare coffee for the guests.

The countess sat upon the old sofa in the front room, giving no indication she thought the décor beneath her. Teresa hesitantly took a chair near the fire. Neil remained standing by the window, looking out at the fine carriage, and Inglewood stood beside him, facing the room.

"When my wife told me about your letter," Inglewood said, voice low and likely meant to be intimidating, "I never imagined you told the truth of your circumstances. Seeing one of your sort dressed like a farm tenant is most unexpected."

Neil said nothing and did not even grind his teeth together. He only smirked. Let Inglewood think what he wanted. His opinion had never much mattered to Neil. He turned enough to watch the proceedings.

"My dear Mrs. Clapham," the countess said, her gloved hands folded and in her lap. "You can see that we are known to Lord Neil. My family, my husband's, and Lord Neil's have known each other for quite some time. We all have ancestral lands in the same area, outside the village of Aldersy, the country seat of the Marquess of Alderton, Lord Neil's father."

Teresa's expression remained neutral, and her posture every bit as correct as Lady Inglewood's. "What brings you to my home, my lady?" she asked, hardly batting an eyelash. One would think she entertained nobility on a regular schedule.

The earl stepped toward Teresa, away from Neil. "Lord Neil recently drew our attention to your circumstances, Mrs. Clapham. It seems he met your brother-in-law, one Frederick Clapham, and was immediately suspicious of the man's behavior, and how your account of your husband's character did not match with what you were told after he died."

At last Teresa looked to Neil, her expression showing confusion. "My husband died a year and one half ago. I am afraid everything is quite settled. His solicitor and my brother-in-law did all they could. They repaid all of my late husband's debts."

"No, my dear." The countess reached across the small space separating her from Teresa, and Neil's shoulders tensed in anticipation. He knew, somehow, exactly what was coming. "Your brother-in-law and the solicitor, a Mr. Doherty, paid all of their own debts with *your* money. They lied to you."

Caroline gasped from the stairway. Neil turned, seeing her young face go pale, and went to her. He held out a hand and the girl hurried down to take it. She stood close to him, listening intently.

Mrs. Godwin stood in the kitchen doorway, her tray with coffee pot and cups rattling. She hurried forward to put the tray on the table before the couch. "I beg your pardon, my lady. What do you mean?"

Mrs. Godwin stepped back and put her hand to her daughter's shoulders.

Teresa's face had gone paler than Caroline's. "You must be mistaken. Frederick assured me that my husband gambled away our funds, including my daughter's dowry and my marriage portion. His solicitor came and showed me the accounts, that the money was all gone."

The countess looked to the earl, and he slowly shook his head.

"It did not take me long to make inquiries, Mrs. Clapham. Mr. Doherty *is* a known gambler. He came from a rather affluent family and was limited to the funds he received as an allowance. When your husband died, your brother-in-law seems to have offered Doherty a handsome sum to pay his debts, under your husband's name, if Doherty would assist him by ensuring the rest of the money left by your husband went into Mr. Frederick Clapham's pockets."

"That cannot—It does not make any sense. I lived in my house, my brother-in-law's house, for six months after the death of my husband. I saw him dismiss servants—"

Lady Inglewood's interruption was gentle. "All the servants who might grow suspicious or help you."

Teresa stood. "Our meals were poor, we were not permitted to entertain."

Mrs. Godwin took her daughter's hand. "He was angry when I arrived, because I was another mouth to feed, he said." She started to tremble and leaned against her daughter. "But he was worried I would help Teresa discover the truth. Wasn't he?"

"That is what I would think." Inglewood looked back to Neil. "The timing of your letter was most fortunate. We received it the day before I went to Ipswich in order to speak to my own solicitor on a legal matter. I told Esther to answer your letter, but I did not think anything would come of it. I was rather dismissive of your story, at first. I owe you an apology for that, Lord Neil."

"I do not care for apologies, only answers for Mrs. Clapham." Neil knew well enough that Inglewood had never had a good opinion of him. What mattered was what the earl had discovered on Teresa's behalf.

Inglewood continued his tale. "My solicitor and two lawyers went to work learning more about the Clapham brothers, and they uncovered the information swiftly." The earl's tone changed, his words meant to reassure Teresa. "Your money, Mrs. Clapham, still exists. It is sitting in the private Cobbold Bank of Ipswich at this very moment. Your brother-in-law has used some of it, and I am afraid a large sum set aside by your late husband was given to Mr. Doherty."

Tears fell from Teresa's eyes. She let them, gripping her mother's hands tightly. "Henry did not leave me destitute?" She looked to Caroline, then Neil. "And Frederick lied about his own brother. Ruined Henry's name."

"A knave if I have ever heard of one," the countess said.

Mrs. Godwin sniffled, then found a handkerchief in her apron to dab at her eyes. "I never liked Frederick."

Caroline looked up at Neil, her hand still in his. "What does this mean?" she whispered.

Inglewood heard and answered with a raised voice. "It means the matter can be taken to the courts. I know my brother-in-law, Sir Isaac, is already in Ipswich setting things up to appear before a judge. He was riled by the tale, Mrs. Clapham. By the time you arrive there, my solicitor and your brother-in-law's will be prepared to make statements and present evidence to the judge. Restitution will be made at last."

"By the time I arrive? But—how will I get to Ipswich?"

THE INFORMATION REVEALED BY THE EARL OF Inglewood had made Teresa's head spin. For more than a year, she had counted every farthing, let her daughter wander about shoeless, and agonized over what the coming winter would mean without sufficient funds and food stored away. All that time, her brother-in-law had held her money and could have ended her anxieties and fears.

The man was heartless.

Lady Inglewood hurried to reassure Teresa. "Ipswich is thirty miles away. A good six hours by coach, and the same road that brought us here will take you there. It is in excellent condition this time of year. We will take you, of course."

"I—I cannot pay a solicitor. And how will I return home again?"

Neil cleared his throat, and when Teresa looked at him, he met her gaze with tenderness in his expression. "Teresa, I cannot imagine Lord and Lady Inglewood presenting this plan to you without having thought out all of these things."

"Indeed not." Lady Inglewood stood. "Lord Neil will accompany us, of course, and when the matter is settled we will send you home with him as your escort. As you are a widow, there is nothing inherently improper about such a thing. And we will see to the necessary arrangements for everything."

The gratitude Teresa felt made her eyes overflow again, and she accepted the handkerchief her mother handed to her. "But— why? You do not even know me, my lady."

"Certainly not because Lord Neil had anything to do with it," the earl muttered, earning a sharp glare from his wife. He cleared his throat. "I happen to be a member of Parliament, and I am uniquely concerned for our county and all who are in it. That this heinous action has been performed, and gone undetected, is an affront to all that is good and honorable. I wish to see to the matter personally."

His wife beamed at him, then went to where Neil stood next to Caroline. "You did well, Lord Neil. Now, you had better pack your things." Then she turned her kindly smile to Caroline. "And you. Are you Miss Caroline?"

"Yes, my lady," Caroline said shyly.

"Lord Neil mentioned you in his letter. I have brought you a gift." She opened the front door, and one of her liveried grooms handed a basket through to the countess.

"Mother, will you help me?" Teresa asked, taking her mother's hand. Her head was pounding with a headache, intermingled with the news and what it might mean for their future.

"Of course, dear." Mother went first up the stairs, at a speed Teresa had not seen from her since the cow escaped her pen.

As she walked by Neil, he lifted his hand just enough for her to touch it as she passed. It was only the barest touch, a brush of her fingers against his, but it sent tiny bits of lightning up her fingers and straight to her heart. Teresa bit her lip and hurried, rubbing her fingers together as she climbed the steps to get to her little room.

Whatever came of the journey to Ipswich, Neil's kindness could never be forgotten.

Mother already had Teresa's trunk open when she entered her bedroom. "I am relieved we did not sell all our best dresses." She took out the overcoat that had belonged to Henry and laid it upon Teresa's bed. Teresa sat down, still muddled, and pulled the coat to her chest.

"Mama," she said, tears threatening to return. She had not called her mother that term since her marriage. "This means Henry never did anything to hurt us. He never kept any secrets." And all the anger she had worked to hide, the forgiveness she had thought she must give, dissipated. She felt rather like her heart had been mended, too.

"Dearest love." Mother smiled where she sat upon the floor, one hand still inside the trunk. "It means a great many things, but I do believe I am most grateful for that. You loved him so, and now his memory will no longer bring pain."

Teresa nodded, running her hands down the sleeves of the coat.

"It also means," Mother continued, turning her attention back to the trunk, "that you can go about finding a new love."

Before Teresa could respond, her mother exclaimed happily and pulled a lavender frock from the trunk. It was a printed fabric with silvery vines and light pink flowers upon it.

Teresa took the dress from her mother's hands. "This will change everything, Mother. If the ruling is in our favor."

Mother arched an eyebrow at Teresa. "You have the full support of an *earl*, child. I cannot see your claim being dismissed." Mother kept rifling around for a second dress. After they had most of her clothing chosen, Mother went to fetch a long spencer from her own trunk, along with a small bag to put everything inside. Teresa changed into a brown gown that would suit travel, the spencer, and a bonnet likely several seasons out of style.

Then she found a pair of gloves, made of soft, buttery leather. For a long moment, she held the gloves in her hand. But her eyes studied her fingers. The backs of her hands were tanned from working in her garden and outside in all weathers. She had callouses. There was nothing soft about her hands anymore.

Shaking away that thought, Teresa pulled the gloves over her hands.

She picked up her bag and the reticule. It hadn't much in it besides a few coins, and it certainly did not match any of her clothing. But it would do.

Mother looked her over carefully and nodded. "When you arrive at Ipswich, be certain to obtain the services of a maid to do up your hair. All will be well, my dear. You will see."

"Thank you, Mother." Teresa embraced her. "Thank you, for being here all this time."

"My darling, where else would I be?" Her mother kissed her on both cheeks. "Now. Downstairs with you. We must not keep Lord and Lady Inglewood waiting."

Or Neil. Teresa's heart swelled with gratitude for all he had done for her. And for the countess including him in the invitation to Ipswich. Teresa could not have asked him to come, though she wished to, without sounding incredibly forward. But there was no one she wanted by her side more. She drew in a breath, bolstering her strength, and left her room.

Chapter Twenty-One

Everything Neil possessed was in his satchel, and it amused him. Never in his life would he have called himself poor. But now... Now he owned but two shirts. He wore the same one he had when the Earl of Inglewood had shown up, the other had been too dirty, but he hoped to have it washed at an inn. His work boots were on his feet and the shoes he had worn when cast out of his father's home were in the bag. As was his dinner jacket, ruined gloves, and crumpled cravat. His hat was on his lap. Truthfully, Teresa appeared far more like a lady sitting on the seat next to the countess than Neil looked like a gentleman.

But then, she always appeared lovely to him.

When she looked up and met his gaze, she smiled. The warmth in the expression went right to his heart.

He shifted and dropped his eyes. She had told him clearly enough, several times over, that they could not be anything more than friends. At last, he began to realize why.

Lady Inglewood had a husband, of course, but had still treated him kindly when his wooing of her had failed. He had decided she behaved that way to be morally superior, and her friendship was valuable given her place in Society. Lady Fox, whom he had first known as Miss Millicent Wedgewood, had been too young to be of interest to him. Yet she had offered her friendship when he'd performed a few small kindnesses for her.

Something about him apparently made it quite easy to make friends with ladies but never attain anything more. Perhaps because his sister, Olivia, had been his only companion for years.

Lady Inglewood had engaged Teresa in conversation for most of their trip. Neil had said almost nothing, and Lord Inglewood had pretended that Neil was not even in the seat directly next to him.

Were it not for Teresa, Neil might have enjoyed antagonizing the earl throughout the journey. But he owed the other noble his good will, and more, for assisting Teresa to such an extent.

There remained two hours of road between them and Ipswich when the sun began to disappear in the west.

"We will have to stop at an inn for the night," Lord Inglewood announced. "There is a large old house in the next village that has been converted into an inn. I have had occasion to stay there before. It will be suitable enough for us."

Teresa fiddled with her gloves. "Thank you, my lord, for thinking of such things."

Neil folded his arms and glowered out the window. It was childish of him, he knew. But why couldn't Neil have done more for her? Not that he wished for Teresa's gratitude. Merely her attention.

I am a complete idiot. He sighed with the thought.

When the carriage stopped, Lord Inglewood climbed out first and then held his hand out first to his wife, then to Teresa. Neil followed, satchel in hand. Teresa put her arm through his as soon as he stepped onto the ground. He looked down at her, raising his eyebrows.

"Are you cross with me?" she asked softly, her eyebrows drawn together. "I did not realize it at first, but Lady Inglewood is the woman you had a tenderness for, is she not? Riding in that carriage all these hours—I hope it did not cause you pain."

After assuring himself that the earl and countess were too far ahead to overhear, Neil bent his head to whisper his response. "It was an idle flirtation, Teresa. My heart was not at stake when she spurned my advances. I am not upset with you, or with them. But Lord Inglewood and I have never been friends, and things were only made more complicated by my indiscretion. It was easier to remain quiet today than to risk his irritation. As he is currently assisting you, I would rather not remind him that I am involved at all."

Teresa smiled, then pressed her lips together as though to try to hide it. "I really should not be amused by what you did to earn his ire. It was wrong of you."

He prepared a flippant statement, ready to make light of the situation, but Teresa had already faced forward again. They entered the old house, now an inn. The innkeeper, a rather rotund fellow with a cheery smile, was speaking to the earl.

"Ah, we have three rooms available at present." He looked over at Neil and Teresa, then back to the earl. "I am afraid not enough for the gentlemen and ladies to each have their own. Perhaps only the two rooms?"

Teresa's cheeks turned red and her lips parted, but Inglewood was already explaining.

"My wife and I will take one room, but I will need the other two for Lord Neil Duncan and Mrs. Clapham."

How strange. His stomach tightened, then warmed as he thought on what it would mean to claim Teresa as his wife. In an instant, he found he could imagine how it would be to introduce her at an inn, to keep her by his side. He swallowed, and when he looked again at her blush, he realized the worst of it.

He wanted to claim her. Not as a friend, or a brief infatuation. But as they followed the innkeeper up the stairs of what had once been a manor house, Neil's eyes upon the way Lord and Lady Inglewood spoke to one another, then disappeared into a room together, it was like a cog clicked into place in his mind.

They came to the first floor and turned down a hall without Neil really taking anything in.

If anyone ever dared to trifle with Teresa's feelings, Neil would call the fellow out. As much as he abhorred violence, nothing would stop him from taking such a scoundrel to task for so much as daring to take advantage of her.

Why hadn't the Earl of Inglewood given Neil a facer when he realized what Neil had been attempting with the countess? Neil had deserved that and worse.

Teresa released Neil's arm, stepping into the room the innkeeper had given to her, key in hand. She had a cheerful light in her eye, but it dimmed when she looked up at him. "Neil, is something amiss? You look upset."

He shook himself free of his thoughts. How had things changed so drastically from the moment they entered the building to now? Not more than five minutes had passed, and yet his perspective had altered severely. He stared at her, then looked to where the innkeeper stood down the hall at another door, waiting.

"Teresa." He picked up her hand, holding it in both of his. "You were right. What you said, downstairs."

She appeared puzzled. He sighed and released her hand.

"I will explain later."

He withdrew, leaving her to watch as he went down the hall to his own room.

It looked as though the room had once been larger, divided by the wall between him and Teresa. He had a window, a decently sized bed, and a chest at his disposal. There was a small table and chair, too. Neil went to the window and leaned his forehead upon the glass.

What had happened to him? The more he thought of his last several weeks, even stretching his mind back further, he began to see his life differently.

The year previous, he had been in an accident with Olivia. Their phaeton had overturned. Olivia had shrieked and carried on over the accident, blaming the other party—a pair of sisters —and declaring it was an insult to the family. He had broken his arm, yet his reaction had been different. He was only relieved that all four of the people involved had walked away from the accident alive.

Neil lowered himself to the chair, scrubbing his hands through his hair. That had marked the start of his change. It must have. He had not entered into any flirtations, any relationships at all, with another woman since then. Instead, he had done a great deal of thinking. For a time, he had even considered pursuing a career. But at his age, was it not too late to attempt gaining employment through the law?

Life had started to feel stagnant. Olivia's petty feuds with social rivals had once amused him, but he found himself caring less and less about them, until she had dragged Miss Wedgewood into a dangerous situation mere months before.

Underscoring everything had been a deep dissatisfaction with his family and their way of living.

He looked down at his boots, his trousers, not at all suitable for a gentleman, much less the son of a marquess.

But he wasn't a son of the Marquess of Alderton. The old devil's blood did not run in Neil's veins. Or Olivia's, for that matter. But was blood alone to account for his change of heart and mind?

Then there was Teresa. Beautiful, warm, and compassionate woman that she was, she had given him a chance without caring about his family or history. And that had changed everything for good. He need not act, nor uphold any sort of reputation for her. Neil only had to work hard, a thing which he had not done since earning disciplinary chores for his delinquency.

Work hard, which he had surprisingly enjoyed, and then be true to himself.

Neil rose and took up his satchel. He took out all his fine

clothing, then left his room in search of the innkeeper. He would have his things washed and brushed, pressed, and returned to him. The fine coat he had worn to dinner long ago would not do, nor would the ruined gloves, but the trousers and a clean shirt, a pressed cravat, would help.

Teresa deserved his best. His best character, his best effort, and everything else.

Though she would not have him, not as he wished, Neil was her friend and her defender.

Neil had given her his heart, whether she knew it or not.

Chapter Twenty-Two

I pswich, though not nearly so large as London, had enough people and carriages to cause crowding. Teresa had not been to a town so large since moving out to Bramble Cottage. She peered out the window of the carriage with interest, and a knot of nerves in her stomach.

"Rest easy, Mrs. Clapham," the countess said. Teresa turned from the window to meet the other woman's eyes. She was so young, and so certain of her place in the world. Teresa almost envied her. "Tomorrow, we will appear before the court. Today, you may do as you please. If you wish to spend the whole of it in bed at the house, you may." They had apparently received permission to stay at a friend's house in Ipswich while the friend was away in the country.

Neil said nothing, the same as the day previous in the carriage. Never would Teresa have guessed him to be able to sit silent for so long. Not that he spoke excessively, but he did enjoy conversation, and she rather missed it.

"Thank you. Perhaps I will take a walk. The exercise may help to settle my thoughts." Teresa stole another look at Neil, but noticed the earl looking in the same direction with a frown.

The two of them truly did not care for one another.

"I think that a marvelous idea. I would offer to join you, but I have missed my son. I intend to spend the afternoon doting upon him." Lady Inglewood smiled wistfully. "I have never been much apart from my child. Leaving him in the care of only his nurse for even a night was too long." The countess smiled somewhat apologetically.

Teresa well remembered what that was like. Removing herself from Caroline had always been difficult. But when she next saw her daughter, it would be with a change in their fortunes. Or so she hoped.

The carriage stopped at a modest townhome; snuggled as it was between its neighbors, Teresa was surprised when they entered the foyer to find it most elegantly furnished on the inside.

"To whom does this house belong?" she asked, looking at the silver and gold wallpaper.

"It is the property of the Countess of Chilton," Lord Inglewood said. "She is my godmother, and has always allowed me to use this residence. She much prefers her rented house in Bath to anywhere else."

Indeed, the servants waited upon Lord and Lady Inglewood with absolute deference. A maid was immediately assigned to attend to Teresa.

By the time Teresa had seen to her things, and tidied herself up, her agitation had only grown. A walk was most necessary, given that there were no weeds to pull to work out her anxieties. Strange, she had never thought how grateful she was to have something to do with her hands when agitated. If she even attempted one of her old pursuits, such as sewing a sampler, she might well stab herself with the needle in her vigor.

Descending the stairs, Teresa saw Neil sitting upon a chair in the foyer, a news sheet in his hands. When her foot landed upon the ground floor tile, he looked up. Instantly upon his feet, he dropped the paper upon the chair and came to her side.

"I thought I might escort you on your walk." He bowed deeply, and she stood a moment to take him in. Cravat. Shirt. Waistcoat. Coat. Everything was spotless, well-pressed, and made him appear more a gentleman than he had thus far. He was clean-shaven again, too. His hair even appeared to have been trimmed, and a golden lock of it had fallen artfully across his forehead.

"I would enjoy that." She took his arm. "Perhaps we could wander in the direction of some of the shops. I would like to find a gift for Caroline."

Neil accepted his hat from the footman near the door, then the two of them went out onto the walkway. Neil instantly put himself between her and the street, his eyes alert and taking in the people passing by.

"Are you looking for someone?" Teresa asked.

He glanced at her, then resumed his visual sweep of the road. "Your brother-in-law, actually. He did not strike me as an honorable man, and now that we have evidence to support my initial assessment of his character, I fear he might attempt to dissuade you from appearing in court tomorrow."

A stab of worry struck her heart. "I cannot imagine Frederick doing more than trying to talk me out of the whole thing. But it sounds as though you are concerned for my physical well-being."

"I am." Neil drew her a little closer to guide her around a puddle, but he kept her there. "Even though I think him a coward, given our interactions, he stands to lose a great deal tomorrow. The money he stole, of course, and his reputation. Though his house, lands, and everything wrapped up in the entailment will still be his, no one will ever look at him the same again. If he is already in Ipswich, he and that solicitor are likely trying to determine how to save themselves."

They fell silent until they turned a corner that brought them to a street full of shops. They passed a bookseller, a stationary printer, glove maker, and then a shop of sundries for ladies.

There, Teresa went inside. Neil followed her but remained near the door while she spoke to the young woman behind the counter.

In a few minutes, Teresa left with a brown packet of buttons and ribbons, new needles, and thimbles. While not the most decadent of purchases, Caroline would love the opportunity to sew a new dress and embellish the older ones with new embroidery.

Even if Teresa won the judge's approval, and what remained of her money, she did not think it would be enough to take them from their life at the farm. She would not count upon it, as that seemed the wisest course.

Neil did not take her down the street very far before pointing out a jeweler's shop. "Would you mind terribly stepping inside with me for a moment?" he asked.

"What business do you have in there?" Teresa gave him a crooked smile. "Have you a pressing need for a stickpin to go with your cravat?"

"Of course," he said smoothly. "An emerald, as large as your thumbnail, to bring out the color of my eyes."

She laughed and followed him inside, grateful for the moment of levity. This time, she remained by the door to give him privacy. From where she stood, looking about at the glass cases full of sparkling gems, the shop was a fine one. A very large man stood near her, ostensibly ignoring her, but she would wager he did a fine job of keeping would-be thieves from wandering in.

When Neil rejoined her, he was tucking a piece of paper into his coat. "There we are. I am to return in two hours."

"Are you?" Teresa searched his face for any clues as to why, but he only gave her a mysterious smile and lift of his eyebrows. "Is it a very great secret that brings you here?"

"A very great one, indeed." He took her hand and tucked it through his arm again. "Where else would you like to go, my dear?"

The endearment made her heart skip. "I have nothing else pressing to attend to. There is a park, I think, near the house where we are staying. Perhaps we can take a turn through there before we return home."

They crossed the street, so as to look through the shop windows there on their return. Neil stopped to show her a curiously worked mantel clock in one window, and she paused before a very elaborate display of hats.

"I would never wear anything that large." She pointed to a hat which appeared to have a miniature boat upon it.

"Perhaps you would, if you were the wife of an admiral," Neil said. Then he made a show of looking from her to the hat and back again. He shook his head. "No, you are right. Even the admiralty could not justify such a thing. Your features are too delicate to be overwhelmed by such extravagance. You would need a topper that did not draw attention away from your lovely face."

Teresa laughed at his flattery and continued walking. "Really, Neil. Now your compliments grow extravagant."

"Do they? I cannot think that I have said anything I did not mean." He grinned at her, then cleared his throat. "But I will desist, as it seems to make you uncomfortable. Ah. The park."

They went down the path lined with stone pavers. The park was not even so large as her vegetable garden, but it had a few trees and flowers, and it was a pleasant enough patch of greenery. As they walked, Teresa felt the tension leave her shoulders and neck. She relaxed and held her packet loosely to her chest.

"This is all happening so quickly."

Neil nodded at her side. "Yesterday morning, you milked your cow. I repaired a broken slat in the wagon. There was a whole list of things to do before dinner."

"And none of the things on that list included a visit from nobility or a trip to Ipswich." Teresa paused beneath a large chestnut tree and pointed to the bench beneath it. "Might we sit a moment?"

"As you wish." Neil walked to the bench and sat down beside her, stretching his long legs out before himself. He crossed his arms over his chest and kept his eyes upon the path.

Teresa watched him, taking in his profile with interest. The man rather reminded her, in that moment, of an especially vigilant shepherd dog. Watchful, calm, but quite ready to raise his hackles and growl if anyone so much as glanced at her. Though no threat was likely to appear, having Neil's protection set her at ease.

Putting her packet next to her, Teresa brushed her hands over the skirt of her gown. "Neil. Thank you for coming with me. I know it was practically decreed by the countess, but you could have said no. I did not realize how uncomfortable it would be for you and the earl to spend so much time in one another's company. I am sorry for that."

"I already told you," he said quietly, still not looking at her. "We will rub along well enough together, for the time being. I have no intention of provoking him." Then he did look at her, from the corner of his eye. "And if they had not invited me, I would have invited myself. Presumptuous of me, I know." He turned a little more away from her. "But how could I let you make such a journey without a friend?"

She had to have imagined the bitterness lacing that last word. Friend ought to be a sweet word in all circumstances. Even theirs. She undid the ribbons of her bonnet, more for something to do with her hands than anything else. "Lady Inglewood is very beautiful. Young, too."

"I believe she is four and twenty," Neil said, somewhat absently. "And yes, quite pretty."

Teresa's eyes lowered to her gloved hands, knowing full well the roughness beneath the soft leather. Teresa was not as tall as Lady Inglewood, and her hair was a great deal darker. She rather suspected herself the darker complected of the two. And she was older, due to turn one and thirty that very winter.

Not that it mattered, how she compared to someone as distant from her socially as Abigail the cow was to a duchess's lapdog.

"I was wondering. If all goes according to our hopes tomorrow, if Mr. Clapham is forced to return to me all that is mine, will it change my arrangement with you?" She bit her lip, her eyes steady on her lap.

"Why would it?" He shifted, crossing one leg over the other and sighing. "You will still need a pair of hands around the farm, will you not? Unless you mean to ask if I will suddenly require payment. I assure you, I have no need of your funds, and I will hold to the original agreement." When she looked up at him, she saw him still staring across the way, his eyes narrowing a fraction. "I will labor for you until my family relents. You may have the worse end of the bargain, madam. They may never wish to have me back." Then he looked at her, dropped a quick wink, and stood.

Teresa's heart warmed, and she stood too, ready to declare herself happy by that idea.

"We are watched," Neil said before she spoke. "Get your things."

She went cold and did as he said. "Where? And by whom?"

Neil took her hand rather than her arm. "Your brother-in-law, at the corner of the park. Do not look. We will return to the house and see if he approaches us."

Swallowing her nerves, she nodded once and fell into step beside him. His fingers squeezed hers gently, then his thumb ran across the skin of her wrist. The gesture calmed her. Neil would look after her.

Not once did she look behind to see if they were followed, though she noticed Neil occasionally turning to look at carriages they passed. He covertly checked behind them.

"Still there," he said when they arrived before the house where they stayed. "Perhaps he only means to find out where you are staying."

"Let us hope so." Teresa hugged her packet tighter, making the paper crinkle against her chest. "I am most upset with him for ruining our walk."

"Is it ruined? I cannot think so. I enjoyed the time with you." Neil spared a moment to turn his most charming smile upon her, one corner of his mouth higher than the other. "But then, I always do."

"Even that time I made you fall out of the cherry tree?" she asked, the conversation proving a much-needed distraction.

"Especially then. Because not five minutes later, something happened that you have made me promise never to discuss, even if I will never forget it."

Her cheeks colored and she turned, lips parted in her surprise. He alluded to their kiss.

They were at the door to the house. Neil knocked, then turned around and stared pointedly behind them. Teresa did not look back. Neil's stance made it clear enough that his stare was a challenge, a declaration to the man following behind them. The door opened, and Teresa went through, Neil just behind her.

"Heavens." She took off her bonnet and put it on the table, then her gloves. "That was somewhat disturbing."

"I doubt he will bother you again." Neil put aside his hat, too. He did not even have any gloves. "Teresa, do you play the pianoforte?"

She looked at his reflection in the mirror above the table, raising her eyebrows. "After what just happened, you wish to know if I *play*?"

"Of course. I think we could both use some music. I have already ascertained that there is an instrument upstairs, in a sitting room."

Teresa turned to face him. "I play. Or I should say that I used to. I have not touched a pianoforte in almost two years."

"Ah, then you are most fortunate to have this chance. Come. I long to hear you relearn the instrument." Neil grinned, an expression she once might have called predatory. But she knew better. He was goading her, for her own good, to turn her thoughts elsewhere.

"Very well. I suppose I cannot disappoint you." Even if she wished to speak of something else. Such as their kiss, as he had nearly done. But he was right. There was no point to it. A marquess's son was far above her, even if she had her funds restored.

Neil followed her up the stairs, and she tried to stop thinking about anything except what piece she might remember well enough to play for him.

Chapter Twenty-Three

With bank notes from the jeweler in hand, and a line of credit that made him rethink everything he once had about the worth of a ten pound note, Neil went directly to a tailor. He had no intention of commissioning a full set of clothing, but if there was anything the tailor had completed for another client, Neil might be able to bribe the clothing and a few alterations out of the shopkeeper. He followed the same successful line of thinking to obtain a pair of gloves. Shoes were impossible, but he had his fine pair from before the marquess's exile. They just needed a bit of attention.

Money made the world an easier place to navigate, to be certain, but he only had so much. And he meant to save most of it. But he would not escort Teresa to the court on St. Helen's street dressed like a pauper.

Neil had nearly left the shopping district when he spotted a shop window full of brightly colored fabrics and a beautiful display of shawls in the window. He went inside and came out a quarter of an hour later with three packages more.

He had chosen a dark blue shawl for Mrs. Godwin, a

rosebud pink for Caroline, and a delicate white shawl for Teresa.

Their family had been kind to him. The shawls were a simple way to express his gratitude. Hopefully, that was what Teresa would think. Their conversation in the park that morning had skirted into dangerous topics. He would not leave her, as he promised, but if they had dwelled on the subject much longer he might have said something imprudent. Such as asking if he could stay indefinitely, if only to be near her.

Foolish nonsense more suited to poets than someone of his age and station in life.

Neil was back upon the street where they were staying when he saw Mr. Clapham again. The man paced upon the pavement across the street from the house. Why did he bother staying there? Teresa would not come out of the house again until morning, and certainly no one would permit the villain inside.

Pretending to ignore him, Neil went up the steps to the house. He deposited his things on the table but kept his hat when the butler came forward to take it. "Not necessary. Tell me, is there a way to get out of the house without being seen?"

"There is a side door that goes into an alley, my lord," the butler said, not batting an eyelash at the strange request. The sign of a well-trained servant.

"Is there a reason you are sneaking out?" Inglewood's voice carried down from above.

Neil glared up at him. "If there were, your shouting about it would hardly help matters."

The earl came down the steps at a leisurely pace, unhurried and feigning disinterest. "I do not generally condone secretive actions, but whether you come or go is of no interest to me."

"Yet here you are, asking as though you wish to know." Neil heard the biting sarcasm in his voice and ground his teeth together. The time for petty disagreements had passed. "Mrs. Clapham's brother-in-law is across the street. He has been there at least two hours. I mean to question him, but if he were to see me coming directly from the door to his place on the walk, he might scamper away before I give him a proper warning."

A most peculiar expression appeared on the earl's face. Complete indifference changed into surprise. "I cannot say I have ever seen you care this much about the welfare of any person other than yourself before this summer. First it was Lady Fox, now an impoverished widow. Neither lady has anything of value to offer you in return."

Impatience mounting, Neil gestured to the front door. "There is a man out there who has made it a point to cheat and lie to a woman under his protection. I wish to take a moment to tell him he is not welcome here. Might I have your leave to do so, my lord?"

Inglewood crossed his arms, appearing to consider the request. "I think I will come with you."

"Have it your way." Neil stalked through the corridor behind the butler, and Inglewood followed. They were out into a narrow alley in moments, where the greater houses could accept deliveries and such. Neil led the way through to the street, around the corner, and then directly behind Clapham. The blasted thief was so occupied with his watch of the house that he did not realize Neil was upon him until Neil tapped him on the shoulder.

Clapham turned, and Neil had the satisfaction of watching all the color leech from his face.

Neil lowered his chin a fraction of an inch, lifting his eyebrows as though surprised. "Mr. Clapham. How unexpected. I did not think to see you until tomorrow. At court."

Moving casually to the other side of the gentleman, Inglewood flanked him. "This is Mr. Frederick Clapham?" The earl's famous stony expression kept him from appearing no more than bored. "Not entirely what I anticipated for one of such low morals."

The nervous gentleman looked from the earl to Neil. He had to know Inglewood's identity, given he had tracked Teresa to this house and whatever information his solicitor had given. But Neil had no intention of making a formal introduction, throwing Clapham even more off balance.

"I had hoped to speak to my sister-in-law," Clapham finally said, looking at Neil. He squared his shoulders and thrust his chin out. "Family should not have to resort to court to work out their differences."

"Family also should not lie, cheat, and steal from one another. Do you not agree, my lord?"

"Certainly. But it seems not all the gentry have learned such a lesson." Inglewood shifted subtly, angling more toward Clapham. His eyes narrowed. "It is such a shame, too. My wife declares Mrs. Clapham is a dear creature, worthy of close friendship. I dislike thinking of all Mrs. Clapham has had to endure these many months. Lord Neil, how has such a gentle woman borne the hardship placed upon her?"

Neil's lips curled upward. "With grace and dignity. Mrs. Clapham impresses me daily with her fortitude in the face of all the adversity she is forced to endure."

The way Clapham drew himself up, puffing out his chest, was almost comical. The man might have every appearance of a gentleman, but as soon as he spoke he revealed himself to be a sniveling coward. "You must let me speak to her. Poor woman merely does not understand the way these things work. I have done my duty by her, of course. I did not turn her out of her house, she chose to leave. Certainly, the courts need not become involved—"

With a wave of his hand, Neil interrupted the buffoon. "I have no interest in discussing any of that with you. Indeed, I had rather not speak with you on any subject." Neil stepped closer, and when the other man tried to back away he remembered Inglewood behind him and stiffened. "I only require you to listen to me, very carefully. Mrs. Clapham is now friends with very powerful people. Not me, of course. You know well enough my situation, as you attempted to use it to your advantage already, but the man behind you has more influence in this county than practically anyone else. You have acted dishonorably, proving yourself a cowardly wretch taking advantage of someone who ought to have had you as her champion."

Neil lowered his voice, speaking with something akin to delicacy. "He can ruin you with one word. And I? I will stand as protector at Bramble Cottage so long as I am needed."

Clapham swallowed. He looked from Neil's glare to over his shoulder at the indifferent expression of the earl.

Inglewood's tone was cold as he spoke. "One hopes you have enough of an intellect to take Lord Neil's warning to heart, Mr. Clapham. Best not to loiter."

Neil stepped back, allowing Clapham to escape away at last. He did so, nearly at a running pace, never looking back.

"I find myself almost inclined to approve of you in this moment, Lord Neil." Despite his words, Inglewood's tone had not changed from how he had addressed Clapham.

"Let us not be too hasty, my lord." Neil relaxed somewhat. "Though I will express my thanks for your part in all of this. I admit, I did not expect you to show any interest at all in Mrs. Clapham's situation. Given that I am the one that brought notice to it."

Inglewood shrugged, then made to cross the street.

Neil followed a step behind.

"I confess, I was more intrigued precisely *because* you were involved. Your assistance this summer with Sir Isaac and Miss Wedgewood confused me. I thought it an abnormality in your behavior."

They stepped into the foyer, the butler there took their hats and acted as though nothing strange had occurred with the two lords running out a side door only minutes before.

"While we have never cared much for each other, Lord Inglewood, I am not as morally lacking as you seem to believe." Neil crossed his arms over his chest and pulled in a deep breath. It was time to do the right thing. Teresa's admonishment from the inn the day before had stayed with him. "There is more I would say to you, if we might step into a private room."

Inglewood raised his eyebrows but gave no other indication of his curiosity. He motioned to a nearby door. "This room will do."

Neil went inside first, but stopped after only a few steps. Lady Inglewood sat in a chair near the window, looking out over the street. She watched them enter, her hands folded in her lap. "I heard your voices downstairs a few minutes ago, but by the time I entered the corridor you had both gone. Imagine my surprise when I came in here only to spy two lords, who are known to dislike each other, across the street together. You both appeared to be on the same side for once."

Neil hesitated and looked to Inglewood, whose expression had cracked enough to show his amusement.

"Interesting, is it not? Lord Neil brought my attention to an unwanted guest." He went to stand by the countess's chair, and he dropped a kiss upon her cheek. "Lord Neil wanted to speak to me in private on some matter or other."

"Should I leave?" She prepared to stand.

"Please, stay." Neil's bravado vanished completely before the young countess. Her presence would actually make easier one of the hardest things he had ever done in his life. "What I have to say is best said to you both."

"Now I am most intrigued," Inglewood murmured, one hand on the back of his wife's chair.

The lady gave her husband a narrow-eyed glare, then turned a more welcoming look upon Neil. He had always liked her. First, he had been intrigued by her beauty, and then by the way her husband had seemingly put her aside as though she was completely unwanted, directly after their marriage. Having been cast off and left to himself, made to feel unwanted by his own flesh and blood, Neil had seen in Lady Esther Inglewood a chance to offer comfort and in turn receive comfort.

Yet now he realized, with a clarity he had never sought, how wrong his actions had been.

"I am well aware that I am regarded by your family and friends with dislike, and no little amount of suspicion. As I have cultivated that view with my actions for the last several years, I will understand now if you have difficulty believing what I am about to say."

"A man's actions speak more to his character than his words," Inglewood grumbled.

"I cannot think that Lord Neil has acted in too many repre-hensible ways, darling." Lady Inglewood looked up at her husband, her expression one of patience. "Let us hear him out."

When the earl said nothing against him, Neil cleared his throat. Then he stood with legs apart, back straight, and hands at his side. He met Inglewood's stare with directness. "I wish to apologize to you, both of you, for my conduct toward Lady Inglewood after your marriage. I approached her with a dishon-orable intention, and I convinced myself what I was doing was not wrong, merely because so many others have acted the same." He saw the earl's scowl darken, and Lady Inglewood's eyes widen.

Neil kept his words firm, speaking with all sincerity of heart. "I have justified my actions to myself more times than I care to count, but I have of late realized the immense stupidity and heartlessness of what I attempted. I should never have risked your reputation, my lady, nor attempted to cause you pain, my lord." He braced himself for Inglewood's displeasure, for his wife's disgust. "I wish to make amends, if possible. I also offer to see myself out of this house, if that is preferred."

For several long moments, no one said anything. Then Lady Inglewood stood and turned to her husband, placing her hand over his where it remained gripping the chair. Neil watched, fascinated to see how they communicated with nothing more than their eyes.

Then Lady Inglewood turned to face Neil again, retaining

her husband's hand in hers. "I never expected you would apologize, Lord Neil. Please know, I forgave you a very long time ago."

"I am not so merciful as my wife." Inglewood sounded curious, if anything. "Why now, Lord Neil?"

They deserved to know, Neil supposed. Though he rather wished to have the whole thing over and done with. He meant what he said. He experienced true remorse upon thinking of how he had flirted with Lady Inglewood, had burdened her with his presence. He had never much cared for Inglewood's part, until he realized the reason behind Inglewood's anger.

"I have only recently learned what it means to protect someone." Neil lowered his eyes to the floor, where an immense rug covered in a swirling pattern of flowers blurred beneath his hard stare. "To care for another enough to stand between them and harm, whether it is the ill-judgment of others or a physical threat. I trespassed upon Lady Inglewood's kindness, I tried to break the trust between you both, and I did not concern myself if anyone was hurt by my actions."

"I understand perfectly," Lady Inglewood said. When Neil looked up, she wore a wide smile, and her eyes glittered with excitement. "You have at last confirmed my suspicions. You are in love with Mrs. Clapham."

Neil said nothing, though he clenched his jaw tight against agreeing with her.

Lord Inglewood actually chuckled, though there was not much humor in the sound. "Poor woman. Out of one hardship and into another. Whatever could a man like you offer her, Lord Neil?"

The earl's disdain made Neil wince.

"Silas," his wife said sharply, a reprimand in the name.

Raising a hand to forestall her protests, Neil looked Inglewood directly in the eye. "I know I am not worthy of her, and she has made it clear she is uninterested in anything outside of our friendship. I intend to remain near her—as a friend—so long as she may have need of me. I have been a pair of hands to work her farm. That is all I will continue to be."

With the shrug of one shoulder, Inglewood took out a pocket watch. "It is nearly time for dinner. I suggest we leave the subject for now. Though I will say"—the earl walked toward Neil, causing him to tense—"I am surprised by your apology. I have seen your behavior shift these past two years and accepted your part in my brother-in-law's happiness with some reluctance. *Perhaps* I will reconsider my opinion of you."

Neil nodded once. "I understand."

Lady Inglewood approached, her hands folded before her. "Thank you for speaking with us, Lord Neil. We will see you at dinner." She took her husband's arm and they left the room.

Neil did not immediately follow. Inglewood's cold question reverberated in his thoughts. *Whatever could a man like you offer her...?* Nothing. Neil was poorer than Teresa had ever been, even with his banknotes in his pocket.

He went to the window, made certain no one lingered upon the street to watch the house, then went to his room.

Having never offered an apology of such magnitude before, Neil could not be certain he had done the thing correctly. But despite the earl's lukewarm response, a weight had lifted from Neil's chest at last.

He had done the right thing. Perhaps he could at last make a habit of that.

Chapter Twenty-Four

T he court proceedings were not at all what Teresa
expected. Not that she had any prior experience to
base such things upon, but she had thought to
witness more of an argument from her brother-in-law's solicitor. But given that the man was taken to task by a barrister who
seemed on good terms with both Lord Inglewood and the judge,
and that he had an entire pile of documents to support the
claims of what the solicitor and Mr. Clapham had done to
Teresa, there seemed little anyone could say in their defense.

Neil had sat beside her the entire time, his steady presence a
true comfort to her. He had surprised her that morning,
meeting her at breakfast wearing new clothing. Though a closer
inspection of his coat revealed it had not been tailored perfectly
to him, he had appeared handsome and gentlemanly, and his
perfect behavior marked him as a man of rank. She felt rather
like a plain country mouse beside him. She wore her second-
best dress. It was gray, and had been a mourning gown she wore
with a black lace collar. Without the collar, it was still a somber
gown. But the color would remind anyone present that she was
a suffering widow.

If she had not been distracted by what she knew she had to face that day, Teresa would have spent more time wondering over *Neil's* change in clothing. When had he procured new clothing?

In the courtroom, her mind was fully taken up by the presented facts. Two hours of discussion, of details, and statements made by all concerned, at last led to the judge's quiet contemplation.

The judge leaned back some in his chair and mused aloud. "I am not usually in this courtroom. It is more common for a magistrate to sit in this chair and make decisions upon the cases presented. I cannot see how any man could listen to this, however, as I have today, and rule any differently than I am about to rule."

Teresa held her breath and reached for Neil's hand upon the bench between them. He turned his hand palm up, lacing his fingers through hers. The confidence she gained from that simple contact made her lift her chin when the judge pointed at her.

"This woman lost her husband to a tragic accident, but it was the intention of two dishonorable men to assassinate the dead man's character. At last we may restore the name of Henry Clapham as a man of integrity and compassion. He did not leave his wife and child destitute. But God help the men who would have done so. Mr. Frederick Clapham, by the authority of the Crown and our laws, I hereby sentence you as guilty of all accusations against you this day. You will make restitution to your sister-in-law." The judge named the amount, and Teresa covered her mouth in shock. It was her full portion, and more for Caroline's future. "You must pay half immediately, the rest no later than a year and one day from today."

Then the judge looked to Teresa, his eyes softening. "Mrs. Clapham, I only wish the law would allow me to give you the whole of your late husband's fortune. But rest assured, if this man does not do as ordered by the court, I will strip him of everything he has."

Teresa's eyes filled with grateful tears. "Thank you, your honor."

The judge went on to deliver a harsher judgment to the solicitor. The man had to pay restitution to the Crown, and was stripped of his right to practice law.

By the time they left the courtroom, and walked beneath the large stone arch of the fortress-like courthouse of St. Helen's Street, Teresa's conflicting emotions overwhelmed her. Her eyes swam with tears, and her knees weakened.

"That was most incredible," Lady Inglewood said, coming to take Teresa's arm. She guided Teresa forward to the carriage, away from Neil. "I knew it would be so."

Teresa shook her head, somewhat woodenly. "I did not even hope for so much. But yes. This is such a miracle. Everything in my life will change."

She wanted to look back, to see Neil's face again. But he walked with head bowed, not looking at her. He had remained calm throughout the proceedings, allowing Teresa to do the same. Without him, out in the air at last, her mind and heart raced with all the new possibilities before her.

They climbed into the carriage with the assistance of a groom, then Lord Inglewood came in and sat across from his wife. He was smiling, almost in a self-satisfied way. "Congratulations, Mrs. Clapham. Justice has been served this day."

Neil entered and took his seat, folding his arms across his chest. He met her eyes, offered one quick wink, then turned his attention to the window. He appeared much more somber than she expected, given that victory was theirs. Or, she supposed, *hers.*

"I thank you, Lord Inglewood, Lady Inglewood, for all your help and support. I cannot understand how it all came to pass, but I know I would never have had the courage to take Mr.

Clapham to court without you. And it all has happened so quickly."

"That is what happens when you know the right people," Neil murmured.

"Thank you, Lord Neil," Teresa said quickly, then laughed when he cocked his eyebrows up at her. "It is knowing you that started all of this. You saved my family."

He gave only the slightest nod, hardly a real movement of his head, and then turned back to stare out the window.

Though Teresa had thought his silence comforting before, undemanding even, it struck her differently in the carriage. With the villain defeated, the hero's reserve confused her. Lady Inglewood gave Teresa's arm a gentle pat, drawing her attention away from the somber man in the corner.

"What will you do now, Mrs. Clapham? Your circumstances have certainly changed drastically. You could likely afford to let a small house in a larger town, if you wish. Procure a few servants. Your daughter, Miss Caroline, may go away to school."

Teresa attempted to avoid that question. "I had not thought quite that far." But Neil's gaze abruptly swung back to her, the slightest downturn to his lips. Bother, could he read her so easily? She had thought of it. A great deal. But she doubted people of the earl and countess's status would understand what she had begun to plan for herself and her family.

"There is time to sort all of that out later." The earl sounded amused, but whether it was with her answer or his wife's enthusiasm, Teresa could not be certain. "Mrs. Clapham, if you determine to seek out a house in town, I hope you will contact me. My man of business in Ipswich, and my assistant in London, would be at your service to ensure you found exactly what you sought."

The offer was kind, and had to be sincere given the reputation of the man before her. "Thank you, my lord. I will keep that in mind, of course."

Neil had turned to the window again, and the carriage stopped before the house.

"My brother and his wife will be here for dinner this evening." Lady Inglewood appeared enthusiastic at that news. "I had a note this morning, but I did not think you wished to be distracted from the matter at hand."

"I look forward to meeting them at last." Teresa had been told the brother, Sir Isaac, had helped sort matters out before the Earl of Inglewood arrived, then he had returned to the seaside with his wife to continue their wedding trip.

The door to the carriage opened, and Neil stepped out first. He extended his hand to help Lady Inglewood down, and then he did the same for Teresa. The moment their gloved hands touched, he met her eyes with his. He appeared most handsome in his new coat and cravat, with his hair shining in the afternoon sun.

Her heart turned over. Warmth flooded her from head to toe. She had to stop reacting that way, or so she told herself as her foot landed upon the pavement. Lady Inglewood linked her arm with Teresa's and swept her up the steps to the house, chatting about dinner that evening. Before they slipped into the house, Teresa looked over her shoulder to where Neil remained standing, Lord Inglewood at his side. Neil watched Teresa, but Lord Inglewood stared thoughtfully at the marquess's son.

Teresa had apparently agreed to sit with Lady Inglewood in an upstairs parlor, without realizing it, as that was where they went directly after removing their bonnets and gloves. She could not remember when the suggestion had been made, but she settled into a chair with a weary sigh.

"Mrs. Clapham, I am absolutely wild with my happiness for you." The countess rang for a servant, then collapsed in her chair with something less than ladylike grace. "But goodness, were you not agitated all the morning long?"

Thinking of Neil's hand in hers, Teresa managed to smile at that question. "Not as much as I should have been, most likely.

But at my age, and with all I have been through, I have learned to be still when nothing I say or do can change the outcome. Though I can promise you that I am quite relieved it is over."

"At your age. You speak as though you are one of those old ladies who chaperone their great-nieces in London." The countess turned her attention to the door as a servant entered. "Will you please bring us tea? And send the nursery maid in with my son."

"I will be one and thirty this winter," Teresa murmured, smoothing the skirt of her second-best dress. She would wear her best gown that evening, to dinner, in celebration of all she had won.

Lady Inglewood shrugged and waved her hand in the air before her. "That is not old, Mrs. Clapham. You are young still. There is much ahead of you, too, that you can yet accomplish. How wonderful, truly, for you."

"While I am most grateful for the return of my funds, I will freely confess that the best thing to have come out of all of this is knowing that Henry did not leave me poor, or lie to me about gambling." His memory had been restored to her with nothing to cloud it, no dark shadows to the brightness that had been his love for her. "I can remember him as he deserves to be remembered, and Caroline need never be ashamed of her father."

Expression and tone both softened as Lady Inglewood spoke. "You loved him very much, I can tell. Love is all too rare. I am glad you may now treasure yours again."

"As am I." Teresa's heart further softened, the emotions of the moment threatening to overcome her. She needed to change the subject, quickly. "You love your husband very much, do you not?" How had Neil ever thought the woman did not adore the earl?

"I do." Lady Inglewood's eyes brightened. "I am quite fortunate. We did not begin that way."

Teresa tipped back in some surprise. "You did not?"

"No. Ours was a marriage of convenience." A knock on the

door halted the lady's explanation, and she rose when a young servant entered holding a delightful little baby, perhaps four or five months old. "There is my little love. Thank you, Matilda."

The nursemaid curtsied, then scampered out the door, likely delighted to have time to herself.

When the countess sat down again, cooing to her son, she returned to the conversation. "Silas and I grew up together. He and my brother are dear friends. But I barely knew him and had never entertained any romantic notions about him. When we married, I determined to be a good wife to him. Love came after. As did little Isaac." She kissed her son's brow.

Teresa smiled to herself, her thoughts turning to a black-haired baby girl. "I remember when Caroline was that tiny. They grow so quickly. I wish I had spent hours more simply holding her close before she grew. You have seen her—she is nearly my height now."

"I was taller than my mother by the time I was fourteen." Lady Inglewood laughed and held her son closer. "You are young yet, Mrs. Clapham. Have you given thought to marrying again? You might have more children, should you wish."

More children. Warmth spread through Teresa's heart. No other children had come after Caroline. No miscarriages or still-births. Her doctor had not known what to make of it, though he suggested once it was Henry and not her to blame, as every-thing seemed perfectly normal. She had never discussed the matter with her husband, as he had declared himself happy enough over Caroline to need no more in their nursery. She had counted her blessings and agreed.

But whether she was capable of filling a new nursery, Teresa could not think on marriage easily. Because when she even briefly entertained the thought, only one man came to mind. But she was not a worthy match for the son of a marquess, whether Neil was in favor with his father or not.

"I cannot think so far into the future." Teresa watched the baby take up his mother's hand and attempt to chew on her finger. "I must go home and sort matters out there, then I may begin to plan."

"That seems sensible. Although, if you do not mind me speaking somewhat out of turn, I believe there is at least one man highly invested in your decision." The sparkle in the countess's eyes, accompanied by her sly smile, left no doubt as to who or what she meant. Teresa's face warmed, but before she could protest, the door opened again admitting a footman and maid with trays of tea and refreshment.

When the servants left, the countess changed the subject entirely to speaking of her family. Teresa relaxed now that she was no longer the topic of choice, and she participated with great interest.

No matter what the countess said, or how much Teresa felt toward Neil, she could not allow herself to speculate on a future with him. His family, his responsibility to them, must come first. And they would never approve of Neil lowering himself to a marriage with one such as she. Even with her case won, the funds at her disposal did not elevate her enough to consider wedding the son of a marquess.

Neil had stated, quite clearly, that he would stay in her life until his family allowed him back into theirs. Asking him to risk the relationships of his family for her would cause still more damage. She would not expect more of him.

Even if she had fallen in love with him.

※

Neil waited in the parlor with Sir Isaac and Lady Fox for their hosts. And Teresa. She had not yet appeared for dinner, either. But the wait was not entirely unpleasant, given that Lady Fox had an especially entertaining wit. The woman was cleverer than most, and she kept the gentlemen entertained by recounting a story about stumbling upon a goat in one of her rambles in the country.

"But enough of my nonsense," she said after finishing the story amid their laughter. "I need to learn more about you, Lord Neil. We have not seen each other in weeks and weeks, of course, but you strike me as much altered since the house party where we met."

Sir Isaac tucked his one arm around his wife's shoulder, as casually as if it was a common thing for a man to show such affection in public. "I must agree with my wife's observation. You are decidedly tan."

Neil glowered at the baronet, but his lady laughed. "I did not mean his complexion, Isaac. I meant his manner. Lord Neil often makes a show of being so relaxed he cannot even bother with proper posture. But look at him now, all stiff and correct, as though he waits for an audience with the king."

As he had no intention of feeding the woman's curiosity, Neil only shrugged and adjusted the ends of his cuffs. He rather missed his clothing being made to actually fit him, rather than making do with something sewn to someone else's specifications. "It has been a trying day."

"Has it? Even though Mrs. Clapham received everything she could hope for?" Sir Isaac smirked, then leaned closer to whisper loudly to his wife, "I see what you mean now, of course. Look how the man fidgets."

Stiffening his spine, Neil crossed his arms over his chest. "I do not fidget. These clothes are ill fitting."

"Ah, yes. The rumors were that you wandered about the country in your evening clothes for a time." Sir Isaac's grin appeared nearly triumphant.

It took effort not to grumble like an ill-mannered youth when Neil answered that remark. "I am pleased my discomfort brings you such entertainment."

"My husband is obviously not feeling compassionate at present." Lady Fox's smile remained undimmed, despite her apologetic tone. "You must forgive him. But do tell me. Is Mrs.

Clapham wonderfully pleased by how it has all turned out? Does she even now plan her new life?"

He leaned against the mantel, uncrossing his arms and trying to relax his posture. "Mrs. Clapham seemed surprised by the outcome, and she is a practical woman. I doubt she will make many plans before the funds are directly in her possession. Life has taught her to be cautious, after all."

Sir Isaac grinned again. "You sound as though you admire that aspect of her."

"One must admire a practical woman," Neil said, tapping his fingers against the mantel. "They are so rare, after all."

"Though that statement sounds rather severe upon my sex, I will agree. When it comes to ladies of Society." Lady Fox actually smirked. "But do see, Isaac, that he readily admitted to admiring our Mrs. Clapham. Do you think, perhaps, the differences we sense in him has less to do with his change in fortune and more with his new acquaintance?"

"Ah, perhaps you have something there, Millie." Sir Isaac tipped his head back, narrowing his eyes as he made a show of studying Neil again.

Neil scoffed and turned his own away to stare at the door. If only he had not readied himself for dinner with such haste. He might have avoided the entire conversation. "You are both imagining things."

"Most unlikely." Lady Fox giggled. "Oh, I can hardly wait to meet her. Do you know, I had not thought Lord Neil the sort of man whose head might be turned by any woman."

Sir Isaac opened his mouth to speak, far too much amusement already written upon his face, when the door opened and Teresa entered.

Not caring who saw, and almost forgetting their audience, Neil approached her at once with one hand outstretched. "Mrs. Clapham. You look enchanting this evening." She wore a dress he had not seen upon her before, with silver embroidery and a lavender color that made her gray eyes appear quite light. Her dark hair was done up in lovely curls and twists, and he saw the ribbon he had procured for her in her hair. It was her only real adornment. She wore no jewels, no silk shawl. Only the ribbon, dress, and cream-colored gloves that had likely come from the days before her husband's loss.

Yet he could not think he had ever seen a more beautiful woman in his life.

"Thank you," she murmured, placing her hand in his and stepping close. Her cheeks turned pink. "I hope no one else will mind that I am dressed all wrong for the occasion." It was true. The gown was simple by the standards he had known. Everyone at the table that evening would be titled, except for her.

"I daresay, no one will care at all." Neil gave her hand a squeeze, then guided her to the now-standing couple in the room. "Sir Isaac Fox, Lady Fox, might I present to you my dear friend, Mrs. Henry Clapham."

"It is an honor to meet you at last," Teresa said as they exchanged the proper greetings. "Thank you for your part in setting things up for court. I cannot possibly express my gratitude enough for all that you have done."

Sir Isaac, standing at attention, bowed to her again. "Mrs. Clapham, it was our pleasure to be of assistance."

"I am well enough aware of what it is like to feel as though no help is coming," Lady Fox said with firmness. "I am only glad that Lord Neil wrote to me and explained the situation. Thank goodness it all turned out for the best."

Teresa looked up at Neil, and he found himself smiling back at her. He tucked her arm through his, resting his hand upon hers. "There is no one so deserving of a miracle as you, my dear."

Sir Isaac coughed suddenly, and his wife abruptly cleared her throat, slanting her husband a disapproving glare.

Perhaps Neil had grown too relaxed, showing his hand in such a way that someone such as Sir Isaac had caught on. With some reluctance, Neil released Teresa and stepped back toward the mantel, pretending interest in the clock that sat upon it. Teresa and Lady Fox engaged in conversation, which he pointedly ignored.

There was no reason to cause speculation, even among people who may never set eyes upon Teresa again after that night. Her reputation was important to him, and his continued affection for her would complicate matters if he did not get it under control.

But how Neil wished he could reveal the whole of his heart to her, without fear of rejection. He had nothing to offer her. Nothing at all. Teresa had the ability to do as she pleased, at last, and did not even need to rely upon his help.

He had been away from his family longer than he once expected. The marquess would not relent, perhaps ever, giving Neil no funds or position to offer a woman. Which meant he would be reliant upon himself to earn a living, and his current employment, his food and shelter, all came from Teresa.

She had the funds to hire help. To move entirely away from the farm, should she wish. Though he depended upon her, as he had at the beginning of their arrangement, she no longer depended upon him. There was nothing he could offer her. Nothing but his love for her. For a woman as beautiful, kind, and compassionate as she, it was not enough. *He* was not enough.

Neil stared at the face of the clock, suddenly wondering exactly how much time he would have left with the woman he loved before he had to give her up forever.

Chapter Twenty-Five

T he Inglewood carriage waited outside for Teresa and Neil early the next morning. They would not need to stop for the night, this time, though the driver and groom would change out the horses halfway through the journey. Teresa's excitement over seeing her mother and daughter, and sharing her incredible news with them, was only tempered by her nervousness at spending six hours alone in a carriage with Neil.

If she did not mind her actions, she knew her feelings might well reveal themselves.

Lord and Lady Inglewood saw them off, with their son in Lord Inglewood's arms. Teresa thanked them once more and promised to write Lady Inglewood to continue their friendship.

Once the carriage door swung shut, and the driver flicked the reins, Teresa leaned into the corner of the vehicle and released a long-held sigh.

Neil sat across from her, in the same clothing he had worn to court. Not as fine as a lord would usually wear, but a perfect match for her subdued wardrobe. Taking his hat off, Neil tossed it onto the seat beside him and stretched his legs diagonally across the floor.

"Home in six hours," he said.

Home? Did he think of Bramble Cottage as home? No, of course not. Most likely he had only meant he understood what she felt. As pleasant as her stay in the house had been, having servants to wait upon her, the lack of things to do to keep herself busy had nearly driven her mad.

The pianoforte had been wonderful. Perhaps she ought to purchase one for the cottage. If they remained at the cottage. It was not precisely fair for her to make the decision on a whim, without conversation or planning. Even if the cottage had become home.

Neil's low chuckle brought her out of her thoughts. "I cannot recall ever seeing a simple statement cause such abrupt brooding."

"Pardon me." Teresa folded her hands in her lap. "I am not certain I will be good company today. I cannot stop thinking about the changes I can make, yet I know it would be imprudent to do anything before the money is in my hands."

"One can always dream, Teresa." He had not called her that before the others, and so she had not heard her name from his lips in days. Hearing it now caused her heart to flutter.

"I have not dreamed in a very long time. I am afraid I am out of practice." Teresa untied her bonnet ribbons and removed her hat, putting it on the bench beside her. "I do not know where to start."

"Where do you wish to live?"

She laughed, without much humor. "I would think that is the most complicated question." Teresa bit her bottom lip.

His eyes softened, and his tone became coaxing. "Not at all. We are speaking of dreams, not what you will do for certain. If you could live anywhere, from a house on Mayfair to a hovel in Northumbria, where would you live?"

Teresa closed her eyes, smiling and preparing to describe a

palace in Austria. Instead, she thought of the cliffs high above the crashing waves of the North Sea. And her cherry trees, blossoming and filling the air with sweet scents.

True, there were the less enjoyable scents of the barn when it needed cleaning. Her nose wrinkled at all of those memories. And yet… Abigail's sweetness, and thinking of Caroline dancing in the loft made all her memories glow golden.

"My farm," Teresa said quietly. "I would stay there. Make improvements, of course, to the cottage. Some to the land. But it has been such a place of peace for my family." She focused her gaze upon him and saw the way he looked at her. His eyebrows were drawn together, not in disapproval, given the way he smiled. He did not seem at all surprised by what she said.

She ought to have been uncomfortable beneath such a knowing look in a man's eyes, but instead she laughed. "What would you have me say instead? That I should like to live in Bath, at a fashionable address? I know no one of fashion anymore, and I have no desire to impress my own importance or lack thereof upon anyone."

With a faint shrug, he lowered his head and rubbed his palms upon the knees of his trousers. "I would only have you in a place where you are happy, Teresa."

Her name again, spoken like a caress, made her heart tighten and trip. "Where would you go?" she asked, though she knew she would not like the answer. "If you could go anywhere to live?"

"I have not recently come into money." He evaded the question quite expertly. "What would you improve about your house?"

"I would add on to it, I think. You have not been upstairs, but there are the four rooms, and they are all very small. I should like to make an addition to both floors. It would be wonderful to have a place for a pianoforte—a small one only, of course. A desk, bookshelves, and things to make it easier to educate Caroline. Then have larger bedrooms, so that there is room for more than a bed to sleep upon. A second chimney on the other side of the house for warmth." Before Teresa knew it, she was describing all the ways in which she could make Bramble Cottage a home fit for a lady and her daughter. Neil nodded, asked questions, but for the most part he did no more than listen.

He sat with his elbows on his knees, leaning forward as though intent upon every word she said.

At last Teresa ended her rambling, not sure how much time had passed. They had moved on to discuss what the money would mean to Caroline's education, and how little Teresa wanted to send her daughter away. Neil appeared to agree with her when she said it would make her happier to educate her daughter at home.

"I haven't a great deal of experience with children, you understand." His grin turned crooked. "But your Caroline is sweetly tempered and has always struck me as intelligent, too. You have done well by her thus far. I cannot see how a school would do better."

"You are in such an agreeable mood today." Teresa yawned, and covered it quickly with her hand. "Do forgive me. I am afraid I did not sleep well last night. I think I was over-excited."

"I cannot blame you for that. Do you sleep well in carriages?"

"Not particularly. How does anyone sleep with their heads bobbing about?" Teresa demonstrated, leaning against her wall. "You see? It is nearly impossible."

A spark of mischief appeared in his eyes. "I know a trick that may help with that."

"I dare not ask, given the way you are smiling at me." Teresa laughed when he changed his expression to one of exaggerated innocence. "Those wide green eyes do not at all fool me, Neil Duncan. Whatever you would suggest, I imagine it would not be helpful in the least."

He crossed his arms, smirking. "You think I mean to tease you?"

"I do. You have no intention of being helpful at all." She tipped her chin up, daring him to prove her wrong.

Neil took her dare. He moved across the carriage to sit beside her, after tossing her bonnet to land next to his hat. Teresa sucked in a breath, her lips parting. It was not entirely scandalous, to sit next to him in a carriage. But he was suddenly so very close.

His arm stretched across the back of the seat, going around her shoulders. "Here. I will keep your head from bobbing about. You may get the rest you need. And before you protest about propriety, I will remind you that no one need ever know of your lapse. I will say nothing. You will take a nap. All will be well."

"You are most difficult, Lord Neil," she said, decidedly not looking at him. He was too close. If she turned her face to his, they would be near enough to touch noses. But that was not, she knew, what would happen.

"Only Neil, please. I far prefer my place as your friend to my place as the marquess's son."

Teresa relaxed, then leaned her head upon his shoulder. "I suppose if you offer me your shoulder—as a friend—then there is no harm in taking a little nap." Not that she thought she would sleep, with his arm around her. She preferred to stay awake. He was warm, and strong. She had seen him work in the fields, trees, and barn, and knew him to be capable of offering her safety and protection.

But the arm around her meant more than those things. He held her carefully, as though she mattered to him. As more than a friend.

She fell asleep, though she could not say when.

And she dreamed all the while of being held.

THINGS HAD TO RETURN TO THE WAY THEY WERE. Neil knew that. Eventually, he must return to his family. There would come a time when Teresa would no longer need him, or when it would drive him mad to not kiss her senseless when she came near. He was not so much of a fool that he dared to think they could keep going on the path they were on and it not lead to liberties taken or trust broken.

He loved her. He had absolutely nothing to offer her by means of funds or position. She deserved more than a man dependent upon her. He must leave her.

But for the time he could, he held her while she slept in the carriage. Her head dipped, resting upon his chest. He bent his head just enough to breathe in her scent. His lips brushed a dark curl.

Teresa did not need him. But he desperately needed her.

Neil swallowed and closed his eyes. If he asked, would she marry him? While he was nothing but a disinherited man with no skills to recommend him? What woman in her right mind would say yes to such a thing?

If he ever found the courage to ask, and then she said no, it would be the end. He could not possibly linger. Not merely because of the blow to whatever pride he had left, which was little enough all things considered, but because of the pain.

Neil woke her when it was time to change the horses, and he moved to his side of the carriage before they stopped. She smiled gratefully as he returned her bonnet to her. While the servants changed the horses, the passengers would take refreshment, and then be on their way again.

"Thank you for that respite," Teresa said when she stepped out of the carriage. "I feel more myself now. I hope it was not too uncomfortable for you."

"Not in the least." Neil tucked her hand through his arm and took her into the inn. "I would gladly offer you such a service again, though I cannot see another occasion for it in our future."

Our future. How he wanted one with her.

The innkeeper bowed to them when they entered. "Good afternoon, sir. What might you and your wife be needing?"

Neil's heart skipped almost joyfully. He did not correct the man's assumption. What did it matter? "A table, some sandwiches, and tea."

"Of course."

"In a private room, if you have one," Teresa added, taking Neil aback. He raised his eyebrows at her, but she kept her gaze upon the innkeeper. "And food for our driver and groom, please."

"Yes, we will certainly see to their needs."

Neil took coins from his pocket before Teresa could offer up payment. She appeared surprised, but then smiled at him. They were shown upstairs, to a room with a table, chairs, and a large window. A small parlor, perfect for two.

When the man withdrew to see about their meal, Teresa took her gloves off and laid them upon her lap. She raised her dark eyebrows at him. "So are we Mr. and Mrs. Duncan for now?" She placed her hands upon the table, as though to smooth the tablecloth.

His heart leaped. *Why not for always?*

"I did not hear any objections downstairs." He took off his own gloves and sat across the table from her. Then Neil held his hand out, palm up. Preparing to make a point. Not really to reach for her. When she slid her bare hand into his, Neil's throat tightened. Her smile was sweet, happy, and lovely. It made his head feel light.

"Neil?" Her smile slowly turned into a frown. "Are you unwell?"

He shook his head and looked down to where he held her hand, running his thumb across her skin. "I am the most happy and content I have ever been. Because of you." He laughed, though the sound was almost choked. "I am not a good man, Teresa. Though I have had a go at reforming myself for a little time now, there is much that needs improvement still."

"I think we might all say the same." She squeezed his hand. "From what you have said about your life before, even about your history with Lord and Lady Inglewood, I have a very difficult time imagining such a man. That man sounds like an absolute scoundrel. You, my wonderful friend, have only a little of the scoundrel in you."

Neil ducked his head, looking down at their joined hands rather than her gentle gray eyes. "You tease me."

"Yes." She sounded amused. "Do you object?"

"No. I rather like it."

A knock on the door meant releasing her, and he called for the person to enter. A maid came in, wearing a clean apron and bearing a tea tray. The innkeeper came behind her with sandwiches and cakes upon a platter. After the man assured Neil that the coachmen were attended to, he left, closing the door behind them.

"Why is it that traveling always makes one hungry?" Teresa asked, pouring tea for both of them. She prepared his cup perfectly, then passed it to him upon a saucer. "I feel I could eat all these cakes myself."

With so simple an interruption, the entire tone of the conversation had changed. Leaving Neil to wonder if he had lost his chance. Or if he had ever had one to begin with.

Chapter Twenty-Six

September slipped into October, and Neil was no nearer an answer for his future than before. He had a routine that kept him busy. Every day for the last week, since returning from Ipswich, he woke up at dawn and fed the animals. He cleaned the barn. Listened to Caroline speak French while he worked and she played with Muse and the kitten. The dog had finally grown comfortable enough to bark in her play, and chase her tail from time to time to make Caroline giggle.

One evening, he sat at the table after Caroline had gone to bed. Mrs. Godwin and Teresa had a notebook between them.

"This coming winter will not be terrible, even if we did not have your funds," Mrs. Godwin said to her daughter. "There are enough stores put aside for food, the roof is repaired, and Mr. Duncan has the barn nearly ready. We only need to purchase our hay and grains for Abigail and Dragon." Caroline had finally named the horse, during Neil and her mother's absence. He hadn't objected to the naming at all, though it smarted him to think of removing the christened animal from the little girl's sphere.

"The first payment will arrive next week, according to the

letter from Lord Inglewood's solicitor." Teresa made a notation in her book. "But I agree. Winter is not so frightening as it was a few months ago." She looked up at Neil, catching his eye and smiling warmly. "Thanks to our wonderful laborer."

He chuckled and looked down into his cup of cider. "I am grateful my inexperienced work has been enough."

"You have been a blessing," Mrs. Godwin said firmly. "With winter coming, however, things must change. I spoke to Teresa of some rather important news this afternoon." Mrs. Godwin looked to her daughter, and Neil saw Teresa's smile broaden, almost unnaturally wide. Whatever the news was, Teresa was pretending more happiness about it than she felt.

"What needs to change?" Neil asked. Perhaps she spoke of his sleeping arrangements. The barn would not be too cold, though he would certainly need more blankets.

"Mother is to be married," Teresa said, grasping her mother's hand. She kept her eyes lowered to the table. "The vicar will read the banns himself, this coming Sunday."

Neil relaxed. Was that all? "Congratulations are in order, Mrs. Godwin. I am happy for you."

The older woman smiled, her beauty still apparent despite her age. Perhaps, one day, Teresa would look like her. All handsome maturity and gentleness.

"Thank you, Mr. Duncan. He has asked several times, but I did not think Teresa could do without me. Now that her finances will be in order, she can afford more help, and the vicarage is not far. Mr. Carter and I will be most happy."

"I wish I had known I stood between you all this time," Teresa said quietly.

"It is not a child's place to know the sacrifices a parent makes, my dear." Mrs. Godwin stood and kissed Teresa's forehead. Neil came to his feet, ready to excuse himself for the evening. But Mrs. Godwin stopped him with a gesture. "This change in our family will have an effect upon you, Mr. Duncan." Despite knowing his title, Mrs. Godwin and Caroline continued to call him by the name he had first given them. "You and my daughter need to talk. Good night, both of you."

Neil watched her go, then looked down at Teresa's bowed head with curiosity. Slowly, he lowered himself back into his chair. "Teresa? Are you upset by your mother's news?"

"No." She laughed, but it was a tearful sound. When she raised her head he could see the shine in her eyes. "I am pleased for her. I truly am. She has given up so much for me, and for Caroline. She has lowered herself to work she had never done before in her life. Cooking, laundry, scrubbing floors. I could not have done all I have without her." She took in a shuddering breath, then started searching her person.

Neil took a clean handkerchief, purchased in Ipswich, from his pocket and held it across the table to her.

"Thank you." She accepted the cloth and dabbed at her eyes. "But it does change things. I intend to hire a cook, and a girl-of-all-work to help in the cottage. But they will be from nearby farms. They will not stay here overnight. Which means that *you* cannot stay. Not even in the barn." Her liquid-silver eyes looked mournful.

"Teresa." Neil chuckled and reached out for her. "I will take a room somewhere, then. I can pay a little for board."

"You would be paying for a room," Teresa said slowly, "in order to come and work at my farm without payment. That makes no sense at all."

Although she was right, of course, Neil forced himself to sound perfectly at ease. He had not expected to leave her yet. It felt too soon. "It makes perfect sense to me, because that is what I want to do."

She shook her head. "But Neil—"

"I promised I would help."

"I can hire someone else—"

"Do you want me to leave?" Though he spoke quietly, Teresa winced. "If you want me to go, Teresa, then you have only to tell me so." Neil ran his hands through his hair, lowering his gaze to the table. He had not meant to sound abrupt and peevish. Yet his frustration had goaded him.

Silence hung between them for a long moment. What must she think of him? Of course she wanted him to leave. She no longer needed him. No one had ever needed him, not really. It had been wonderful while it lasted, more so because of *her*.

"Teresa," he said quietly, treasuring her name upon his lips. "I will leave. Though I must tell you, I would rather stay here. With you." He looked up at last, though it had taken all his bravery to say that much. He, who had never struggled with a turn of phrase, to speak words that could cut or praise a person as he saw fit. What had happened to that eloquence?

When her gaze met his, steady and soft, he knew at once that he was lost.

"Your family will relent, Neil. Eventually, the marquess will relent." Teresa fidgeted with the handkerchief, but kept her eyes upon his. The soft glow of the lamp made shadows dance around them, transforming the familiar kitchen into something different. Something special. "The son of a marquess cannot want a woman farmer."

"I am not the marquess's son. Not by blood, and I believe I can safely say he will never welcome me back. What woman would want a man as useless and poor as I am? It is you who outrank me, love." The last word came out choked, almost entirely withheld. But her lips parted and a light came into her eyes.

She bit her lip and looked down at the table, a dozen emotions appearing and disappearing on her beautiful face. "Neil. I could never—. You must know. I do not think of you that way. You have given me so much. You are dearer to me than I can possibly say."

His heart sped up. Perhaps she was only being kind. Yet there was nothing left to lose. Nothing for him, at least. He must speak, or leave in three weeks' time.

Neil rose slowly, so as not to startle her, then came around the table to her side. He knelt upon the floor and gathered up her hands between his. "Teresa. My dear, my darling, my love. I want you, forever and always. Were I the son of a duke, or a fishmonger, or anything else, I would want you." Her eyes brightened, though a tear slipped down her cheek. Neil could not help smiling through the tremble in his own words. "Though I am not worthy of your kindness and patience, I would beg you to be my wife. I can offer you nothing. Not a title, not a fortune. Only my heart. Please. Tell me it is enough."

"Neil." She shivered and shook her head. "Neil, I cannot— your family—"

"I do not care about the marquess." Neil kissed her fingertips, his heart aching for her answer. "I care about *you*. I want you, and Caroline, to be my family. If you will have me. If I am enough." He had never been enough. Not as a son, a brother, a friend. No one had wanted him. But his love for her gave him hope.

At last, she smiled. And laughed. The sound was like music to him, as beautiful as when she sang as she worked. "Enough? Neil, you are *everything* to me."

"I love you." He had never expected to speak those words aloud. Not to anyone. Love was for fools, for people too poor to know there were other ways of finding pleasure in life. Or so he had thought, before he found the richness in loving Teresa.

She put one hand upon his cheek. "I love you, Neil."

He stood, bringing her to her feet only to sweep her off of them, holding her close as he kissed her. She loved him. He need never doubt anything again. Somehow, despite everything that made him unworthy of love, he had found the one woman who could see him as the man he wished to be.

Her lips sought his with as much longing as had been in his heart for weeks. He held her close enough to feel her heartbeat against his chest, one arm keeping her near while his hand held her, fingertips in her hair and thumb brushing her jaw. Teresa's kisses were like rain, and he was a man too long in a draught.

Teresa deserved every happiness he could give her. Neil slowed his kisses, becoming more tender. He parted from her, hardly able to hear her ragged breathing over his own.

"Will you marry me?" She had not yet answered, and he had to hear it.

"Yes," she whispered. "As soon as possible."

He chuckled and pressed another kiss to her forehead. "I agree. The week after your mother exchanges vows with the vicar. Can you wait until then? We cannot take her day of happiness."

She pulled back and looked up at him, her expression bright. "You are the best man I know, putting my mother's happiness before yours that way."

"I have another motive," he confessed, purposefully putting on his most wicked grin. "It means she will be married and living at the vicarage, so we can send Caroline to her after our wedding."

Teresa laughed, and even in the lamplight he had the great pleasure of watching her blush.

Chapter Twenty-Seven

T he day before Teresa's wedding, she lingered in the orchard with Neil. The leaves were beginning to change colors, and there was nothing to keep them there except for their desire to be with one another.

Arm in arm, they walked beneath the trees. "Tomorrow," she said, "I will be Mrs. Duncan. I never thought I would love someone again. Not like this."

Neil raised her hand to his lips and kissed it. "I never thought I would love anyone at all. Thankfully, I have you as a most excellent teacher in such matters."

Teresa was fully prepared to reward him for that compliment with a kiss, but a clatter of hooves and wheels made her pause. They turned, together, to face the house. A carriage had appeared on the road, and turned into their lane.

"Goodness me," Teresa breathed, hand going to her mouth. She recognized the coat of arms only because Neil had recently drawn it for her. A dark blue background with a black swan upon it declared for all to see that the carriage belonged to the Marquess of Alderton.

"They would turn up now," Neil muttered, sounding rather

cross. "My family enjoys stomping upon the happiness of others." He kept Teresa's hand in his, but stalked toward the cottage and their unexpected visitors.

Teresa kept up with his long-legged stride, trying to keep her dread at bay. Neil loved her. Nothing his family said or did would change that. She knew that.

One of the men atop the carriage had climbed down and opened the door. He reached inside and helped a most elegant woman to alight. Her hair was the same honey-blonde color as Neil's, and though she had to be older than Teresa's mother, there was a handsomeness about her that suggested she had once been a great beauty.

The woman who stepped out next was a younger version of the first, closer in age to Teresa. "Dear me. What is this horrid place?" she asked, her voice clearly ringing through the air.

Caroline had appeared in the door, her grandmother behind her. The vicar and his new bride had come to visit and help Caroline pack a small trunk for her stay with them.

"Mother," Neil called as they stepped upon the newly laid gravel between house and barn. "Olivia. Welcome to Bramble Cottage." He gave Teresa's hand a squeeze when the marchioness turned toward them. "Allow me to present Mrs. Clapham." Teresa curtsied, undaunted by the chilly glares from both women.

Though they were Neil's family, she saw at once they held no warmth in their hearts for her. Perhaps not for anyone.

"I received your letter," Lady Alderton said. "You are quite determined to wed this woman?" She did not at all mention the other letters Teresa knew Neil had sent her, every week since he had come to Dunwich and the cottage.

Had she only come to prevent her son's wedding?

Neil drew Teresa closer and looked down at her, his expression determined. "I am. I love her." He looked up. "You are welcome to stay for the wedding tomorrow."

Lady Olivia huffed and stamped one foot, a childish display

of temper even Caroline had given up years before. "Neil, how could you? And what are you dressed like? A peasant?" Her lip curled. "Papa was on the verge of relenting until your letter arrived."

Teresa swallowed and looked at Neil again.

He shrugged. "I doubt that."

With slow, purposeful words, Lady Alderton spoke. "He has written you entirely out of his will. You will receive nothing more from him, even after his death."

For a moment, Neil's expression fell. But not with regret. With sorrow. "I hope his anger has not hurt you, Mother."

That statement seemed to surprise his mother. She looked at him more carefully, then at last looked to Teresa. "And what do you have to say to this, Mrs. Clapham? My son is penniless. For the rest of his life."

"It is fortunate that I am not, then." Teresa began to relax. There was no threat in the woman's words. Indeed, she seemed only curious. "And we have the farm. We will be well enough, my lady."

"Living in the dirt," Lady Olivia said with a snarl. "How could you debase yourself like this, Neil?"

"Olivia." Her mother turned to the young woman, her tone cold. "The situation is not as I thought. Take yourself back to the carriage. I will speak to your brother." She raised both eyebrows. "And Mrs. Clapham."

With a scowl, Lady Olivia flounced away. Muttering unkind things as she went, which Teresa chose not to hear.

Neil appeared to take it all in stride. "What is it you wish to say, Mother?" he asked, all politeness. Teresa knew he cared for his mother and had always respected her as a good son ought. But there seemed to be no great love or tenderness between them. Not like what Teresa shared with her mother, or Caroline with her.

Lady Alderton gestured to the orchard. "Might we walk through those trees? They are quite lovely."

"Of course." Neil offered his free arm to his mother, and she took it. Though Teresa's mind rather felt like a hive of bees had been loosed inside, buzzing about with her thoughts and nervousness, she remained silent upon Neil's other arm.

"The marquess is not your natural father, as you know," Lady Alderton said without preamble. "The man who sired you is dead, and of no worry to any of us." She spoke coldly, but Teresa wondered if it was from habit rather than lack of sentiment. "He was killed in a duel, shortly after Olivia was born. The coward who shot him fled to the Continent shortly after."

Neil's arm stiffened, and Teresa drew nearer to him in support. He had only wondered aloud once, to her knowledge, who the man might be.

"He was a philandering cad." Lady Alderton spoke without emotion. "But he was kind to me, and I was lonely. I tell you this not to hurt you." She withdrew her arm and stopped them beneath the first of the trees. "But so you know, once and for all, that you have always been your own man. The marquess was harsh with you, and you have never so much as boxed the ears of one of your brothers. Your natural father cared little for anything but his own pleasure, and you have always put your sister and I first. Though I do not claim to understand this"— she gestured between him and Teresa—"I want you to know that you have been a good son to me. The marquess would leave you penniless. I would see you happy."

Teresa's heart went out to the woman. Though she spoke so calmly, only years of pain and sorrow could have produced a woman with such a fortified heart. When Teresa looked up at Neil, she saw the same knowledge in his eyes.

"Thank you, Mother."

After making a brief, dismissive gesture, her ladyship looked over the orchard. "This is a pretty place. I am glad you have found it. Perhaps, someday, I might come visit you both again."

The surprise on Neil's face made Teresa hasten to answer for them. "We would like that, your ladyship."

The woman nodded. "That is all I wished to say. Neil, I have brought you some of your things. I could not liberate much from your rooms, but there are a few books and clothes."

Neil swallowed, a grateful smile appearing upon his face. "Thank you."

"And one of your dogs. That favorite male hunter of yours."

It was that revelation that made Neil's eyes tear up at last, and Teresa leaned her head briefly upon his shoulder to offer comfort. He had told her of the dogs, the kennels he spent hours in every day, and how his only solace had been those animals. That his mother knew him well enough to bring him such a prize spoke of greater understanding than Teresa had thought the woman to possess.

The marchioness tipped her chin up, her eyes blazing as though she dared her son to thank her again. When he only nodded, she returned it with the dip of her head. "May God go with you, Neil. And you, daughter-in-law."

Teresa curtsied, Neil bowed, and the marchioness swept by them to return to her carriage. Neil did not follow, and Teresa remained next to him. She wrapped her arms about his waist and rested her head against his chest. They stood motionless until the carriage left.

Caroline came running out to them. "Mama, Mama. Who was that? Why did they leave a treasure chest in the house?"

Neil chuckled, and when he pulled away Teresa saw evidence of tears in his eyes. "A treasure chest? You must be mistaken, Cara-love."

The girl giggled and grabbed his hand. "Come look. Was that a queen? Grandmama says no, but the woman looked like a queen."

"That was a marchioness," Neil said, holding Caroline's hand in his, and offering Teresa the other. "I suppose we better go inspect that treasure chest."

"Will you be all right?" Teresa whispered when they reached the cottage and Caroline darted inside ahead of them.

"I have you. So the answer to that question will always be yes." Neil kissed her on the cheek.

The vicar and Mother were inside, and Teresa could see the questions boiling inside them. She slipped to her mother's side and whispered only, "I will explain later."

Caroline's gasp drew everyone's attention to the very large trunk in the middle of the floor. Neil had opened it and stood, mouth open, staring inside.

"It *is* a treasure chest," Caroline said. "I was only making a joke. I thought it would be clothes."

Teresa came forward at the same moment Neil fell to his knees. "What is it?" she asked, then had to cover her mouth to keep from gasping.

There were clothes, of course. And books. But across the top of everything were necklaces studded with precious jewels, earbobs, bracelets, and a velvet bag with more spilling from within. Neil choked on a laugh, then looked up at Teresa with a shaky grin. "These are my mother's jewels. I have seen her wear all of them."

Teresa lowered herself to her knees beside him, and he tucked her against his chest.

It seemed his mother would not allow her son to go without an inheritance after all.

Epilogue

SEPTEMBER 1816

Despite the brittle wind and unseasonably cold weather, Neil walked hand-in-hand with his wife up to the Dunwich cliffs. Caroline went ahead of them, Muse and Hunter with her, and three puppies behind them. The only members of the family missing, Neil thought ruefully, were the other barnyard animals.

"I will end up carrying all of you back," Neil said.

"Nonsense." Teresa kept her arm through his for balance, her free hand upon her slightly swollen middle. Somehow, despite Teresa's certainty that they would never fall pregnant, she carried his child. A child he hoped would have his mother and sister's ebony hair and loving hearts.

The sky hung heavy with clouds above them, yet nothing could dampen Neil's happiness. The year had been strange, with reports of snow throughout the countryside in the middle of summer. Their crops had not suffered too terribly, likely because of their proximity to the sea. Yet they had dipped into their carefully saved funds to provide work for others not so fortunate. They had paid for new thatch roofs for several neighbors, and Neil assured each of them it was only repayment for all the assistance the neighbors had given first Teresa and then himself.

"I received a letter today, from Lady Inglewood. Did I tell you?" Teresa asked.

"What did the countess have to say this time?" Neil helped her over a rock, then looked up to whistle to the dogs. Caroline turned too and waited for them to catch up, as he knew she would.

"We are invited to come to a house party." Teresa grinned at him. "Before the baby comes. Esther wants to see us, and she wishes to examine Caroline's artwork."

The countess had taken to sending Caroline supplies and pieces to study, tutoring her from afar. One day, perhaps, it would be Lady Inglewood who sponsored Caroline in Society—if Caroline wished. The twelve-year-old girl gave little thought to her future, reveling in her idyllic childhood.

Neil grumbled. "A house party? I thought I had managed to get away from those things for good, becoming a farmer."

They had made it to the top of the rise, the cliffs only a few yards away.

"Papa, look at what Prince can do." Caroline held a stick up in the air near one of the puppies, and the furry creature wasted no time in leaping directly over it. The girl laughed and looked to see Neil's reaction.

His heart warmed and he returned her grin. Hearing her call him Papa had become one of his favorite things about his new life. They still spoke often of Henry Clapham, as Neil had no wish to replace the man who had loved both Teresa and Caroline before him. Neil hoped, fervently, that Henry would approve of all Neil had done to make their family happy.

They stood together, his arm around Caroline's shoulders and Teresa's waist, looking out to sea. Both women wore the shawls he had purchased for them in Ipswich the year before, and they served well enough to ward off the chill. Yet Neil made certain Teresa's covered her shoulders fully, then bent to kiss her temple.

"I love you, Teresa," he whispered in her ear. "My darling wife."

She rested her head upon his shoulder and sighed with contentment. Caroline nestled against his other side, humming to herself the song she had begun learning on the pianoforte.

Though he never would have thought he deserved such happiness, Neil's gratitude knew no bounds. He had every intention of living a long, joyful life with his dearest love and their family.

IF YOU ENJOYED *REFORMING LORD NEIL*, MAKE CERTAIN YOU read Sally's other complete Regency series, *Branches of Love*. Or go back to the beginning of Inglewood's romances with *Rescuing Lord Inglewood*.

Sally also has an upcoming Historical Western Romance series, starting with the book *Silver Dollar Duke*.

Keep up with all of Sally Britton's publishing news by signing up for her newsletter on her author website, www. AuthorSallyBritton.com.

Acknowledgments & Notes

Dunwich is a very real place, and one I hope to someday see. There really is a sunken city off the coast of the little town, including churches and large buildings that have disappeared beneath the North Sea.

Lord Neil's story has been on my mind for over a year. I wanted to write a character who reflected the ideas and social hypocrisies of the time, yet chose on his own to be someone better. You may have realized by now that the title of this story made it seem as though someone else would *reform* our hero. But I believe that people cannot change other people, only present them the opportunities and forgiveness needed to allow them to change.

The majority of this book was written during the early days of the COVID-19 pandemic. It was a struggle to put my mind into the world of romance and love stories while it felt like the real world crumbled before my eyes. I could not have focused or found the energy to write Neil's story without help from my own hero, my wonderful husband. Thank you, my darling. You saved me.

Thank you, wonderful readers, for making it this far in the

journey with me! Since Neil's story was first announced, several of you have expressed excitement to have a chance to read it. Thank you for encouraging me to continue writing about this character I was certain only I would love! Thank you especially to those who are part of my Sweet Romance Fans on Facebook.

Many thanks to my creative team of editors, proof readers, and my incredible designer. Thank you Jenny, Shaela, Molly, and Carri. Each of you make this author-stuff a lot easier.

Writing isn't easy. No matter how hard an author tries, they can never be perfect. I have yet to publish a book completely devoid of typos or minor mistakes - even the largest publishing houses in the world usually have what they call "an acceptable error rate." No book is perfect, because no author, editor, or proofreader, is perfect, either. So I am all the more grateful for the wonderful people on my team who help me polish my drafts until they shine.

Also by Sally Britton

Heart's of Arizona Series:

Book #1, *Silver Dollar Duke*

The Inglewood Series:

Book #1, *Rescuing Lord Inglewood*

Book #2, *Discovering Grace*

Book #3, *Saving Miss Everly*

Book #4, *Engaging Sir Isaac*

Book #5, *Reforming Lord Neil*

The Branches of Love Series:

Prequel Novella, *Martha's Patience*

Book #1, *The Social Tutor*

Book #2, *The Gentleman Physician*

Book #3, *His Bluestocking Bride*

Book #4, *The Earl and His Lady*

Book #5, *Miss Devon's Choice*

Book #6, *Courting the Vicar's Daughter*

Book #7, *Penny's Yuletide Wish (A Novella)*

Stand Alone Romances:

The Captain and Miss Winter

His Unexpected Heiress

A Haunting at Havenwood

Timeless Romance Collection:

An Evening at Almack's, Regency Collection 12

About the Author

Sally Britton, along with her husband and four incredible children, calls Texas home no matter where her adventures take her.

Sally started writing her first story on her mother's electric typewriter, when she was fourteen years old. Reading her way through Jane Austen, Louisa May Alcott, and Lucy Maud Montgomery, Sally decided to write about the elegant, complex world of centuries past.

Sally graduated from Brigham Young University in 2007 with a bachelor's in English, her emphasis on British literature. She met and married her husband not long after and they've been building their happily ever after since that day.

Vincent Van Gogh is attributed with the quote, "What is done in love is done well." Sally has taken that as her motto, for herself and her characters, writing stories where love is a choice.

All of Sally's published works are available on Amazon.com and you can connect with Sally and sign up for her newsletter on her website, AuthorSallyBritton.com.

Made in the USA
Middletown, DE
19 June 2020

10141169R00154